D0342613

Also by Erin Bowman

Taken

Stolen: A Taken Novella
Available as an ebook only

A TAKEN NOVEL

FROZEN

ERIN BOWMAN

An Imprint of HarperCollins*Publishers*

HarperTeen is an imprint of HarperCollins Publishers.

Frozen

Copyright © 2014 by Erin Bowman

Tree photograph by iStockPhoto

www.epicreads.com

Library of Congress Cataloging-in-Publication Data

Bowman, Erin.

Frozen / Erin Bowman. — First edition.

pages   cm

Sequel to: Taken.

Summary: "Gray Weathersby and a small team of rebels set off on a frozen, icy journey in search of allies to help them take down the cruel Franconian Order—but they quickly learn that no ally or enemy is truly what they seem"— Provided by publisher.

ISBN 978-0-06-211729-8 (hardcover bdg.)

[1. Adventure and adventurers—Fiction.   2. Brothers—Fiction.   3. Government, Resistance to—Fiction.   4. Fantasy.]   I. Title.

PZ7.B68347Fr   2014   2013015447

[Fic]—dc23   CIP

                                                                          AC

Typography by Erin Fitzsimmons

14 15 16 17 18 CG/RRDH 10 9 8 7 6 5 4 3 2 1

❖

First Edition

For my husband:
who shows me the road when I'm lost,
and the woods when I need to wander.

PART ONE
OF TREKS

ONE

WE HAVE BEEN WALKING FOR two weeks. Nothing tails us but snow and crows and dark shadows of doubt. The days grow shorter, the evenings frigid. I thought I'd be able to handle the cold.

I was wrong.

Back in Claysoot, our winters were hard, but while our homes were drafty and crude, we still had shelter. Even if I had to bundle up and head into the woods for a day of hunting, I could always return to a house. I could light a fire and put on clean socks and cling to a cup of hot tea as though my life depended on it.

Now it is just endless walking. Endless cold. At night we have only tents. And exposed fires. And blankets and jackets and countless additional layers that are never enough to chase the chill from our bones.

It's funny how Claysoot actually looks good on some days. When it's freezing and no amount of blowing on my hands seems to warm them, I can't help but think of the comforts of my old home. I have to remind myself that Claysoot was never a home. A home is a place you are safe, at ease, able to let down your guard. Claysoot is none of these things. It will never be these things. The Laicos Project made sure of that, starting the day Frank locked children away to serve his own needs, corralling them like cattle, raising them to create the perfect soldiers: Forgeries. Human machines to do his bidding. Perfect replicas of the people he imprisoned.

And now we march to one of those prisons, a forgotten group in the Western Territory of AmEast's vast countryside. We'll look for survivors at Group A, invite them to join us in the fight against Frank. See what secrets they've learned in all their years of hiding. Ryder's holding out hope that Group A might make a decent secondary base, help us extend our reach to the opposite end of the country.

I look at my hands, dry and chapped. Snow is falling again, drifting through the early-morning light as delicate, gray flakes. I'm supposed to be doing something. What am I supposed to be doing?

I see the footprints, and I remember. Clipper.

He's been drifting from our team lately. We'll settle down for the night, or pause for a water break, and then someone will notice that he's missing. I always get saddled with the honor of retrieving him.

I stand and pull my gloves back on, return my focus to tracking him. I crest a small rise and there he is, leaning against a pale birch tree.

"We need to keep moving. You ready?"

"Gray," he says, turning to face me. "I didn't hear you."

I force a smile. "You never do."

"True." There's an unmistakable heaviness to Clipper's voice. He sounds older. Looks it, too. After Harvey died—was murdered by Frank—the boy took over as the Rebels' head of technology. All the added responsibility seems to have aged him.

"I miss her," Clipper says, touching a twine bracelet I watched his mother give him when they said their good-byes two weeks earlier. "And Harvey." He kicks at a snow-dusted rock at his feet. "He was . . . I don't know how to put it. I just feel lost without him."

Harvey was like a father to Clipper. That's what he means to say. I know it, and so does the rest of our team. It's painfully obvious.

"You've got me, at least," I offer. "I'm the one who races after you every time you take off. That has to count for something, right?"

He laughs. It's a short, quick noise. More of a snort than anything.

"Come on. Everyone's waiting."

Clipper straightens and takes one last look into the endless forest of tree trunks. "You know I'll never actually leave you guys, right? Sometimes I just need some space."

"I understand."

"But you always come after me."

"It makes my father feel better. We'd be lost without you, and as our captain, he sleeps better knowing you're not running away."

Clipper frowns. "I might get scared, but I'm not a coward." He folds his arms around the location device, clutching it to his chest as we head for camp. Clipper's spent so much time staring at the thing lately, I've started to think he believes Harvey is out here somewhere, waiting in a snow-filled gully that Clipper can get to if he only plugs in the right coordinates.

Even though my father has been pressing us at a grueling pace lately, the camp is still not broken down when it comes into view. Tents as bright as grass speckle the snow, and a fire sends a thin line of smoke through the tree branches.

Xavier and Sammy are pulling their tent stakes from the frozen earth, but everyone else is huddled around September, a mean-looking girl in her early twenties who is actually far sweeter than her angled features let on. She's dishing out a breakfast of grits. This has been our fare since we set out. Grits in the morning. Whatever meat we manage to catch throughout the day for dinner. And little rest in between.

Bree spots Clipper and me first. She shoots me a smile, wide and shameless. It's a good look on her. Refreshing, even, since she seems bent on scowling most of the time. She elbows Emma, who stands beside her, a wool hat pulled over wavy hair. Even from a distance I can hear Bree's energetic words. "They're back. I told you not to worry."

Emma looks up and raises a hand in a shy sort of greeting. I don't return the wave. I wish I could forgive her. For replacing me so quickly when we were separated earlier this year—me on the run from Frank, her stuck under his watch in Taem. For moving on as if what we had was meaningless, as if we never talked about birds and pairs and settling into something that feels right. I know it's foolish to hold a grudge, but I've never been the forgiving type. I've never been able to look past people's faults or bite my tongue or be generally decent. I am not my brother.

Clipper runs ahead to retrieve a cup of grits from

September and my father shouts to me from across camp. "Took you long enough!"

"The wind covered his footprints," I lie. I don't want to mention that, like Clipper, I experienced a moment of weakness alone in the woods. That I stopped to ponder it all: the grimness of what we face, the bleakness of our journey so far.

My father swallows a spoonful of his breakfast before narrowing his eyes at Clipper. "I won't have this anymore, Clayton." Hearing Clipper's true name makes the entire team freeze. "We waste time whenever you take off. Gray has to find you. We all have to wait. And we can't afford delays like that—not when our mission's details could be spilled at any moment."

Just three days after we left Crevice Valley, Rebel headquarters, Ryder radioed to tell us one of our own fell into enemy hands. We're now well out of communication range, with no way of knowing how much information, if any, the Order acquired. Still, we spend a lot of time glancing over our shoulders as we hike. Fear is an ugly thing to have chasing you.

"I need you to start acting like a soldier," my father adds, jerking his chin toward Clipper. "You hear me?"

"Oh, go easy on him, Owen," Xavier calls out, securing his broken-down tent to the underside of his pack. The act reminds me of when he taught me to hunt in Claysoot, him loading up his gear and signaling for me to follow him into the woods. "He's just a kid."

Clipper frowns at this, obviously disagreeing that a boy of almost thirteen is nothing but a child.

Sammy stops wrestling with his pack. "Yeah, he's just an immature, no-good, brainless computer whiz who can take any piece of equipment and make it do his bidding. Actually, on that note: Clipper, can you fabricate a time machine so we can get to Group A already? My toes are about to fall off, and I could really benefit from an accelerated schedule."

This gets a light chuckle from the group. I met Sammy over a game of darts back in Crevice Valley, but it wasn't until this mission that I truly came to know him. He's good-natured, endlessly sarcastic, and has a quick-witted sense of humor that's been a welcome distraction.

"We all know you're cold, Sammy," my father says sternly.

"I'm not just cold, I'm freezing," he responds, wrestling a hat down farther over his pale hair. "And think of what this wind is doing to my face! How am I going to win over any girls when I have these windburned cheeks?" He pats them with his palms.

"The only girls you'll be seeing for the foreseeable future are the three in our group. And they're not interested."

Sammy raises his eyebrows as if he means to accept Owen's words as a challenge, and my father adds, "Don't get any ideas."

"Let's start moving," Bo says. "Standing still only chills a person further." His customary twitch surfaces—a forefinger tapping frantically against his mug of grits—and I decide he looks the coldest of us all. His aged frame appears thinner and paler with each day. He's younger than Frank, in his early sixties, but the years he spent cramped in Taem's prison weren't kind to his body. Sometimes I'm amazed Bo's made it this far without complications. I half expected him to turn back to Crevice Valley during the first few days of hiking. I'm pretty certain Blaine would have expected the same.

But of course Blaine isn't here to confirm or deny the theory, and sometimes, his absence hurts worse than the cold. I always feel slightly lost without my brother, my twin. Next time I see him, he'd better be back to his old self. I miss the brother who could keep up with me while hunting, and run without getting winded. I even miss his disapproving, judgmental looks, although I'll never tell him that.

September spreads out the coals and the team scatters to break down the rest of camp. We've all become so proficient at the process that in mere minutes, our bags are packed and we're falling into a thin line.

I tell my feet to move, one in front of the next. Bree joins me, assuming her usual place at my side.

"Think it's too late to turn back?" She says it like she's joking, but I can see the seriousness on her face.

"What? Why would you say that?"

"The more I think about it, the more I worry we won't find anything. I mean, the Order confirmed Group A extinct years ago. Maybe we saw what we wanted to in Frank's control room."

"No. There were people moving through those frames. We both saw it. Bo and Emma, too. We didn't *all* see something that wasn't there."

She lets out a long exhale.

"And it was the most advanced of the test groups," I add. "Even if we find it empty—which we *won't*—we're still going to see if there's anything we can salvage. Ryder thinks—"

"It could make a good secondary base. I know. He yapped about it enough before we left. There's just that small problem about it being without power."

"And that's why we've got Clipper. He'll work his magic."

She nudges me with her elbow. "When did you become so positive?"

"When I decided Sammy alone wasn't enough."

She grins at that and even though I know Emma is behind us, I throw an arm over Bree's shoulder and pull her closer.

It's late afternoon and we're staring at a town that shouldn't be nestled in the base of the valley before us, at least according to Clipper. He's been using his maps and location device to steer us down the least populated routes. Sometimes we'll cross an abandoned, deteriorating stretch of road, or spot a town so far away it looks like a minuscule set of children's building blocks on the horizon; but this community, practically at our feet, is a first. Surprising, too, since we left the Capital Region a few days back and have since entered the Wastes, a giant stretch of mostly unpopulated land that Clipper claims will take close to two weeks to cross. At least it's flatter. The mountain pass that filled the first week of our journey was so brutal I still have sore calves.

Owen pulls out a pair of binoculars. "No lights or movement that I can see. Deserted, probably."

"Maybe we should hike around it," Bo offers. "Just to be safe."

People this far west are likely harmless—average civilians trying to make a life for themselves beyond Frank's reach—but we've been extremely cautious about revealing our presence to *anyone*, especially since Ryder called about the captured Rebel.

I'm as surprised as anyone when my father stows the binoculars away and says, "We're cutting through. The town's abandoned, and we could all do well with a night inside four walls."

I'm thinking about sleeping in comfort—being *truly* warm for once—when I spot the crows. There are dozens of them, circling over the buildings waiting ahead. I don't like the way they hover, or how their shrill cries echo through the valley.

Owen pushes open the wooden gate that borders the community and waves Bree and me in first. We pass beneath a sign reading *Town of Stonewall*, weapons ready. The crows' shadows glide across the snow as we walk up the main street.

The homes are in rickety condition, but not because they've been long abandoned. There are signs of life everywhere: an evergreen wreath on a door, hung in recent weeks given how lush it still is. A wheelbarrow on its side, as though it was dropped in a hurry. Clothing, strung up on a warmer day, now frozen and stiff, that creaks on a line.

Something crunches beneath my boot. I look down.

Fingers, hidden beneath a thin layer of snow.

Fingers that attach to a hand, an arm, a torso. I step back quickly. Then I spot another. Human remains slouched alongside a well just ahead. And suddenly, they are everywhere. Mounds I thought to be snowdrifts are bodies, rotting and festering and rigid in death.

Bree uses her rifle to roll over the one at my feet. Two hollow eye sockets stare back. When she speaks, it is nothing but a whisper.

"What happened here?"

TWO

MY FATHER MAKES A FEW swift gestures, ordering Xavier and Sammy down a side street, September and Bo down another. He nods at me and Bree to continue up the main one, and heads into the nearest building with the others to check interiors. We all know his order, even if he never said the exact words: *Spread out. Look for survivors.*

Somewhere in town a wind chime is clinking, singing an uneven melody as Bree and I move up the street. The road dead-ends before a whitewashed building, tall, with a cross on its peak. Its heavy wooden doors hang open. There's a dog between them, copper in color, and on the brink of starvation, given his thin, wiry frame. He bares his teeth, a low guttural growl escaping him, and then runs inside. Bree and I glance at each other and dart after the dog, taking the stairs two at a time.

The inside of the building is composed of a single room, large and cavernous and shaped like a *t*. Snow has drifted up the aisle we stand in, which bisects rows of benches. The seats are burdened with the dead, heads resting on shoulders, hands clasped as they sleep eternally. Even in the intense cold, the air smells like spoiled meat.

"Gray?" Bree nudges her rifle toward a raised platform at the front of the room. I follow the motion and I see him.

A boy, tucking candles into a tattered bag. He is young. And scrawny. And dirtier than a wild animal, with dark skin, and hair that stands up in all directions.

"Hey," I call out. "Are you okay?"

He jumps, twisting toward my voice. When his eyes find us, they linger on Bree's weapon and he backs away slowly, until he's leaning against the far wall. His dog stands before him, growling.

"What happened here?" I ask.

"Sickness," the boy says, lip trembling. "One got sick. Then another, and another. They died."

Bree lowers her rifle. "From what? What kind of sickness?"

"Don't know. Mama said it came from the east—a city under a dome. She said they brought it here knowing we would die."

Bree and I exchange worried glances. Not more than two months ago, we infiltrated Taem to track down a vaccine that would protect the Rebels against a virus engineered in Frank's labs. We feared he'd capture one of our own and send him back infected, eliminating all the Rebels in the process.

"Who brought it here?" Bree asks. "The sickness?"

But the boy just sinks to the floor, hugging his dog around the neck. He's so scared he's shaking, or maybe he's just cold.

Bree walks up the aisle, pausing in the center of the t. The dog growls, and she decides not to risk the stairs. "Come on," she says, holding out a hand to the boy. "We can get you warm. Help you—"

"No!" he says. "They carried weapons, too. I don't trust you!"

Bree looks at me for help, but I'm as confused as she is. She turns back to the boy, cautiously walks up half the stairs.

"Go away!" he shouts. "You're like them. You're just like them!" He keeps screaming like she's attacking him, which causes the dog to lunge at Bree. She jumps back, barely avoiding a bite.

"Look, we're offering to help you," she snaps, sounding like she wants to do anything but.

"Can't you see you're scaring him?"

The voice startles all three of us. We twist, and find Emma

standing in the building's entrance.

"I'm not *trying* to scare him," Bree says through her teeth.

"But you are." Emma walks up the aisle, passing me and slowing only when she reaches the stairs. The dog growls a bit more adamantly now that there are two potential threats to his master. "Maybe only one of us should do this," Emma says.

Bree rolls her eyes. "Fine." She stalks over to me and mumbles, "This will be fun to watch."

I don't say anything because I already know that Emma will be successful in calming the boy. Emma's voice sounds like a fresh snowfall, whereas Bree's comes out like a slammed door. And Emma moves the way a deer might in an open field, cautious and smooth. I'm not sure she could startle someone if she tried.

Bree and I watch Emma climb the stairs and sit down an arm's length from the boy, seemingly unaware that the dog is baring his teeth more than ever. She tosses her wool hat toward them.

"Take it," she says to the boy. "Go on. You must be cold."

He moves so quickly, I nearly miss it. A hand juts out, grabbing the hat. He wrestles it over his disobedient hair.

"I'm Emma. What's your name?"

The boy blinks, eyes wide. "Aiden," he says finally.

"How old are you, Aiden?"

"How old are *you*?"

Emma laughs, and a smile spreads briefly across the boy's lips. "I'm eighteen. Just had a birthday last month."

The boy counts on his fingers. "I'm eighteen minus ten."

Emma compliments him on how smart he is and Bree crosses her arms. "Lucky," she says to me. "I could have gotten him to talk if I'd had more time."

"Sure you could have." Bree shoots me a look and because I don't feel like being punched in the shoulder, I add, "I couldn't have done much better, you know. Emma's good with people."

"And we're not?"

Bree's eyes are narrowed and she looks like she wants to kick something.

"No. Definitely not."

Ahead, Emma is offering a hand to Aiden. "We're going to make a fire and cook some dinner. Would you like to eat with us? Get warm?"

He nods and slowly takes her hand. As soon as Aiden has chosen to trust Emma, his dog seems to trust her as well. Not fully, because he won't stop growling, but he trots behind them as they walk up the aisle, his teeth no longer visible.

Aiden freezes a few paces from us. "I don't like the one with the gun," he says.

Bree snorts. "See? I was doomed from the start."

Emma drops to her knees alongside the boy and takes both his hands in hers. "Aiden, I don't know what happened to you here. And you don't have to tell me—not unless you want to—but just know that not everyone carrying a gun is bad. Some people let the power of a weapon go to their heads and they do terrible things with it. We are not those people."

Aiden nods, peering up at Bree and me. "What's for dinner?"

"Meat of some sort," I say, and my stomach growls at the thought of it.

"With potatoes?" he asks. "And fresh bread?"

"You're dreaming, kid."

We find the rest of the team in a building that looks like some sort of woodworking shop. It has a vaulted ceiling and a series of workstations lining the walls. They are covered in sawdust and half-finished projects. Carving knives and planes wait patiently, as if they suspect the carpenter simply stepped out for fresh air.

Someone has cleared out the center of the room, save for a few chairs and benches, and September has started a fire on the slate floor. She's found a large pot from one of the abandoned houses, and based on the smell, several cans of chicken stock as well. The broth is boiling while a skewered chicken sizzles over the fire.

"Where did you find chicken?" I ask.

"There were a few still alive in a coop down the west side of town," Xavier says, poking at the fire. His eyes fall on Aiden. "Where did you find a boy?"

"I didn't think there were any survivors," my father says, looking up from the maps he's examining with Bo and Clipper.

"There aren't," Aiden answers. "It's just me and Rusty." The dog bounds forward, ecstatic.

"I told Aiden he was welcome to join us for dinner," Emma explains.

My father frowns but says, "Of course."

Not much later we are huddled around the fire, feeling warm for the first time in days and devouring chicken soup that tastes so delicious no one bothers with talking.

"They came three weeks ago tomorrow," Aiden announces suddenly. "I've been carving lines on my bedpost to keep track of the days."

My father pauses, a spoonful of soup halfway to his lips. "Who came?"

"Men. In black uniforms. They said they needed our water. I was upstairs in my bedroom when they arrived. Mama told me to stay there."

Aiden looks at the door as though the black-suited men may be waiting there.

"The well is right outside our house," he says finally. "I sometimes lean out my bedroom window and shoot pebbles into it with my slingshot. Sophie—she was my cousin—played, too."

Was. The boy has already adjusted how he refers to people who just three weeks ago were alive.

"The men walked right up to our well and started hauling out the water," Aiden continues. "Mr. Bennett, who worked at the blacksmith shop, came running and tried to stop them. He said bad words, a lot of them. The man in black said something about the country needing our water, and when Mr. Bennett didn't stop yelling, the man took out his gun and then Mr. Bennett was dead."

The room is so still the crackling fire sounds as loud as gunfire. Aiden starts shaking again, so Emma pulls him into her lap.

"They pumped the well dry and left. The next day, people started getting sick. Mama got a cough and locked me in my room with our last jug of water and a bunch of bread and cheese. I thought I'd done something bad because she had a handkerchief over her mouth and wouldn't look at me. She told me to keep my window shut and made me promise not to open it.

"I didn't. Not even when I saw them walking around town,

crying and coughing. Their skin peeled. Their eyes went yellow. Some of them got on their horses and left. Most went to the church and prayed. I watched them all from my window, but I kept it closed, just like Mama told me to. I didn't touch the window until it was silent, and when it was, I pushed it open and climbed out.

"Everyone that stayed was dead. Mama was in bed. I wanted to bury her, because I know that's what you're supposed to do, but I wasn't strong enough to move her. The only ones I could manage were the small ones. The babies. And Sophie. I buried Sophie, too."

He keeps talking, about how he lived off canned fruit and chicken eggs. How he melted snow for water and gathered clothes and blankets from other houses to keep warm. How he goes back to his house only once each day to record a nick on his bedpost, but never lingers because of the smell of decay. I don't understand how someone so young can go through so much alone.

"Rusty and I stay in Mr. Bennett's house because it's empty," Aiden explains. "I'm running out of food, though. And it's getting hard to feed all the chickens and horses—most are sick or dying. Are you going to leave me here? In the morning?"

"Of course not," Emma says, but no one else speaks up.

Bree has this pained look on her face and I know she's thinking the same thing I am: An eight-year-old boy is going to slow us down.

Owen runs a hand over his head and gazes at the fire. "We're on a strict schedule."

"You can't be serious."

"It's not like I want this, Emma, but we have to average around twenty miles a day. There's no way he'll keep up with us."

"So you're just going to leave him here?" She's almost shouting now. "You can't! We can put him on a horse if pace is your concern." My father remains quiet, refuses to make eye contact. Emma turns to me. "Tell him, Gray. Please. If anyone can talk sense into him it's you."

She looks even more desperate than she did when I found out about her and Craw, when she apologized to me again and again and again. I wonder if siding with her now will make our conversations come easier. They've been forced at best, even when we've been trying so hard.

But my father is right. We still have another two weeks of travel before we reach Bone Harbor, a small town that sits along a stretch of ocean cutting north through nearly half the country. A boat is waiting to ferry us closer to Group A while simultaneously keeping us out of the Order's eye. Without the boat, there's a domed city we'd have to pass near.

Haven, I think Clipper called it. Either way, Aiden will slow us drastically.

I glance at the boy and his face is hopeful in the firelight, his eyes as wide as Emma's. I don't want to let either of them down.

"If we leave him, we're as good as letting him starve to death," I say to my father.

He sighs, rubs his forehead. "You're right. You're both right." He looks at Aiden for a long while. Exhales again. Then finally: "You can come, but only until we find somewhere safer, a place you can settle with the living."

"Oh, thank you," Aiden exclaims. "Thank you! Can I bring Rusty, too?"

"Why not? It will be good to have a dog around. They're clever creatures, good judges of character, fantastic on watch."

Sammy frowns. "Sir, I'm honored you think so highly of me, but I'm a little offended you've mistaken me for a dog."

The group dissolves into laughter.

"Bed," Owen orders. "Everyone. Now. Breakfast is at first light and then we're moving again."

THREE

TONIGHT I HAVE SECOND WATCH, which means I might actually get a decent night of uninterrupted sleep. We rotate the order and it's the middle shifts that are the worst—I never feel rested the following day.

Outside it is cold and gusty. I have the woodworking shop at my back, blocking most of the wind, and Rusty at my side, keeping me company. He's a good guard dog, just as my father suspected. Twice he hears something before I do, his ears perking up, and both times it is nothing but a raccoon coming to feast on the dead.

I watch the minutes go by on a wristwatch that Clipper says runs on "solar power." He walks with it strapped to the outside of his pack each day, allowing the sun to warm its face so that it can tell time throughout each evening. When my hour's up, I head back inside, where everyone is cramped around the makeshift fire pit, fast asleep. I find Bo, who always follows me on watch, and shake him awake. He grumbles, pulls on his jacket, and heads out.

I creep around the fire and slide into my sleeping bag. Bree is on one side of me, my father on the other.

Despite being properly warm for the first time in ages, I can't fall asleep. In the darkness of the woodshop, all my doubts seem magnified. Group A seems so far away still, and Blaine farther behind with each day of hiking.

Bree rolls over, nudges into me for extra warmth. I can feel her pulse even with the sleeping bags between us. I smile, close my eyes, and suddenly sleep is easy.

The sound of Rusty barking jolts me awake. My father scrambles for the door, Sammy and Xavier trailing him. A moment later there is shouting outside and I know something is very wrong.

I grapple for my gear, but can't find one of my boots and end up being the last person to sprint outside. It's maybe an hour before dawn, still dark enough that it's difficult to see. I can make out several things in the bouncing beams of flashlights: Rusty, still barking like mad, and Aiden trying to restrain him; my father, surrounded by the rest of the group, shouting; and two strangers, one of whom has a gun to the other's head.

The hostage is young and lean and has a look on his face that appears more vicious than terrified. The other man is Blaine.

I skid to a stop. "How did you . . . Who is . . ." I have a million questions and they're all overlapping to the point that I can no longer get my mouth to work.

"Hey, Gray," Blaine says, beaming in my direction.

Sammy jerks his rifle at the hostage. "What the *hell* is going on? Someone better start talking or I'm putting bullets in you both."

Rusty barks savagely.

"The only person you want to put bullets in is this rat," Blaine says, pushing his handgun more firmly against the stranger's head.

"No one is putting bullets in anyone," my father yells. "Blaine, lower your weapon."

My brother grits his teeth. "Can't do that, Pa."

"Why's that?"

Rusty yelps and lunges against his rope.

"Because this piece of scum will attack us the second I do."

"It's not true," the stranger says. "I wouldn't—"

Blaine strikes him across the back of the head with his gun. "You lying piece of filth!"

I don't think I've ever seen Blaine so angry, so furious. It makes me fear the stranger he's holding more than I've feared anyone in my life.

Rusty keeps barking.

"Will someone shut up that dog?" my father snaps.

Emma grabs Aiden and helps him guide Rusty back to the woodshop, glancing fearfully over her shoulder as they leave. My father stares at Blaine and the stranger for a moment longer, eyes narrowed, then pulls his rifle up so fast I barely see it happen.

Blaine yanks the stranger in front of him as a shield. "What are you doing?"

"What any captain would do when two men walk into his camp without explanation: I'm protecting my team. You have to understand that this looks very odd, Blaine."

My brother stays sheltered behind his hostage's shoulder. "I left headquarters just three days after you did," he explains, "right around when one of our own got taken into Order custody. Ryder wanted to put Elijah on your tail, just in case the Order extracted mission details from our man and decided to send one of their own after you. Basically, Ryder wanted to send a Rebel shadow for the possible Order shadow.

"I kept telling Ryder it wasn't right, that I was healthy enough and I should be with the team, with you and Gray.

Family. Ryder ran me through a final endurance test—which I passed—and agreed to let me go in Elijah's place. I've been putting in twenty-five-plus miles a day just to catch up with you guys."

"Which means . . ." Owen's eyes go wide as he looks at the stranger before Blaine.

"Ryder was right. Frank got some mission details out of our man, because this guy"—Blaine shakes the hostage—"is with the Order. I've been hiking for about an hour already today, and I caught him just outside Stonewall, loading his handgun." Blaine tosses the extra weapon to Xavier.

"Is he the only spy?" my father asks.

"I think so. At least, he's the only person I've seen between headquarters and here."

"Your name?" my father asks the prisoner, whose skin is pale in the first light of dawn. He looks about my age and is perhaps just as reckless, because rather than answer my father's question, he spits on his boots.

Blaine shakes him forcefully.

"Jackson," the Order spy grunts. "My name is Jackson."

My father raises his weapon. "Well, Jackson. Any last words?"

"You can't kill me."

"That's an interesting theory. Perhaps we should test it."

"Oh, I'll die," he says, smiling slyly, "but Frank will know.

As soon as he loses my reading, he'll send someone to replace me. You're better off keeping me with you so that he thinks I'm still tailing your team."

I frown because he's right. Frank puts tracking technologies in all his soldiers, Order members and Heisted boys alike. One was unknowingly injected beneath my own skin last summer. Clipper removed it, living up to his nickname just moments after I met him. Once free of the device, Frank believed me dead. At least until I marched back to Taem with Harvey and Bree for the vaccine.

"I think we'll take our chances. You dead gives us a head start. A big one." Owen's finger reaches for the trigger and Jackson's face washes over with panic.

"Okay, wait-wait-wait," he sputters. "Let's talk this through for a minute. I don't know what your mission is; the Order couldn't get it out of the guy we captured. All we know is you're heading west, so I was sent to intercept you, learn the details of your mission, and try to uncover the location of your headquarters in the process. But let's just forget all that for a second and instead think about how useful it could be to have an Order member with you on this trek. Right? Eh?" He glances around for takers. "I can speak up for you in any Order-patrolled towns, help you avoid Frank's eye. You can even take out my tracker if you're willing to chance someone else being sent after the team, but don't kill me. Okay? *Please* don't kill me."

The team looks around at one another, startled by Jackson's willingness to fold.

"It's a sign of weakness," Owen says, weapon still poised, "betraying your kind so quickly."

"Only if you believe your life is worth less than the success of your mission," the spy says. "And I don't. I put my own life above Frank knowing why a handful of Rebels are on a hiking trip. Some would say self-preservation is the very opposite of weakness." He smiles. Wide.

"Knock him out," Owen says to Blaine.

Blaine strikes Jackson with his gun harder this time, sending the prisoner crumpling to the ground. Xavier rushes to bind his hands and feet, but my father keeps his weapon aimed at Blaine, his finger dangerously close to the trigger.

"Now holster that gun," he says.

Blaine does, but even still, Owen won't lower his. "I need proof," he says, jabbing the barrel in Blaine's direction. "I need it or I have to pull this trigger."

My brother looks stunned. "What more can I give you? He admitted he's with the Order!"

"Yes, and now I need proof that *you* aren't with them, too."

I know where this is headed, but it can't be true. I'd be able to tell. This is Blaine—scared, anxious, furious at a spy who was about to attack us—but it's him.

"Pa," I say, taking a step toward him. "It's Blaine. It has to be. He mentioned the conditioning test, and Ryder, and—"

"The Rebels have been deceived by Forgeries before. These are dangerous times and we can't be too careful." He glances back at Blaine, eyes narrowed. "Your brother has a few scars. Name them."

Blaine stifles a small laugh. "A few? He has more than a few."

"And if you are truly my son, you know Gray better than anyone in the world and this question will not be a problem."

Blaine looks at me. His blue eyes, the only feature that differentiates us, seem so colorless in the poor lighting that he could be my reflection. I give him an encouraging nod, and he starts listing off scars. A nick on my upper arm from a misfired arrow—his fault—when we were kids. The line on my palm from a poorly wielded knife—my fault—when whittling. A mark on my chest from falling on a jagged branch, stitches that scarred my chin after a fight with Chalice, the line along my neck from when Clipper removed my tracking device.

"And on his forearm," Blaine says. "Burns from the public square in Taem that scarred real bad."

I touch my arm, remembering my trip to Taem in the fall. Bree shot me with a rubber bullet so that I didn't have to execute Harvey on Frank's orders, and I ended up immobilized on a burning platform until Bo dragged me to safety. My father must have been waiting for Blaine to speak of this scar—a detailed account of an injury that healed within the safety of Crevice Valley, away from Order eyes—because he finally lowers his rifle.

Owen yanks the collar of Blaine's jacket back to reveal a small, thin scar. Clipper's work, done the same day he tended to my tracking device. Then Owen clasps a hand on either side of Blaine's face. "I'm sorry I had to interrogate you like that."

Blaine winks. "Like what?"

Owen pulls him into a quick hug and then turns to address the rest of us. "The spy makes a good point. Having someone to cover for us if we stumble across the Order gives us an advantage we can't pass up. And so long as we have his life as a bargaining chip, he should remain loyal. Soon as we clip him, Frank's bound to send another in his place though, so let's eat quickly and get back on the move."

The group disbands for breakfast, and I'm left alone with Blaine, still staring in disbelief.

"You're really here," I say.

He flashes me a smile. "I have to look after you, don't I? You wouldn't last long without me."

Almost the same words he said when he woke from his

coma. The joke he makes over and over because while the two of us are perfectly self-sufficient, we both know we're better together.

"You're full of it," I say, but I pull him into a hug anyway. His arms are stiff, his clasp weak. When I step back he looks exhausted. "You okay?"

"Yeah. Just tired. And sore. And my chest's been burning the last few days. Maybe Ryder was right all along. Maybe I wasn't ready for this."

"You absolutely weren't."

He shoves me and I'm sent stumbling through the shallow snow, laughing. "Stop that right now," he says. "I'm supposed to be the big brother."

"You're older by a couple minutes, Blaine. Get over it."

"Never." He smiles and it brings some of the light back into his eyes. They momentarily look the way I remember—brilliant and bluer than a summer sky. "Now, did someone say something about food?"

"It's only grits."

But you'd think I'd said bacon and eggs from the look on his face.

FOUR

WHILE THERE IS NO BACON, breakfast does end up including some luxuries. September has decided that if we are leaving the town and Aiden is coming with us, there is no need to let a stocked chicken coop go to waste. I have to admit: Grits taste far better when paired with eggs.

Emma wants to bury the deceased, or at the very least make a pyre, but my father says it would take far too much time to gather all the remains, not to mention the fact that a giant plume of smoke puts us at risk of being spotted. So Sammy retrieves a small, black book from the building where we found Aiden, and we stand around the well while he reads about giving rest to the labored. It's odd to hear Sammy's voice so serious, to have it stir up feelings like remorse and compassion when until now it's drawn out only laughter.

As soon as Sammy closes the book, Blaine escorts Jackson from the woodshop. He's conscious now, but still bound and gagged. Blaine wrestles him to the ground and Clipper pulls the clipping device from his pack. The entire thing is over in a matter of seconds, but Jackson screams and writhes for far longer.

Watching from beyond the well, Emma is cringing. Like the rest of us, she knows the pain. She underwent a precautionary clipping when I brought her from Taem to Crevice Valley after securing the vaccine. I was surprised when Clipper found a tracker in her, but the boy pointed out that while Emma never served as a soldier in Frank's Order, she *did* work in his hospitals, and Frank has never been one to take his security lightly.

When the clipping procedure is over, we pack our bags and ready ourselves for another day of travel. Xavier rounds up the healthiest two horses from the stables. Aiden is set to ride a dapple gray named Merlin while the second steed, a white mare called Snow, is loaded up with hay and grain for the both of them.

Sammy bursts from the woodshop, Rusty in tow. The dog is bounding playfully—at least until he spots Jackson, at which point his ears fold back, and he starts growling.

"This dog," Sammy grunts, tugging to restrain him. "I

thought the kid said he was good."

"He is," I say, looking between Jackson and the dog. "He doesn't like the spy. It's like he can sense he's up to something."

"I haf a name," Jackson grunts through the handkerchief in his mouth.

"Your name's Jackson," Aiden says from Merlin's back. "I heard everyone talking about you during breakfast."

Jackson starts, staring at the small boy. "Yeah. It is."

"Whatever," Sammy says. "The dog hates him and I'm going to have to keep this thing leashed, and at a distance, or even a deaf man will hear us coming." Rusty lunges, snapping, and Blaine and Jackson skirt out of the way to protect their heels.

"Great," Blaine says. "I stand too close to the scum and the dog doesn't trust me either."

"Jackson," the spy says through the gag.

"Right," Blaine says. "Sorry." But he doesn't look it.

We start walking, our growing team again on the move. I glance back only once. The crows are already diving, anxious to return to their feast.

At midday we pause to give Owen, Bo, and Clipper a few minutes to discuss our route. There is a small town ahead according to Clipper's location device, and after the fiasco

Stonewall became, my father is desperate to avoid it.

From the back of his horse, Aiden has taken to playing a hand game he calls Rock, Paper, Scissors with, of all people, the Order spy. Jackson still has his mouth gagged and his arms tied behind his back, so he has to shout his selection as Aiden pushes his hand out to reveal his choice. The spy looks pretty miserable about the entire affair.

Aiden counts, bobbing a fist up and down to the numbers. "One . . . two . . . three!"

"Pahpur," Jackson says, and at the same time, Aiden's fist opens to form scissors. He snips them at Jackson, beaming.

"Again. One . . . two . . . three!"

"Roch!"

Aiden's fist is now flat.

"You're chea'in'," Jackson mumbles through the gag.

"Nuh-uh."

The spy frowns. "Den you're rea'ing my mind."

They get in one last round, Jackson again losing, before Emma pulls the boy from Merlin's back.

"Let's not get too fond of the prisoner, Aiden," she says.

"But he plays with me. No one else does."

Sammy bursts through the snow, being dragged by Rusty, who is barking at Jackson yet again. "I'd play if it wasn't for this crazed animal. I think my forearms are going to give out."

Emma laughs at this and Aiden relieves Sammy of the dog; the boy's touch seems to be the only thing to calm the animal. Rusty curls up at Aiden's feet, but he doesn't take his eyes off the spy.

Sammy links his fingers together and pushes them into a stretch. "Who'd have thought I'd spend my twenty-first birthday like this: cold, frozen, and being tugged through the forest by a manic dog."

"Today's your birthday?" I ask.

"It's the eleventh, isn't it?"

I try to count back to when we left. The date sounds right, but I'm not positive.

"Clipper!" Sammy calls across camp. "What's the date, genius?"

The boy doesn't turn around to face us—he's too deep in conversation with my father and Bo—but he holds his hands overhead, each with a pointer finger raised to the sky.

"The eleventh," Sammy says. "Yup. Twenty-one today."

"Another December birthday," Bree chimes in. "I'm the twenty-third."

I'm shocked to discover that until now, I didn't know Bree's birthday. How has such a basic detail never come up?

"We should do something," Emma says. "You know, to celebrate."

"Find a pub and I'm in," Bree deadpans.

Sammy snorts. "Me, too, Nox. Me, too." He jerks his head at Emma. "Have any backup plans, Link? You know, since there are no drinks in sight?"

Sammy has a habit of calling people by their last name, but for some reason, it bothers me when he refers to Emma this way. Emma and Bree both have harsh-sounding last names, but only Bree's suits her.

"Yeah, actually. I do." Emma grabs a small sack of grain from Snow's back and sets it on the stump of a fallen tree about twenty paces away. "Archery match," she says, pointing at the target. "Right now."

Sammy's eyes liven. "Oh, you're on. Who else is in?"

I raise a hand. Xavier and September come join us.

"Hey, Blaine? You playing?" I call out.

He shakes a thumb at Jackson. "Have to hold this rat so he doesn't run off."

"I'll watch him," Bree says.

"You're passing up an archery match?" I ask, shocked.

She shrugs. "A bow and arrow is not my preferred weapon of choice."

"So you're saying you can only fire that thing," Emma says, eyeing the rifle in Bree's hands.

"Is that a challenge?"

"Maybe."

September and Xavier let out a series of *ooohs*, and Sammy starts whistling.

"Fine," Bree snaps. "I'll play."

Xavier and I are the only two in the group who opted for a bow when we left Crevice Valley, so ours are passed around as the match progresses. There are six of us playing and we agree to knock off two people with each round. The first round is shot from twenty paces. To my surprise, September, who is deadly with a firearm, doesn't even come close to hitting the target. Everyone else strikes true, including Emma. I'm proud to think that I trained her months ago in Claysoot, and I compliment her form. Sammy's arrow ends up being the farthest from the sack's center, so he joins September off to the side.

I fire a perfect shot in the next round. Xavier slips in the snow and shoots wide, but both Emma and Bree strike close to my arrow. Bree is a tad high, Emma a tad low.

"Not bad," I tell Emma again. Bree snorts from behind me, but if she expects praise for *missing* a bull's-eye, she's crazy.

"Aiden wants to help judge!" Sammy scoops the boy onto his shoulders and comes racing through the show. Once we're all gathered around the target, Sammy points at the two outlying arrows. "All right, Aiden. Which of these is closest to the center one?"

Aiden screws up his face in concentration and finally points at the arrow below mine.

Bree throws up her hands. "Of course he'd pick Emma's. He hates me!"

"We didn't tell him which arrow was hers," Sammy points out.

"Ugh, whatever. I'd slaughter you all if this was a spear-throwing match. We didn't use arrows much in Saltwater, you know. A spear is far more effective for catching fish."

"But it's *not* a spear-throwing match," I say, nudging her with my elbow.

She scowls at me, furious, and stalks off. I should have known better than to joke with her during a competition.

"Don't you want to see who wins?" I call after her.

"I couldn't care less."

"Moody thing, huh?" Xavier says. "Must be that time of the month."

Sammy smirks. "Yeah, these next few days should be downright peachy."

September and Emma glare at the both of them.

"What?" Sammy asks innocently. "Can't a guy speak his mind on his birthday?" Xavier buckles with laughter.

Even I can't help smiling.

"What time of the month is it?" Aiden asks from atop Sammy's shoulders.

"Forget it, Aiden," Emma says. "They're just being boys."

"But I'm a boy! I want to know."

"How about we finish the game? You can judge the final shot, too, if you'd like."

"Okay," he agrees.

But when we get back to the shooting spot, Rusty is trying to have another go at Jackson, and Blaine is somehow stuck in the middle of it. His pack is held out like a shield, protecting him from the dog's jaws. The Order spy stands safely behind him, laughing through his gag. Aiden calls Rusty off and Blaine throws his pack in the snow.

"That dog needs to get it through his thick skull," he snarls. "Yes, the prisoner is with the Order. Yes, he's no good. But he's going to be with us for a while, and I'm not okay with losing a limb because the dog feels like attacking *me* in the process of getting to *him*!"

"Blaine, are you feeling all right?" Emma asks. She reaches out to him and he shrugs away. "You're not one to get worked up over something so small."

"He would have killed me just to get at the spy, Emma. I swear it," he says. "That's no small matter."

"All right!" my father calls out. "Clipper got us straightened away. We need to cut south for a few miles."

"But the match," Sammy says. "Emma and Gray have to play the final round."

My father looks between us. "Gray would win—no offense, Emma—and we have a pace to maintain. This is not negotiable."

We start walking again, but tensions are high. Clipper's worried about the nearby town; my father, our pace. Sammy's sullen and Blaine, suspicious. He keeps glaring at Rusty and holding the spy in front of him as protection. And Bree's ill temper is transmitting in waves so thick it could knock a person over.

When I ask her if she's okay, she rolls her eyes and walks faster.

Somehow, I feel like I'm at fault, even though I obviously have no control over any arrow fired but my own.

FIVE

THAT NIGHT AFTER DINNER, WE disperse into smaller groups around the fire. My father and Clipper are deep in conversation, likely discussing our path. Again. Xavier is hard at work drying out his socks—he's stuck them on the end of a forked stick so he can dangle them over the fire like roasted meat—and Aiden is back to playing Rock, Paper, Scissors with the spy.

Someone removed Jackson's gag and retied his hands in his lap so that he could eat, and he's now able to make hand gestures back at the boy. He has a look on his face that almost appears big-brotherly as he plays with Aiden, not at all like the blood-hungry Order-spy-on-a-mission that we know he is. Blaine hovers nearby, watchful. Rusty, too, while not barking, hasn't stopped snarling in Jackson's direction. If I were the spy, I wouldn't make a single sudden move with that dog around.

I'm sitting with everyone else, listening to Sammy ramble about his childhood in Taem. Bree, who hasn't said a word to me since the archery match, has taken especial interest in his story. Mostly, I think, so she has an excuse to not make eye contact with me. Emma, on the other hand, seems to have zero interest in Sammy's words. She keeps twisting around to check on Aiden, her shoulder knocking against mine each time.

"He's fine," I whisper to her. Blaine's been looking at the boy the same way he looked at his daughter, Kale, back in Claysoot. Like he wants to show him the world and teach him everything he knows and protect him with his own life if it comes to it. I don't understand how Blaine can care so much for a person he's only recently met. More proof that he's a better person than me.

"I just worry about him," Emma says, as if I didn't already know this. She hasn't taken her eyes off Aiden since he joined our group, and he hasn't wandered far from her side either. The fact that he's sitting with Jackson—farther than an arm's length from Emma—is a small miracle in itself.

"Well, you're wasting your energy. He's with Blaine. He's as safe as he'll ever be."

Emma gives me a look that seems to say, *You know I can't help worrying.*

". . . I was barely six when he died," Sammy says, and we're both pulled back to the conversation happening beside us.

"Who died?" Emma asks.

"My great-grandfather. He lived through the Second Civil War and watched Frank come into power nearly fifty years ago. Man, the stories he would tell."

"Like?" I prompt.

"They're not really fireside material."

"And this isn't a typical campfire in the woods," Bree points out.

"Fair enough, Nox," Sammy says. "Fair enough." He tosses snow at the fire for a moment, listening to it sizzle.

"He used to talk about how chaotic things were in the years between the Continental Quake and the Second Civil War. That was his favorite word for it all—*chaotic.*"

"Well, it fits," September chimes in. "We learned about it all in middle school. Decades before the Quake, scientists were predicting massive shifts in the Earth's plates. Plus, the climate was changing. Getting hotter, drier. There was less rain and more droughts, and the ocean levels were rising like crazy. A lot of major cities were in jeopardy of flooding. That's where Robert Taem came in."

"Taem like the city?" Bree asks.

"People forget it was named after him," Bo says. He starts tapping on his knee, his fingers unable to stay still, and September nods in agreement.

"Taem was the engineer behind the domed design—nearly indestructible, safe from harsh suns, better air quality. The government contracted him to make it, and then the capital ended up beneath it, farther inland and safe from the rising ocean. Voilà! The city of Taem."

"My great-grandfather used to joke that Robert Taem knew what was coming, but he couldn't have," Sammy says. "Not really. Taem died young, long before the War."

"I don't even think he saw all the other domed cities spring up," September adds. "But they did, all based on his original design."

"I thought we were talking about the years between the Quake and the War," Bree interjects.

"I'm getting there, Nox." Sammy takes a swig from his waterskin before continuing. "My great-grandfather had enough money to move to Taem with his fiancée. It was expensive to buy your way under a dome, but he got lucky, especially with the timing. Two months after his move, the Continental Quake hit: a half dozen widespread earthquakes in the course of three days. The coasts pretty much all fell into the ocean. The gulf ate its way up the center of the country. Rivers and streams flooded with salt water.

Roads were upturned and cities toppled—including some domed ones. If the ground falls out from beneath a place, it's not going to stay standing no matter how indestructible its outer shell is.

"People obviously panicked. My great-grandfather said the world outside still-standing domes became like a war zone. Everyone was looting abandoned stores, stealing from neighbors. Law enforcement was stretched too thin. Hospitals were over capacity. And then when the flooding didn't slow, the government started barricading and controlling freshwater resources. Clean water went to the capital first, then the surrounding areas."

"And it was taxed like crazy," Bo chimes in. "I heard people muttering about that during my time in Taem. The farther water had to be shipped, the more expensive it was."

"Not exactly how disaster relief should work," Sammy says. "The West got furious—threatened everything imaginable, including secession. The capital ignored it all, and that, according to my great-grandfather, was when they attacked."

"The virus?" Bree prompts. I know the one she's referencing—the virus AmWest used to initiate war on AmEast—the very same virus that Frank's lab workers transformed into the threat we faced in the fall.

"A Western movement dropped it in Big Water," September

says. "They were trying to take control of some water sources in that territory, but the damn thing mutated, spread, took on new forms. Even killed a bunch of the West's own soldiers. Domed cities went on lockdown, but outside, people were dropping like flies."

"And so began the Second Civil War," Bo says rather casually, which makes me wonder how many times he heard these stories in Taem to become so numb. "The East staged a counterattack. Millions of lives were lost—to bombs, to disease. Point is, the country tore itself apart from the inside until two separate nations emerged: AmWest, their secession complete, and AmEast, led by Frank's father, Dominic Frank."

"And your great-grandfather was in Taem during all that fighting?" I ask Sammy.

"Yup, and the way he told it, Dominic was a decent ruler. It was only when Frank took over that things fell apart. Frank didn't trust the people, so he stripped away everything he saw as a risk to a unified AmEast. Books, music, art—anything that could encourage debate or confrontation was declared illegal."

"That doesn't even make sense," Bree says. "Debate's a good thing. And why didn't Frank focus on AmWest? They were clearly the enemy, not his own people."

"Look, Nox," Sammy says. "I get it. Really, I do. It's messed up."

"There has to be a reason. A motive. *Something*."

September leans forward, firelight dancing on her face. "A few years after the War, when Frank was at college in Taem, his father—his mother and younger brother, too—were murdered. They were distributing water to communities in AmEast's Western Territory—not far from where Group A now stands. AmWest soldiers stormed the square, shot Frank's family and every Order member in sight. Then they took off with the water. The people of AmEast did nothing to stop it, and if there was a moment that caused Frank to snap, I'd imagine that was it."

"That's not the way my great-grandfather told it," Sammy says. "His cousin was there that day; he said AmWest was only looking to take out the Order, but Frank's family was killed in the crossfire. When the bullets stopped flying, AmWest apparently gave a speech about how the Franconian Order wasn't the solution to rebuilding the country. It was a brand-new division back then," he says quickly, reading the confusion on my face, "aimed at instilling peace between the two countries."

"Regardless of its goals, AmWest never liked the Order," Bo says. "They always felt that the people should rebuild the country together, not have it forced upon them at gunpoint by law officials wearing black. Sort of admirable, I think."

September scoffs. "Well, they're not teaching Sammy's

great-grandfather's version of the event in school."

"Of course not!" Sammy says. "Frank wants us to all believe the version where AmWest mercilessly assassinates his family. It paints him as an advocate for justice."

"Are you saying you think AmWest isn't despicable?" September counters. "After the virus that started the War? The fight they continue today? I mean, they just attacked Taem over the summer!"

Sammy rubs the back of his neck, but doesn't answer.

"I think the point here is that Frank stepped into his father's shoes with motives more deeply rooted in revenge than justice," Bo says.

"But it's the people of AmEast suffering most under Frank's rule," Emma points out. "People not even responsible for his parents' death."

"I know that. You know that," Bo says. "But if it had been you in Frank's place, do you think that day might have broken you?"

Months ago, when I was first in Taem, I saw an image of a family on Frank's office wall. I understand now that Frank was the older of the two boys. His mother was smiling, her arms on his brother's shoulders, his father looking stern. Frank's family hangs there, always reminding him, always motivating him. I wonder if Frank's ever noticed that his goal of avenging them has slipped into a territory that can no longer be considered admirable.

"So then he started the Laicos Project," I say. "He began growing his soldiers, boys he could later replicate to fight against AmWest, to serve in the Order."

"And girls," Bree points out. "Boys *and* girls."

Sammy nods. "Yup. You lot are just another piece in the puzzle of a man spiraling out of control. But of course, no one has stopped him. He is still bent on demolishing AmWest, and he fights that battle daily. And although he's restricted the lives of people in AmEast, he's also managed to keep up the work of his father, getting water to almost everyone in need. Rationed and highly taxed water, but still. Plus the Order is loyal to him, as are the majority of citizens in his cities. They know life's far worse outside the domes."

"Yeah, like in Stonewall," I say. "Where he takes their water and gets them all sick in the process."

"I never said it was right," Sammy says.

"None of us have," Bo adds. "But I can understand his motives in some weird, twisted way."

I hate to admit it, but I can, too. I look over at Blaine, who is smiling as Aiden beats Jackson in yet another round of their game. I've already lost my mother to illness. I remember what it felt like to lose Blaine to the Heist. If they'd been taken from me all at once—murdered—I know I'd spend the rest of my life trying to avenge their deaths.

Aiden turns to play a round of his hand game with Blaine. The boy reveals scissors; my brother, a rock. Blaine reaches out to clunk Aiden with his fist, but he moves too quickly, or too forcefully, because Rusty lunges. Blaine is thrown backward into the snow. It's not until he starts screaming, wrestling against the dog locked on to his forearm, that I'm jolted into action.

I sprint across camp. Aiden is trying to call the animal off, but it clearly has no intention of letting go. I throw myself onto the dog, latch my hands in his mouth, and tug. I'm bleeding almost immediately, but I pry harder, attempting to loosen the animal's grip. His paws slash at me; his teeth clamp down. And then I feel someone else tug at the animal's jaws. Jackson. His hands are still bound and yet he's helping me force open Rusty's mouth. The dog's grip gives, and Blaine scrambles backward, cursing and clutching his arm to his chest.

"That dog is crazy!" he shouts.

Aiden puts a hand on Rusty, whispering until he calms. "He thought you were attacking me, that's all."

Blaine mutters a few curses as I kneel next to him. His forearm is a mess of blood and shredded clothing. I call for Emma, but she's already there. Clipper hovers, flashlight poised.

Emma cuts Blaine's sleeve open. She works swiftly,

disinfecting the wound, washing away the blood, and dressing his arm in bandages. She takes the flashlight from Clipper to better inspect the rest of his arm—the minor cuts and scratches from the dog's paws—and then focuses the light on Blaine's face, his eyes.

"Blaine?" she says, her hand resting on his forehead. "Do you feel okay?"

He blinks rapidly. "It's too bright."

She looks at him hesitantly. "He'll be fine." Then she moves on to me and Jackson, examining our hands, shining her light in our eyes as well. She still looks confused when she finishes with the spy. Shaking her head, Emma packs up the gear and walks away to clean the used equipment.

The team is discussing what to do with the dog, which Aiden hugs as though it is harmless, but I'm staring at Jackson. He's on the outskirts of camp, gazing into the trees like he's thinking of running for it. The gag, which Emma loosened when she attended to him, hangs around his neck.

"You helped," I say.

"Was there a reason I shouldn't have?" When he looks at me, his eyes are too bright. Hopeful. I step away from him.

"We're still keeping you bound and gagged. This doesn't change anything."

He shrugs. "It was worth a try."

SIX

LATER, WHEN THE COMMOTION HAS died down and people have settled back around the fire, I approach Blaine. We sit shoulder to shoulder, staring through the branches that scrape at the sky. The moon is bright, nearly full, and it makes the stars seem minuscule.

"I used to do this sometimes in Claysoot," I say to him.

"Get bitten by dogs?"

I laugh. "Stare at the sky. When you were snoring too much, I'd sneak out to the crop fields."

"I used to do the same," he says.

"Really? I didn't know that."

"That you snored, or that I used the same escape?"

"Both."

Blaine glances at my hands. "You going to have another scar to add to the list?"

"Nah. They should heal all right. What about you?"

He touches his bandaged arm and winces. "Not sure. But the dog's dangerous. We should put it down."

"Pa already discussed it. Rusty stays. He's so astute, he'll be able to warn us if the spy is up to something."

"And he might chew someone's limb off in the process."

A star streaks across the sky, and we point to it at the same time, Blaine gasping at the pain the movement causes.

"If Pa thinks we should keep him, we're keeping him," I say.

Blaine turns toward me and even with the shadows obscuring his face, I can tell he's hurting.

"You're gonna side with Pa?" he says. "Over me?"

"If the dog attacks again, I'm on your side. You come first. Always."

He turns back to the stars, smiling. "Always."

I wake to Xavier's foot jabbing at my sleeping bag.

"It's your watch."

I feel like I only just closed my eyes. "But Sammy always follows you."

"Owen gave him the night off. Special birthday privileges."

I grumble and pull on a few more layers, feel around the

corners of the tent for my hat. Bree stirs beside me. Like most nights, she came to my tent just a few hours earlier, only this visit she was uncharacteristically sweet. I think she was trying to make up for her attitude during (and following) the archery match.

I know the two of us shouldn't let our guard down so much in the evenings, but sleeping alongside her is the only small comfort that exists on this mission. It melts my fears, silences the constant worry, makes me brave in a way I've never experienced before. It also doesn't hurt that I like the feel of her lips on mine—like the feel of her in general.

"Is it your hour?" she mumbles.

"Yeah. I'll be back soon. Don't go anywhere."

But even as I crawl outside I know she will. She never stays through a full evening. She'll sneak back to her own tent before I return from watch. Just like how she always darted back to her room on those nights we fell asleep together in Crevice Valley, leaving me to wake up alone, the only sign of her an impression on my pillow.

I head for the fire pit, where Xavier left the watch propped up on a stick. Fifty-eight minutes until I can wake Bo to take over. Three more minutes go by and my eyelids grow heavy. Another two and it's a struggle to keep them open at all.

I hear the gentle crunch of snow. Bree, sneaking back to her tent as I predicted. But no, the sound is coming from the opposite side of camp. Near Blaine's tent. He's been pitching it at a distance because he's been tasked with keeping an eye on Jackson, and if they stay too near Rusty, the dog spends the entire night growling.

A moment later, I hear whispers. Worried the spy is giving my brother trouble, I steal toward the voices. The nearly full moon makes crossing camp relatively easy and I spot Blaine standing just beyond his tent. Sure enough, he's arguing with Jackson.

"The dog is no good," Blaine is whispering, his voice tense.

"I'm not killing it," the spy answers.

Blaine thrusts a knife at him. "It's just a dog. Do it."

"But Aiden . . . It will crush him."

"He'll think a wolf got to it. Or a coyote."

"If you want it done so badly, do it yourself."

Blaine must be scared senseless, asking Jackson to kill the dog in the middle of the night. Why wouldn't Blaine come to *me* if he was so worried? I promised I was on his side just earlier.

"Blaine?" I call out. He sees me and grabs Jackson's arm, yanking him closer. "What's going on?"

"Nothing." But his voice quavers slightly. "The spy had to take a piss so I was escorting him."

Why is he lying to me?

"I know what's really happening here," I say, looking between him and Jackson. "Why can't you just tell me, Blaine?"

He laughs. "Tell you? I couldn't tell you!"

What could be so terrible about admitting you're scared of a dog? I pause, wondering if I've misinterpreted something, when he adds, "And you can't tell anyone either. I won't let you."

Footsteps approach, and I turn to see a sleepy Emma walking to meet us. "You guys are going to wake the whole camp if you can't keep it down," she says.

What happens next unfolds so quickly I blink and nearly miss it. Blaine shoves Jackson aside and grabs Emma. He pulls her into his chest and brings the knife to her neck. All I can do is pull my bow up instinctively, an arrow already nocked, and aim at my brother.

"You figured it out, you sly little weasel," he snarls at me. "How did you know? *When* did you know?"

"Blaine," I say slowly. "I don't know what you're talking about."

"Yes, you do," he hisses. "You said so yourself: *I know what's really happening here.* What tipped you off?"

"Blaine," I plead. "Put the knife down." He's gone crazy. The dog must have been sick, and then he bit Blaine, and now Blaine's sick, too. Emma is shaking, her hands clutching at Blaine's bandaged forearm, which pins her to his chest.

"I kn-knew it," she stutters. "They're wrong. Both of them."

"What?"

"It's their pupils. They don't dilate properly."

"Shut up," Blaine says, and he presses the knife to her neck.

"And the dog."

Blaine shakes her. "That's enough."

"The dog hates them both. Neither of them are right."

"I said that's enough!"

Neither of them are right. Are they both sick? Are they—

And then, I see it. Blaine always passing off the dog's aggression as a hatred of the spy. Blaine hugging me in Stonewall, his arms stiff. I didn't notice anything odd about his pupils, or Jackson's, but Emma must have, when she'd tended to them just earlier. Even still, I don't want to believe it. It can't be—not when Owen interrogated Blaine the way he did, checked for his clipping scar.

"Blaine," I say, hoping that something in my voice will resonate with him. "Please?"

I take a small step forward, and he pinches the blade into Emma's neck. Blood blooms against the weapon, against her pale skin, and when she cries out in pain, I know this is not my brother. Not really. Blaine would never force me into this position. He would never hold a knife to Emma or spill even a drop of her blood.

We've been deceived. We are not dealing with one spy; we are dealing with two.

And they are Forgeries.

I do the only thing I can think of: I let my arrow fly.

It strikes true. Blaine's head whips back, and he falls, releasing Emma. She staggers to me, collapses against my chest. My arms go around her, squeezing, hugging tighter and tighter until it sinks in. What I've just done.

Jackson is standing over the darkening snow, a smile tugging at his lips. I shove him aside and then I'm yelling, screaming. I drop to my knees.

The camp is awake now. Someone is trying to nurse the fire to life. Owen is shouting orders. But my hands are moving of their own accord, checking Blaine's neck, finding the same thin scar my father did. It doesn't make sense. I pick up the knife and cut open the leg of Blaine's pants. There is no scar on his thigh, no sign of an arrow wound when there abso-lutely should be. My brother was hit when we fled through the Great Forest over the summer. This thing, now dead in the snow, was made without knowledge of that injury. And whoever put the mark along his neck was not Clipper.

I throw a fist into his chest, curse him, start choking down sobs. Why couldn't I see it? How could I not sense something so wrong in my own brother? I look at Blaine's face for the first time, the arrow in his forehead. I throw up in the snow. I cough and pant and heave and scream until Owen drags me away from the body.

SEVEN

JACKSON IS SHOVED INTO THE snow before the fire.

"Explain." It is a one-word command from my father and Jackson yawns at it.

I lose control and punch him as hard as I can. "Blaine brought you to us with a gun to your head! And now you're on the same side?"

Jackson smiles but doesn't say anything. I hit him again and my knuckles split open. At least he's bleeding now, too: a bloody nose. I hope I broke it.

"Answer us, Forgery," Owen demands.

Jackson rolls his eyes, like we're boring him. "Blaine brought me in because we planned it that way. He pretended I was the enemy because we planned that, too. Everything we did we planned, except for, well . . . this." He jerks his head toward the body in the snow.

"But Blaine had a clipping scar," my father says. "He was flawless when I questioned him. He even knew about the burn on Gray's forearm. How could he—" Owen exhales sharply. "Our man! The one the Order captured." His eyes snap to Jackson. "Your people got information from him. How much, exactly, do you know?"

Jackson shrugs and this time it is Owen who strikes him. He shakes out his hand, opening and clenching his fist repeatedly. "You will answer my questions without cheek or I will make sure you regret every moment from here on. Is that clear?"

Jackson spits a mouthful of blood onto the snow.

"Let's try this again." My father kneels before him and I'm struck by how terrifying he looks in the moment. I've never before seen this side of my father, a man who someone should fear. "Explain everything."

Jackson glances at my father's fist and sighs. "You're right, okay? The Rebel we caught leaked information when pressed accordingly. He was willing to lose a few fingers, but not an entire limb." Another coy smile, as though the Forgery finds this detail amusing. "He told us a small group of your people was heading west on a specialized mission. The boy who infiltrated Taem to steal the vaccine would be a part of the team, while his twin"—Jackson's eyes flick my way—"who was still recovering from a coma, would not. We gathered as much information on Gray as possible—learned that he sustained injuries to his arm and that he wanted his brother with him on the trip, but Blaine had failed to pass conditioning tests. The prisoner was willing to die rather than divulge the goals of your mission, though, or the location of your headquarters, so that's exactly what he did: He died."

"And you were sent after us?" my father asks.

"Blaine and I were already out patrolling the Great Forest when we got the call. We were given orders to track your team, uncover your plans, and stop them as necessary, all while trying to determine the location of your headquarters. That was the main goal: getting the coordinates and relaying them as soon as possible.

"We picked up your trail easily enough. It was the hiking that was rough—ten days of nearly nonstop pursuit. When we caught up with you at Stonewall, infiltrating seemed smartest, especially since Blaine would be recognized, so we agreed on a cover: I'd be an Order spy in his custody. We each played a part, and he, clumsily, botched his."

"And Blaine's scar?" my father prompts. "The one on his neck?"

"Oh, he's had that ever since Gray came back to Taem for

the vaccine. Frank saw Gray's neck, knew the Rebels had found a way to remove tracking devices. He marked some of us after that—anyone he suspected to have fallen into your hands." Jackson's eyes dart over each of us in turn, like he's waiting for someone to congratulate him on how deceitful he's been. He's suddenly so different from the desperate spy we met in Stonewall. Cool, calculating, unfazed.

"If I'm smart about things, I can still complete my mission," he adds.

"Like hell you can," Xavier snaps from the other side of camp.

Jackson laughs. "Why not? I've already uncovered your mission details by simply listening. The whole thing's ridiculous! Group A? Frank gave you too much credit—the way he assumed you'd try to extend your reach into the west, strike up allegiances. But fine, I'll keep tagging along on your pointless crusade. And when the time presents itself, I'll slay you. One at a time. Slowly. Until someone divulges headquarters' location."

"You realize you were one of us once, right?" I say through clenched teeth. "The real Jackson spent his childhood behind a Wall. He was Heisted to make *you*. You're Frank's puppet, and you're doing everything the real Jackson wouldn't want."

"It doesn't matter what you say," he says quietly. "My mind

can't be changed. I know what I have to do."

I believe him even though I don't want to. Harvey told me as much. The difference between a Forgery that can think for itself and a Forgery that blindly does Frank's bidding is a piece of code—software as smoothly integrated with the replica's brain as the blood that runs through its veins.

"I can change your mind," I say.

"I'd like to see you try."

I have an arrow nocked before Jackson even finishes speaking.

"You won't fire that. Not with what I know."

"What you know?" my father echoes.

"I'm a soldier. A technologically enhanced soldier over-loaded with secrets. Do you have any idea how much confidential information is swimming around in my head? City maps. Computer passwords. Access codes to safes and storage units and maybe even Outer Rings."

No one says anything. Jackson's grin grows wider.

"What were you planning to do when you reached Group A? Push the Outer Ring's wall over?" he says. "It's taller than the interior Wall—surrounds the whole place. You need me or you'll just stand there, staring at a dead end."

Bo steps between Sammy and Emma on the opposite side of the fire. "You said *maybe*," he calls out. "Access codes to storage units and *maybe* Outer Rings."

Jackson grunts. "I can't very well tell you how to open the door now. It's my only leverage."

"Then maybe you're lying and we should just get this over with," I say, raising my bow.

"Shoot me now and you're already doomed to reach a dead end. But if you keep me alive, things can go one of two ways: I open the Outer Ring for you and you actually have a chance to complete your stupid mission. Or, I was lying all along, you hit a dead end later rather than sooner, and shoot me then instead of now. Your pick."

Bo shifts uncomfortably. Emma is shivering behind him—still in shock or maybe just cold. Sammy puts his coat on her shoulders. And Jackson keeps smiling. That arrogant, cocky smile that I want to wipe right off his face.

"The Forgery lives," my father announces. "We believe Clipper can get us into the Outer Ring, but on the rare chance he *can't*, this is a solid backup plan and we'd be foolish to waste it. If the Forgery is lying about what he knows, it's just like he said: He'll die then instead of now."

Owen turns and asks Emma to show the team what she recognized in Jackson's and Blaine's eyes. Sammy is in the process of bandaging her neck, but she agrees to explain everything when he's finished.

"I still can't believe it," Bree says next to me. "Blaine. Even after we interrogated him. It's—" She stops, touches my arm. "Hey, are you okay?"

Sammy's brushing Emma's hair to the side so he can better see the cut on her neck. He must say something funny because she lets out a small laugh. Bree follows my gaze and frowns.

"Gray?"

Xavier shouts for Sammy to help him move Blaine's body away from camp, and I feel nauseous all over again.

"I just need a minute," I say to Bree.

I want to be alone right now. *Need* to be alone. She has the decency to not give me a hard time about it.

I wander away from the tents, slip between the trees. When I find a fallen pine, I sit on the trunk, cringe at the sting of an oncoming headache. The moment I close my eyes, I see it all over again: Blaine's head whipping back from the force of my arrow, his body in the snow; the way he lay, broken, with one arm crushed beneath his weight.

A little while later, my father finds me. "How are you holding up?"

I want to tell him how sick I feel, but he seems so formal in the moment. More captain than father.

He sits beside me. "It wasn't him, Gray. That wasn't your brother."

"I know. But I still . . . I feel like . . ."

I don't know how to put it into words. Like I ate spoiled

meat and my stomach is writhing? Like I have a headache that pounds at the slightest movement? Like the wind's been knocked out of me and I can't get an ounce of air into my lungs no matter how deeply I breathe?

"You did the right thing," Owen says. "Emma would be dead right now if you hadn't acted so quickly."

"How is she?"

"Fine. Nothing but a nick on her neck. She's showing the others how to identify a Forgery, although the sign is so subtle. Clipper's the only one having any success." A quick pause. "I don't know what it means. Not even Harvey seemed to know about this giveaway, and he made the damn things."

Owen leans forward, resting his arms on his knees. I run a hand over my bloody knuckles.

"I don't get it," I say finally. "What the Forgery said—Frank giving us too much credit for heading west. That's *exactly* what we're doing."

"I think our final destination surprised him, that's all. I'm sure when Frank heard we were traveling west he expected us to be gathering more supporters, and of course he has a reason to fear that. With more numbers we have more power, and with those numbers spread out, more people doubting him in more locations. He could have an uprising on his hands, one that would be difficult to fight if it broke out in and around all his cities at the same time. It's his biggest fear: losing control over his people." Owen pauses for a second. "Frank probably never mentioned Group A to the Forgeries when he briefed them, and why would he? The place is a wreck and there are no numbers there to help our cause as far as he's concerned. Of course, that's exactly why it's so alluring to us. It's under the radar. Never thought of or looked at twice."

"There are still cameras watching it."

"Once we get the survivors on our side, Clipper will see to them. Remember his discussions with Ryder before we left—that idea to take several hours of video footage and loop it indefinitely? To anyone watching from Taem's control room it will *look* like Group A is as deserted and dead as always, only we'll be able to start recruiting beyond the survivors still there."

"And the Forgery?" I ask.

"We'll get rid of him as soon as we're through the Outer Ring. The Order will think we're anywhere but Group A 'extending our reach,' and he'll be dead before he's able to discover and give them headquarters' location."

I nod silently. I heard these plans, all this logic, a dozen times over—mostly in meetings before we left Crevice Valley. I've even repeated some of them to Bree when her reservations about the mission get the best of her. But now, as I sit here listening to my father, thinking about Blaine's body back in the snow and how quickly life can get thrown off course, I catch myself feeling doubtful. There are so many details in our plan that could go wrong as easily as they could go right.

Owen turns toward me, his features extremely calm given all that's happened. "You positive you're okay?"

No.

But I don't say it. Because I want to be unfazed like him. I want killing that Forgery to have no weight on my conscience.

"If you decide you want to talk about it," he says, "or about anything, ever, you just say the word. I'll make time."

If he were Blaine he'd know I want to talk right now. He'd be able to read my silence as well as my words. But my brother is not here. And right then, another fear hits me.

Frank wanted Harvey back in order to make the limitless Forgeries. That was always his goal—a Forgery that could be replicated over and over. But when I brought Harvey to Taem in the fall as a decoy, Frank casually mentioned that he didn't need Harvey's help anymore. Which makes me wonder if he's already accomplished it. The limitless variety.

"What if I have to kill another Forged version of Blaine?" I blurt out. "I don't think I could do it."

"You can," my father says. "You will do what you must and you will do it without hesitation."

"An order; how reassuring."

"It was meant to be a compliment. I'm saying that you are a stronger person than most because you do what needs to be done even when those actions are unpleasant." Owen scratches at his chin, stares into the sea of trees before us. "It's supposed to hurt," he adds. "Seeing something like that. *Doing* something like that. If it didn't hurt, you'd be no better than a Forgery yourself."

He stands and drops a square of cloth into my hands. "Clean yourself up." A smile flickers beneath his beard. "You look like hell."

EIGHT

THE NEXT DOZEN DAYS PASS as imitations of one another. We wake in the morning and break down camp. We walk for hours that seem as endless as the Wastes itself. Xavier guides Jackson now, who spends half his time staring off into the trees like he might run for it and the other half eyeing our team members with a look so vicious it gives me chills. I can't figure him out, though, because each evening after raising our tents, the first thing he does is play a round of Rock, Paper, Scissors with Aiden. One night Rusty even calms long enough to let the Forgery scratch him behind the ears. It makes Jackson smile—a true, genuine smile—and for a split second it's like I'm seeing through the replica and into the real Jackson. The one who must have grown up in

Dextern, seeing as neither Bree nor I recognize him as one of our people.

Emma continues to lead the horses, but Sammy will sometimes lift Aiden from the saddle and carry him on his shoulders. It always sends the boy into a fit of giggles. Watching the three of them together reminds me of a funeral in Claysoot. Emma stood at my side, and Kale slept in my arms, and something about it felt right, made me think I might actually want a family of my own someday. Not yet. Definitely not yet. Although when Sammy glances at Emma and gives her his goofy, joking smile, I start thinking I could be ready if I had to. I could be whatever Emma needed, so long as she would stop smiling back at him the way she currently does.

I fall in line beside Bree when we hike. She's back to her old self, the bitterness from the archery match and the surprising tenderness that followed it that evening both replaced with constant heckling. I mention that I have blisters from my boots and she tells me to stop whining. I offer advice in a team meeting and she counters it just to watch me frown. I climb a tree to check the trail behind us for pursuers and she criticizes my form, shouts out grip advice from the snow below like I can't see the handholds myself. The only time she doesn't seem to have something to say is when I bring up my showdown with Forged Blaine, wondering aloud how doing something right can also feel wrong. She just squints at me, her face somewhat pained, before turning to stare off at the horizon.

Still, she comes to my tent each night to fall asleep beside me, and each time I return from my watch she's gone. There's always a sting in my chest when I find my sleeping bag empty. I start wondering if she's leaving me, drifting away just like Emma. Before I can ever make sense of it, a new day will break—one where Bree and I are back to our typical banter, as comfortable and familiar as a pair of worn gloves, wearing each other thin.

The landscape grows flatter and sparser, forests trading themselves for rolling plains and valleys. The snow thins beneath our feet until we can finally see earth again. Frozen earth, but visible. I think it is warmer, too, but I'm so numb after weeks of exposure that I could be tricking myself into believing it. I pull off my hat and let my jacket hang open, relish in the fact that it no longer hurts to draw a deep breath.

"We *are* heading a bit south these days," Clipper says when I ask him about the temperature. He shows me on his location device, which he's been using sparingly to prolong its battery life. The Wastes ends soon, butting up against a massive chunk of blue that spreads north through about two-thirds of the country. Clipper calls it the New Gulf. The

AmEast–AmWest borderlines run along the Gulf's western shore, and at its northernmost end, the water forks into two bays, long and narrow, like rabbit ears. Group A is supposedly located somewhere between them, in AmEast's Western Territory.

But for now, our destination is Bone Harbor. I spot it on the eastern edge of the Gulf, miles south from where the water forks into those two ears. No one has said anything in days—not even Clipper, who sees how close we are—but we can all feel it: hope.

Reaching Bone Harbor means a good meal and a bath, but above all, it marks a crucial turning point in our trek. We will be over halfway to the end, the hardest part behind us. I've never been on a boat, but I'm excited for the experience, if only to give my legs a rest. Bree warns that the passage across the Gulf could make me ill, and I laugh in her face.

"It's only water. I've swum in it. Why would sailing on it be any different?"

"I'll remind you of that when you're throwing up over the side," she says.

The evening before Clipper estimates we'll arrive at the Gulf, I have my only conversation with Bree that doesn't include her arguing with me or criticizing my faults. In fact, it's rather civil, completely void of judgment.

The team is relaxing around the fire after dinner when she sits down next to me and says, "It's terrible afterward. The feeling. You walk through it again and again and wonder what you could have changed, how you could have acted differently, if you missed something that would have spared them."

It takes me a moment to realize she's talking about killing someone, finally responding to my comments about the Forgery of my brother.

"That is exactly what I'm going through," I admit. "Every day I reanalyze it."

"The analyzing will stop eventually. The nightmares might not. I still dream about my first sometimes."

"What happened?" She's never told me the details and I'm suddenly curious. "Unless you don't want to talk about it."

"No. It's fine." But she stares at the flames for a long while before she speaks again. "I was on a scouting mission with the Rebels. We'd all split to go our own ways and had orders to meet up two hours later. I got turned around and couldn't find my way back to the rendezvous point, so I dropped my gear and climbed a tree to get my bearings. When I came down, there were two Order members standing there. I don't know how I didn't see or hear them coming.

"They had their guns on me and one of them pinned me against the tree. I've blocked out what he looked like, but I remember his breath was hot when he said—I'll never forget the words—'She's awful pretty, Mack. Maybe we should have some fun with her first.'"

I can't believe she's never told me this before. I'm gaping at her, horrified for what comes next.

"The instant that guy reached for his belt, I kneed him in the gut, pulled a knife from my boot, and slit his throat. The second guy ran off as soon as I snatched up my rifle. I didn't even bother following him because I was too busy crying like an idiot and staring at the man who was bleeding out at my feet.

"For weeks I kept blaming myself for being so careless, leaving my weapon in plain sight, not hearing them coming. I visited the hospital in Crevice Valley a couple times for meds; my headaches were so bad I couldn't sleep. I just wanted a do-over. I wanted to repeat the whole day so it could turn out differently."

"That creep had it coming, Bree," I say firmly. "He deserved what he got."

"So did the Forgery you killed, but that doesn't mean you wanted it to happen." She turns so that she is looking directly at me. Her blond hair is dark with sweat, her cheeks caked with dirt. She looks wild in the firelight. "I'm not happy you had to kill someone, Gray. But I am glad you did it before he killed Emma. Or worse, you."

She stands up quickly, and before I can say another word, she is gone.

We've been keeping up a blistering pace since dawn, and it is at midafternoon the following day, when my feet feel as though they might dissolve to dust, that the land before us stops. We crest a bluff and the earth drops away, revealing pebbles and sand and blue. Blue, as far as the eye can see.

The New Gulf.

Its surface is darker than the sky and speckled with white rifts that build and surge and throw themselves at the shore as though they are alive.

"Waves." Bree sighs, and she opens her arms to the wind. It is salty when I breathe and the air feels wrong against my skin, but Bree seems so at home in these elements.

"This is the best birthday present ever," she says to no one in particular. I realize I have again lost track of the days. It is the twenty-third already, a year to the day after her Heist from Saltwater. Today she is seventeen.

"We're only a few hours from Bone Harbor," Owen announces, "but let's set up camp for the night. We'll head in tomorrow morning with the traders to draw less attention."

By the time the tents have been raised and dinner eaten, the group is in nothing short of good spirits as we sit around a dying fire.

Sammy and September are singing in harmony from across camp, him tapping out a rhythm on a piece of driftwood while Emma bobs her head to the beat. Even Bree hums along as she cleans her rifle. To my left, Bo has fallen asleep with his feet dangerously close to the fire. Jackson gives Aiden a piece of tall grass to tickle Bo's nose. Each time Bo bats at it like he's swatting a fly, Aiden descends into a fit of giggles.

I catch myself smiling.

Because there's a sense of tranquility among us, an optimistic current you can't ignore.

We've almost made it. We're nearly there.

PART TWO

OF OCEANS

NINE

AS THE TEAM BEGINS TO retire, Xavier takes his post for evening watch. Sammy guides Emma to her tent, his hand on the small of her back. She smiles, looking shy, but not trying to avoid the contact either.

I glance away and catch Bree stalking from camp. She slides down a bluff, disappearing from view as she makes for the ocean. I dart after her.

"And they say you're a quiet tracker," she says, turning on me almost instantly. "I heard you coming a mile off."

"What are you doing? Everyone's settling in for the night."

"That's exactly what I *am* doing." I stand there, confused. "Come on," she says. "I'll show you."

I scramble down the bluff. The moon is waning but the

sky is cloudless, and being free of the forest, its light seems to go on forever. There's a dark shadow on the beach. Bree's tent. It's facing the water, far enough back that the surf can't swallow it, but close enough that the ocean is an endless roar that ebbs and flows.

"That's your tent," I say.

"Good work, genius."

I'm about to ask her why she chose to set up camp so far from the others when something she admitted during a game of Bullshit hits me. "You haven't been able to sleep well since your Heist," I say. "You miss the sound of waves."

"You remember that?"

"I remember everything you said that night." Her lips press into a sly smile, like she's impressed. Or amused. "So you're planning on falling asleep with the ocean, then?" I add quickly.

"Yup." She raises an eyebrow, jabs me in the chest. "You should stay with me."

"Does this mean you'll be sneaking out of your own tent before dawn, then? Or am I supposed to go back to mine after my watch?"

Bree frowns. "I really don't want to argue tonight."

But that's what we do best, I feel like saying.

"Let's just sit for a while," she offers. "Deal?"

I have plenty of time before my watch and since I'm not terribly tired, I agree. We start a small fire and sit facing the ocean, the tent at our backs. The salt is strong on the air and the waves endless. They seem too restless to help a person sleep. Just when one has fully died out, a new one comes crashing against the land: a constant disruption.

Without warning, there is a noise out on the water, a mournful call. It is solitary and eerie, drawn out. And then there is another, in response. The two echo each other, wailing into the evening.

"Loons," Bree says. I'm not familiar with the bird, but she identifies their call so surely I don't question her judgment.

"They sound sad."

"But a sort of peaceful sad, don't you think?"

They call out again and I suppose I can see what she means. There is something bittersweet and melancholy to their cries.

"If a pair gets separated, they call for each other until they're reunited," she explains. "We had them during the summers in Saltwater. You could always hear them when dusk fell. Their songs helped me sleep, just like my waves, but the birds migrated away for the winter—warmer waters, I think. It doesn't seem warm enough here, to be honest, but then again, this water didn't always exist.

Maybe the flooding changed their habits."

The loons call out again. Bree clasps her hands together and blows on her thumbs. The whistle she produces is strikingly similar to the birds' cries on the water. Beautiful and haunting and stark.

Bree shows me how to shape my hands, the way to bend my thumbs, where to place my lips. She makes it look so easy but after many attempts, I've done nothing but blow soundlessly into my palms.

"This is impossible."

She shoots me an unforgiving look. "It took me almost a month to learn how to do it when I was a kid. If you picked it up after two minutes, I'd be furious."

"Knowing how rare it is to see you angry about something, I don't want to miss this opportunity." I dramatically roll up my sleeves and cup my hands together. I blow on them without success, but a loon wails at the same exact moment. "Look at that! Perfection."

I expect a snide comment but it never comes. I turn and find Bree staring at the burn scars on my left forearm. They look more pronounced in the firelight: the rippled portions of skin deeper, the slight discolorations more severe. I wonder what state my arm would be in if Bo hadn't pulled me from the flaming platform as quickly as he did. When Emma first tended to me, she said I was lucky and that the scarring wouldn't be too drastic. Even still, my arm has never looked the same.

Bree presses a hand to my skin like she hasn't seen the burn before, like she didn't spend our first night together running her palms over the scars and kissing from my fingers to my elbow.

"I wish there had been a way to get you out of that square faster," she says. "It kills me that this happened to you. That I let it happen."

"It wasn't your fault."

"It feels like it was."

"You did an awful lot of good that day, too," I say, thinking about how I was staring down the barrel of a rifle at Harvey moments before her rubber bullet hit me. "You saved me from pulling the trigger. I don't know if it's possible to repay someone for a thing like that."

"I didn't do it so you'd owe me, Gray. And I didn't do it to save you from shooting Harvey, either. I did it because it saved you. Period."

I feel a smile creep over my lips. "You see why *thank you* doesn't seem like enough?"

She elbows me and the loons start crying again. Bree calls back, and I try to do the same, failing to make a noise that even slightly resembles their wails.

"This was a perfect way to end my birthday," she says, resting her head on my shoulder.

"We should have done something as a group, like we did for Sammy's."

"No, this is better. Just you and me."

Yes, just the two of us, I think. *Always for a few hours. Always when no one is looking. But never for an entire night.*

Bree tilts her chin toward me, offering me her lips. I hesitate and she sits back, frowning.

"Why are you fighting this, Gray?"

I glance at her fingers still resting on my skin.

"Tell me," she demands.

It's only now that she's asking—willing to talk about us in the open rather than hide behind all our jokes and teasing—that the truth seems so painfully clear.

"Because . . ." I look out to sea, terrified to say it to her face. "Because maybe we're not right, Bree." A wave crashes against the shore. "You and me . . . Maybe we're too aggressive for each other. We're either at each other's throats or we can't keep our hands to ourselves. We fight and yell and argue. We shove each other around. We never stop critiquing what the other is doing. It's exhausting. And that's not a real relationship. That's not how it should be."

"Yes, it is," she says firmly. "That's exactly how it should be. We're a team. We push each other. If it's not honest and truthful and challenging, what's the point?"

"To find a balance, maybe? A counterweight? Someone who is the things you're not."

"Like Emma?" She is staring right at me, but I'm too much of a coward to look at her. I can face Frank and Forgeries and Walls, but a girl half my size terrifies me.

"Maybe. Or someone like her. I don't know. It's just that Emma helps me fight my weaknesses. She calms me. I could probably use someone like that."

"Emma makes you boring, Gray. She makes you safe."

Those words are spoken with such bitterness that I'm suddenly brave enough to look her in the eye. "What?"

"You heard me. She takes all the things I love about you and stifles them. She doesn't mean to, but that's what happens when you're with her. You fizzle. You die. You become quiet and guarded and cautious and not yourself. I hate it. I hate how I accept you in your entirety—the good *and* bad—and you do the same for me, and yet you're still fighting it. Trying to act like you can't feel what I feel. Like this won't work." She motions between us.

"Well, look at us. All we do is argue. Maybe it *won't* work. Maybe it was *never* going to work."

"Bullshit," she spits. "A part of your heart has always belonged to her, so don't you dare tell me this won't work when you haven't even tried. Not truly."

"*I* haven't tried? Really? Me? Because last I checked, *you're* the one rushing out every night, running back to your own bed."

"Oh, sure—blame me, Gray. Make this *my* fault. My defenses could never be because I sense your hesitation. Because I catch you watching her. Because it's been this way since the day we met. No, I should gladly hand my heart over so that you can stomp all over it."

"I have no intention of—are you even listening? This is exactly why I just said everything I did. Because we're not right, Bree. We self-destruct! Can you not understand that?"

She throws sand on the fire and the beach goes dark. "Oh, I understand. I understand so well I swear I'm in your head! I knew this was coming. I knew it all along. Do me a favor, will you? The next time a girl wanders into your bedroom, think real hard about what you're doing before you pull back the covers for her. I'd hate for her to get *confused* and *misled* by your oh-so-clear intentions."

"I'll go, then," I say, because she is furious, and a wildfire cannot be controlled, *will* not be controlled. A civil conversation is not going to take place tonight.

I stand and she jumps to her feet, squares her shoulders to me.

"Yeah, great. You go! That's just perfect! It really was a

lovely birthday, though, Gray. I appreciate the effort."

And then she is storming toward the waves, hair whipping in the wind, jacket flailing. I think of following her, but know it's useless. The only words she wants to hear are words I'm not sure I can give her without lying.

TEN

BREE WON'T TALK TO ME in the morning. She won't even make eye contact. When the team heads north along the shore toward Bone Harbor, she runs ahead to walk with Xavier and I feel her absence from my side more deeply than I expect to.

It is another cloudless day, warm enough for us to forgo our hats and let our jackets hang open. It's liberating to walk in so few layers after weeks of frigid temperatures. Clipper says the change is a combination of things: the Gulf trapping warm air and the fact that we are farther south than we were when we set out from Crevice Valley. But I don't care to make sense of the change, not when I can finally feel the sun again.

Bone Harbor appears well before noon. It is unlike Taem

in every way possible. The town is tucked back into a cove, no dome protecting it, no glamorous signs or flying trolley. Docks clutter the shoreline. Shanty buildings along the water are discolored with growth from the sea. The ones set back farther hunch as though the wind has crippled them, paint peeling. The entire place smells like fish, and a rowdy species of white birds hovers overhead, screeching endlessly.

"Is it called Bone Harbor because it looks like death?" Sammy asks as we enter the town from the south.

"Course not," Bo says. "It was the backbone of the fishing industry for a while after the Quake; hence the name. But the flooding continued and the Gulf crept closer to Haven, so now Bone Harbor is just a forgotten waterfront community where those not fortunate enough to buy their way under a dome make do the best they can."

"You know something about everything, don't you?" I say. "Did they let you read a history book on AmEast when you sat in Frank's prisons?"

Bo stops tapping at his pack's straps long enough to wink. "It's phenomenal how much a person can learn if they only listen."

"Um . . . guys?" Bree waves a hand to get everyone's attention. When I see what she's pointing at, my stomach lurches.

Plastered against the walls of the back alley we're walking

through is a series of posters. Most threaten arrest for any-one caught harboring, trading with, or even conversing with an AmWest citizen. Several announce the recent capture and execution of Harvey. But one is larger than the rest, hung dead center, overlapping a curfew warning.

WANTED ALIVE FOR CRIMES AGAINST AMEAST INCLUDING LARCENY, SEDITION, ESPIONAGE, AND HIGH TREASON.

And above the crimes is my name, and above that, my face, staring out into the street with the gray eyes for which I was named. It's a recent picture, probably taken by Frank's cameras when I returned to Taem for the vaccine. I will most certainly be recognized in Bone Harbor.

"Oh hell," Sammy says. I think he's reacting to the poster, but I follow his gaze and just when I think things can't get any worse, they do.

The Franconian Order. Two of them, ahead in the alley, questioning an older woman who's wiping her hands nervously on her apron.

Xavier turns on Jackson. "The damn Forgery sold us out."

"Me?" he says, startled. "How? Telepathy? Magic?"

"You got ahold of our gear! Radioed someone!"

"We had a deal: You keep me alive and I get you into the Outer Ring. I still don't have what I was sent for—your headquarters' location—so why would I risk my own life to call the Order, who may or may not be able to get me out of this mess?"

Xavier looks furious. "Oh, I don't know, maybe to—"

"Clipper and Xavier, stay with me and the horses," my father orders harshly. "Everyone else, split up. I don't care how you do it; just do it now. We'll meet at the docks. After sundown, if we can manage."

"But the Forgery," Xavier says. "He—"

"Not now," Owen snaps. "There isn't time."

We scatter not a second too soon. I somehow get stuck with Jackson after Xavier shoves him at me. The two of us run for the nearest side street—or rather, I run and Jackson refuses to cooperate, so I have to drag him behind me. I shoulder my way into the first building we come to. It is a single-level home, set on the corner of the side street and the alley we just fled. It's currently vacant, but there are clothes hanging on a drying rack and a few dishes set out on a table that also holds a bowl of fruit. Someone will be back eventually.

I move into the kitchen, where a window looks onto the alley. My father is just coming into view.

"You're going to get caught," Jackson says, a note of humor in his voice.

"Shut up."

"I'm just stating the facts."

I shove him against the wall. "I mean it. Not another word."

Outside, my father has pulled his hat back on even in the comfortable weather, but I know he's done it to cover his hair. Between the hat, and his blue eyes and full beard, he no longer looks like an obvious father to the boy on the wanted posters. Xavier holds the reins of the two horses at his side and Clipper has his hands on the straps of his backpack, gripping them so tightly his knuckles have gone white.

The Order members flag them down as they approach. The red triangles on their chests are screaming danger, and I want my father to turn and run. Nothing good can come of these people.

"Morning, folks," one of them says. His words are murky through the glass window, but I can hear well enough.

"Morning," Owen echoes.

"What brings you to Bone Harbor?" the second asks. A female. Her face is square and angular, her neck so thick she almost appears not to have one.

"What makes you think we are only visiting?"

"There's not much need for horses around here," the woman says, eyeing the reins in Xavier's hands.

"We plan to trade them," my father answers. "They were necessary to get here, but we need a boat now, not horses."

"Where are you headed?"

"Haven," Clipper says.

"You're pretty far south of home. Where are you coming from?"

"Even farther south, ma'am," Clipper continues. "A small town in the Southern Sector. We have family there."

"So you're all related?" the male asks.

"My son and nephew," Owen says of Clipper and Xavier, which is believable enough.

"And you chose to travel by boat and horse from Haven all the way to the Southern Sector?"

"Not everyone living under a dome can afford to power a car. And a trip through the Wastes is desolate, too easy to get stranded without fuel. I don't mean to pry, but was there a point to this questioning?"

The stocky woman frowns. "Yes, there is." She holds out a copy of the wanted poster. "We're looking for this boy. We have reason to suspect he was heading west, possibly through this town or one of the others along the New Gulf."

Owen takes a moment to examine the photo. "I haven't seen him."

"You're positive?" the woman says, folding her arms across her chest. "This boy can be quite persuasive when necessary. If he promised you anything in exchange for silence, you should know he won't keep his side of the bargain."

"I assure you we have never seen him," my father says, "but if that changes, we'll alert someone immediately. It's no good, having a criminal like that running around."

"Too true," she responds.

"Are we free to go now? I'd hoped to trade these horses by midday."

"Yes. Thank you for your time."

They pass by, horses in tow, and I feel like air is finally returning to my lungs. Not a second later the door of the house is thrown open and Emma and Aiden stumble inside.

"What are you doing?" I hiss at her as she closes the door.

"We were one house over, but the owner came home and we had to sneak out a window."

I peer back onto the main street. The Order members are turning the corner, pointing at houses as they head up our side street.

Emma reads my face. "They're coming, aren't they? This way?"

We hear footsteps, boots against the hard-packed earth. Then a knock on our door.

Jackson looks momentarily amused. He sold us out after all, just like Xavier suspected. But then the Forgery notices Aiden shaking in fear and his demeanor changes to something so close to worry that I reconsider the theory. Maybe the Order is simply doing what Jackson and Blaine were sent to do: intercept us.

Another knock.

"Don't say anything," I whisper. "They'll leave eventually."

"Franconian Order!" the woman shouts from outside. "We're sweeping all houses in this alley. You have twenty seconds to open your door or we will assume no one is home and open it ourselves."

"Let me talk to them," Emma offers.

"What? No!"

"I'll tell them I saw you across town or something. I can do this. It will be easy."

She looks so sure of herself, so confident. It's her eyes: brilliant with hope, so steady she seems unstoppable. But I can't have Emma risking herself like this for us. Frank might suspect she followed me back to Crevice Valley last fall, and just because I've only seen posters with my face on them doesn't mean Frank didn't create additional signage featuring hers.

"Take Aiden into the back room," I tell Emma. "Find a closet or something and stay put until I call for you."

"Let me do this." Her voice is hard. Almost desperate.

The door trembles under another pounding.

"Emma, please don't make me ask again."

She exhales sharply and takes Aiden into a side room just as the Order woman starts counting backward.

Ten . . . Nine . . .

The quarters are too tight to fire an arrow, so I grab a knife from the kitchen and face Jackson. "Open that door and tell them you saw me on the other side of town."

Eight . . . Seven . . .

He eyes the knife in my hands. "You won't be getting access codes to Group A if I'm dead."

Six . . . Five . . .

"We keep you alive, and you help us if we run into Order members," I remind him. "You said that back in Stonewall."

Four . . .

"Do you *want* them to search this house? Find Aiden? Punish him because he's here with me?"

Three . . .

Jackson's eyes dart between me and the door. "I'll handle it."

Two . . .

I cut the ropes binding his wrists.

One . . .

He opens the door. It swings inward, blocking me from the Order's sight.

"Sorry about the delay," he says. "Was in the bathroom."

"Not at all," replies the woman. There's a rustling of paper. "We're looking for this boy and checking in on citizens while we're at it. Making sure he's not holding anyone against their will."

"I think . . . Yes. I saw this boy just earlier, peering into a window down that alley." Jackson's voice is surprisingly convincing. "I thought he locked himself out of his house, but maybe he was looking for a place to hide."

I hear the woman take the poster back. "This alley, you say?" Jackson must nod or point in clarification because she says, "Thank you."

The door closes and I'm breathing again, weight lifting off my chest. I grab the Forgery—who's rubbing his forehead like the entire encounter has given him a headache—and push him into a chair in the sitting room. "Emma! It's safe."

She looks angry when she reappears with Aiden. It's not an expression I'm used to seeing on her face and I know why she's shooting it my way; deal or not, I momentarily put our lives in the Forgery's hands. But it paid off and I don't regret a thing.

I rebind Jackson's wrists, covering the rope burns he's beginning to develop. "Thanks," I say to him. "For helping us like that."

"I was helping the boy, not you. I'll do what I need to, eventually: get the location I came for. I don't have a choice."

"Every action is the result of a choice. Even a Forgery's."

He grunts skeptically. I look over to Emma, who has a hand on Aiden's shoulder.

"The others?" I ask her. "Did you see where any of them went?"

"Sammy has the dog, and he just sat in the open. Smart, really. Bo and September hid in a house across the way."

"And Bree?"

"I don't know. Last I saw, she was running along the roofs. Alone."

But these words are reassuring, because if Bree is on her own, I know, without a doubt, that she is absolutely fine.

ELEVEN

WE TAKE TURNS BATHING. THE water that comes from the faucet is tinged with salt, but I'm clean at the end of the process and that is enough to make me happy. There is no window in the bathroom and I feel comfortable letting Jackson have some privacy after I've emptied the room of razor blades and anything else I think he can get too creative with.

The owner of the house still hasn't come back, but the sky is starting to lose some of its color. We should leave soon, but Emma insists on cutting my hair first.

"I like it better long," I argue.

"It's not about what you like, Gray. It's about making you look less like the face on those posters."

I reluctantly stand near the sink in the bathroom while

Emma hovers around me with scissors. I'm not sure why parting with something as meaningless as hair hurts a little. Nothing has been the same since I climbed the Wall with Emma over the summer, and I feel most comfortable when my hair curls over my ears, falls into my eyes, grazes the back of my neck. These things remind me of Claysoot: a reassurance that I haven't lost myself in all that's happened.

"What's Jackson doing now?"

Emma glances out the open door and into the sitting room. "He's playing Rock, Paper, Scissors with Aiden. Just like he was the last five times you asked me to check."

She smiles at me in the mirror and then pushes me to my knees so she can better attack the rest of my hair.

"What will you do when this is all over?" she asks, cutting my bangs back so they no longer fall into my eyes. "Group A, Frank, everything. What then?"

"I haven't thought that far ahead. It almost feels dangerous to be so optimistic."

"I'll go back to Claysoot," she says. "I miss my mother. And I want to find Laurel, too; tell her that I was never crazy to believe there was more, even though she laughed at all my theories when we were younger."

I picture the reunions. Emma's mother and best friend dissolving into tears, hugging Emma so tightly she can barely breathe.

"Will you stay there?" I ask.

She shrugs. "It depends. It might have too many tough memories, of being a prison and a lie. But then, it's still home, and maybe it won't seem so bad when we can cross the Wall freely."

"I'll go with you. To see Blaine, because I know he'll go there immediately, looking for Kale. And then maybe I'll fight with Chalice for good measure, just to watch you stitch her chin up again."

Emma grins and puts the scissors down. "You are *not* good with grudges."

"I know," I say, standing. "I'm terrible with them."

"Well, no one's perfect. Least of all me."

A few months ago I would have said that Emma was as close to perfect as a person can be. Kind, helpful, confident. Loyal. But now, even though I've known her my whole life, she feels like a stranger.

"I really am sorry." She looks at me, and her eyes are terrifyingly doubtful, like she fears we're ruined forever. More than once, I've had the same thought myself.

"Whenever you decide I deserve that second chance, I'll be ready," she adds. "I hope you know that."

She brushes past me and into the sitting room. I squeeze the lip of the sink with both hands, stare at myself in the mirror. I wish I knew how to forgive her, wish I could love this Emma the way I loved the one in my memories.

I fetch a blade from the other room and shave. It will make me look more like the face on the wanted posters, but I don't care. I just want to feel like myself.

By the time I step into the sitting room, Aiden has grown tired of his hand games. He's lying on the couch, his head on Jackson's lap, eyes struggling to stay open. Jackson has an arm draped over the boy in an almost parental manner. The Forgery: a pillow, a protector. It's so ridiculous I almost laugh.

I gather my gear, tell the others to do the same. Aiden yawns and says something about using the bathroom first, and I snap at him to hurry. Emma gives me a chastising look, but the sun is setting. I don't feel like pushing our luck in the house much longer.

I flip through a handful of letters lying on a cluttered desk while we wait for Aiden. They are handwritten in elegant script, all smooth arcs and flourishes. I find the most recent one, dated a week back, and read.

Carl—
Badger told me he won't run our letters anymore, even if you are trading with him. He says it's getting too risky. The Expats are gaining momentum—I know some of their

stories have made it to Bone Harbor—and Order troops along the borders have doubled as a result. Ships on the Gulf are being stopped more and more often. They're looking for reasons to arrest people, Carl. So long as it's a blow to the Expats—dulls enthusiasm—they won't hesitate.

Badger claims these notes hold too much damning evidence. I've pleaded with him, said we can change names, places, anything—we'll talk in code if we have to—but he refuses to be our courier.

This is my last letter.

I'll be fishing with Charlie where the catch is good the week of the holidays. You know the place: our favorite spot southwest of the Gulf. Meet us, won't you? You can come west for good. We'll give up fishing and head for Expat protection. I know you've never liked my brother, but this was all Charlie's idea: getting you out, having you join us. We can even sink your seiner, make it look like you went down. No one will come after you.

Please, Carl. The Order has taken everything

from your people: their hope, their resilience, their freedom. Don't let them take your heart, too.

You know where to find me.
All my love,
May

I realize then what I hadn't before: the clothes on the drying rack are not the slightest bit damp; the fruit on the kitchen table is beginning to spoil. The owner of the house—Carl—is long gone. And he won't be returning.

Also on the desk are dozens of paper scraps, edges ragged as though Carl tore them from a larger source. There's a story about Order troops being stationed in gulfside towns as additional border control, an announcement on freshwater taxes, a note mandating curfew, another saying all ships are subject to random search upon leaving and entering port. The Franconian emblem sits at the end of each story.

A crumpled piece of paper catches my eye because it's a different shade from the others—more tan than ash gray. I skim a few sentences about water prices and black markets. Badger's name appears twice. There is no Franconian mark on this paper, merely a line at the bottom that reads *The Bone Harbor Harbinger—burn after reading.*

I frown at the conflicting stories, run my thumb over Badger's name.

Aiden steps from the bathroom, and I slip the *Harbinger* and May's letter into my pocket. I'll show them to my father later, but at the moment, we need to move.

TWELVE

THE STREETS ARE QUIET AS we steal through them. We pass a building with a cross on its peak. People are singing inside, and a single candle burns in each window. Most other buildings in town lie dark and seemingly vacant, and we spot only one Order member on our way to the harbor. He stands with his back against a brick wall, staring at the stars instead of the streets he should be watching.

When we get to the docks, the rest of the group is already there. The horses are gone and I assume this means my father had success selling them.

Bree greets me with a curt nod. "Nice haircut."

"I thought you weren't talking to me."

"I'm not. But it's good to know you aren't dead." She pivots and stalks off to join Xavier and September in a discussion about something called *high tide*.

My father is scanning the town, binoculars to his eyes. Clipper does the same. "Three flames in the highest window, one in all the others," Owen says to him. "That's the signal."

"There," Clipper exclaims, pointing at a tiny house set back in the cove.

"It's a good thing everyone is preoccupied with holiday eve celebrations," Bo says. "Otherwise getting to that house unseen would be a difficult task."

"Yeah, hooray for holidays," Sammy mumbles behind me. "This is exactly how I like to spend them." Rusty yaps in agreement, and half the team hushes him all at once.

When we get to the marked house, my father raps on the door, a funny little pattern that I'm sure is another signal. The door is yanked open and light floods the alley. The man standing before us is plump and lively, with bushy eyebrows and an even rowdier mustache. A pipe is rooted between his teeth as though it grows there.

"Merry Christmas, friends!" he says. "Come in. Come in! It's nearly curfew."

And then we are ushered into the warmth of his cramped home for a series of introductions, the cry of the ocean shut out by the door.

The captain, Isaac Christopher Murphy, is the most super-stitious person I have ever met. He nearly faints when he learns that there will be women on board his ship.

"This weren't part of the agreement," he spouts. "Ryder didn't mention no women. I won't have it! Wouldn't've taken the job if I'd known."

Isaac paces around the small sitting room, puffing on his pipe and claiming the females will sink his boat. It's not until a small girl walks into the room and points at Isaac's tabby cat, which has curled up in Bree's lap, that Isaac finally calms.

"Look, Pa," she says. "Dixie likes the lady."

"Well, it changes things a bit," Isaac says after some con-sideration, "but I still ain't fond of the idea. Lunacy this is, bringing women on board. Especially with the state of things! Order members increasing their presence in town. Tensions rising along the borderlines. When I was fishing with my regular crew on the western shores of the Gulf a month back, we heard wind that AmWest is trying to convince AmEast citizens to come to their side. 'The real patriots are Expats,' they've been saying. Have you heard this chatter?" I'm about to mention May's letter when Isaac gasps, the pipe tumbling from his lips.

"There will be thirteen of us! Thirteen, including Dixie.

More bad luck. Not to mention it ain't comfortable with over ten, but thirteen! No, I won't have it."

"It's fourteen, actually," Bree says. "If you count Rusty."

"You don't count dogs," Isaac says, as if this should be obvious.

"But you counted the cat."

"Course I did. Cats are good luck on a ship."

"Hold on a minute," my father says. "Not everyone continues from here, so the number won't be a problem. September will be setting up a post in Bone Harbor."

"I will?" September says, as surprised as I am by this news.

"We agreed to take Aiden as far as the next town, and the upcoming leg of our journey is no place for a young boy. But since we can't just dump him on the streets, I'm hoping that you, September, can find him and Rusty a good home. Then we'll need you to sit tight until we are able to send word for you to join us. So that drops our number down to ten, Isaac. Eleven, if you insist on counting the cat."

"We've established the cat's counted," he grumbles. "I still don't feel good 'bout the women, but I suppose I ain't got a choice in the matter. Can't very well strand friends of a friend." He puffs on his pipe a moment longer and adds, "I don't suppose you ladies would be willing to remain naked on board? A bare woman is good luck, you know."

"You're dreaming," Bree says. "We're coming and we're

keeping our clothes on and everything is going to be fine."

"What about you, then?" Isaac raises his bushy eyebrows at Emma.

She just blushes and stares at her hands. Bree nudges her shoulder and whispers, "Go on, Emma. Don't let him make you uncomfortable. Tell him to shove it."

But before she can, Isaac's daughter and Aiden erupt with squeals. The girl has been teaching him a new hand game—one where they join fists and battle to pin each other's thumb down.

"Catherine, child. Bed!" Isaac motions toward the hallway. "If you're expecting Saint Nicholas to come with even the smallest of holiday tidings you'll be asleep before I count to three. One . . . two . . ."

But Catherine is already gone. Emma leads Aiden after her.

"My sister'll be here early to take care of Catherine. I'd prefer to be gone before she arrives—that woman'll talk our ears off—so rest while you can." Isaac stares at me, as though he is seeing me for the first time despite the fact that I shook his hand when we arrived. "You . . . You're the boy on the posters."

I nod, and he pulls a set of curtains closed hurriedly.

"I don't like it," he says yet again, which leaves me thinking Isaac doesn't like much of anything. "It's a bad time to be smuggling fugitives 'cross the Gulf. It's a bad time to be on the Gulf in general." He blows out the candles in the front of the house and yanks those curtains closed as well.

"Ryder said you were a man we could trust," my father says. "If this is true, I'm sure you don't believe everything you read on Franconian signage."

"Course not," Isaac mutters. "How could I when the Order keeps patrolling our streets like we're criminals and taxing our drinking water like it's gold? They're gonna make me broke. I've had to start buying off this guy that goes by *Badger*. Man's shifty as they come but his water's clean and cheap, and I ain't turning down that sort of deal. Even if he *does* live in AmWest."

"AmWest?" Bo echoes. "I thought water was even harder to come by out that way."

"Supposedly is, but they'll trade for the right price: information. Anything Franconian they can get their hands on, so long as it's trustworthy, and I know a boatload about the Order's shipping habits from all my time on the Gulf. They're planning something. Don't know what, but if it knocks the Order 'round a bit, gets them outta my hair as much as theirs, I ain't complaining. You know, sometimes I catch myself wondering if those AmWest guys are just like us, only caught on the opposite side of a line drawn in the sand."

Isaac pulls the last set of curtains closed. "We'll leave well before dawn," he announces to the room. "Pack your black clothes away—they won't be worn on my ship—do not utter the word *drown* on deck, and when you step on board, lead with your right foot, else you'll brew up a storm and bury us in the Gulf. Is that clear?"

Everyone nods, but when Isaac retires to bed Bree mumbles, "What a load of crap."

We spread out in the tiny house, sleeping bags practically overlapping. Those in the group who have not yet bathed take turns using the washroom. I'm squished between Bo, who is humming his song about red berries, eyes closed; and my father, who is cleaning his rifle. I show him May's letter and the *Harbinger* story. He reads silently, forehead wrinkled.

"What's it mean?" I ask when he hands them back.

"I don't know. Could mean a lot of things. The *Harbinger* is clearly an underground paper published by people here in town, so its facts are only as good as rumors, which is to say, not good at all. And the letter? It's just one girl's words to a fisherman she likely met on the sea and fell for."

"But the rumors in the *Harbinger* match most of May's letter, plus some of what Isaac said earlier. And besides, wouldn't rumors have some basis in truth?"

My father nods and frowns in one motion. "A very good point."

I watch him run a cleaning rod through the rifle. "I just . . . I think we'd be stupid to *not* look into it."

He puts the weapon down. "Let me see those again." I hand him the papers and he reads through them. Twice. "We'll talk to Isaac again tomorrow. Try and get more out of him. I think I might have September poke around town after she gets Aiden settled, too. See if she can confirm any of these rumors."

I nod, settle deeper into my sleeping bag. I'm not sure what will come of it, but it seems the right thing to do: follow these odd stories until the truth unearths itself. I'd still be sitting in Claysoot if I hadn't done the same after my doubts about the Heist surfaced.

Behind me, I can hear Dixie hissing as Jackson tries to coax her into his lap. It took him forever to win over Rusty. I don't know why he'd expect to have success with the cat. Forged Blaine flashes through my mind, how I couldn't sense his true nature, and I feel a little pathetic for having worse instincts than a house pet.

"You sure we should take the Forgery on the boat?" I ask my father.

"It would be too easy for him to tip off the Order in Bone Harbor. And I don't want to regret leaving him behind if Clipper ends up having complications with the Outer Ring."

Dixie hisses at Jackson again and I worry that he will be a

greater risk to us than ever once we are on a boat and Aiden is left behind. The child miraculously brings out a semblance of humanity in him.

"You should sleep, Gray," my father says. "It might not come as easily once we're on the water."

I roll over and try to block out Bo's humming. Outside, wind surges against the house. The ocean is a distant noise now, practically drowned out by the creaking of floorboards and drafty walls. It seems like my eyes have closed for only the briefest of moments when someone is shaking me awake.

It is time to greet the sea.

THIRTEEN

ISAAC IS FRANTIC IN THE morning.

"Let's get going," he urges. "The Order's been inspecting boats at random before they push off these last few weeks and I want to disappear before they start crawling the shore. Hurry, hurry!"

We are rushed through our good-byes. September promises to take care of Aiden and find him the very best of homes. We all peer into the bedroom before leaving, even the Forgery. Aiden's dark hair is splayed out against his pillow, Rusty curled up at his feet.

We gather our gear and head out, Isaac mumbling about early departures and how we're bound to get flagged down if we don't pick up the pace. By the time we reach the docks, most of the team is stressed. Even Sammy seems flustered.

The vessel is larger than I expect, a looming giant emerging from thick morning fog. Sammy says it's a fishing boat, a *trawler*, to be exact, but I can't imagine sneaking up on any animal in something so massive. He laughs at this and says the boat is midsized, but when I look through the harbor, not many of the vessels surpass Isaac's in scale.

The sky has barely started to lighten, but I can make out *Catherine* painted on the boat's side. I wonder if the ship was named after Isaac's daughter as a token of good luck or simply because he loves his child so much that her name helps him feel near her when he's at sea. The captain left fruit by the fireplace when we set out this morning, along with a doll and wooden top, which makes me suspect the latter.

Isaac won't let us board until he's spit in the sea—yet another ritual for luck—and warned us again about leading with our right foot as we step on board.

"He's something else, huh?" I say to Bree as we shuffle along the dock.

She stares ahead, hands grasping the straps of her pack.

"The captain," I clarify. "All those superstitions."

"I'm sorry," she says, her face full of mock concern. "Were you saying something?"

"Bree, you can't avoid talking to me forever."

"Watch me," she snarls, marching toward the boat.

"Ah-ah-AH!" Isaac scolds. "Your right foot first. Your *right!*"

Bree throws her hands up and even with her back to me, I'm positive she's rolling her eyes. She switches her footing and continues forward.

Sammy nudges my shoulder. "What's going on with you two?"

"Nothing. Just Bree being Bree."

He looks doubtful. "She scares the crap out of me, man. I don't know how you put up with her."

Bree's arguing with Isaac now, something about *ridiculous rules* and *delusional superstitions*.

"She scares me, too," I admit. "I think she scares everybody."

Sammy gives me a look I can't fully read. "Come on. Let's board before Isaac finds something unlucky about us standing on the dock and delaying the departure."

On deck, we are immediately put to work. Sammy and I end up struggling with the thickest ropes I have ever held, coiling them into organization as Isaac hurries off to start the boat. He keeps glancing at the shore, but with the exception of a few other fishermen, the town is still sleeping.

The boat rumbles to life a moment later and then we are pushing out to sea. The land fades away; Bone Harbor's buildings shrink in height. Soon the people on the shore are nothing but minuscule silhouettes. I blink and they are swallowed by the fog. It's just us and the boat now, battling against the choppy water as we sail northwest.

To be surrounded like this, blue in all directions, makes me feel like I've fallen into the sky. I get a little paranoid by the idea that the only visible "earth" is the deck I stand on. The whole thing makes me queasy and I take to wandering with Sammy as a distraction.

Everything making up the boat has a common enough name, but the words seem to take on new meanings out on the water. There is a bridge, but it doesn't span anything, just serves as a raised section of the ship where the captain can command the vessel and oversee the main deck. The bridge is made up of what Sammy calls the wheelhouse— which is not a house at all, but a room protected from the elements and filled with navigational equipment, a captain's chair, and a table currently covered in maps—and a small deck that encircles the wheelhouse and its many glass windows. There are multiple sets of stairs leading between the ship's decks, but Sammy refers to them as ladders. Given how steep they are, this seems just as well. The crew quarters below are full of bunks, which turns out to be a fancy word for beds stacked one on top of another.

The boat lurches without warning and my stomach reels.

"Air," I tell Sammy. "I need air."

Back on the deck, the wind is whipping fiercely. I pull my hat on and cling to the railing, trying to steady my breathing. My feet are planted firmly on the deck and yet I feel like they are bobbing independently of each other.

"You look green." Clipper has joined us at the railing.

"Nah," Sammy says, smiling. "He's pale as a ghost. The color's drained out of him completely."

"Not. Helping." The two of them look so chipper I forbid myself to lose my breakfast. It figures that Bree would be right about the sea making me sick. Why did she have to be right?

"You think this is rough?" Clipper says. "Just wait 'til there's a storm."

Sammy grins. "Maybe we should put him in the lifeboat and drag him behind us." He motions to a small boat strapped down on the deck that wouldn't hold more than five people. "Then he'll realize how good he has it, how this thing cuts through waves like a knife."

They stalk off, laughing at my misfortune. I hate them for it, but at the same time it's oddly comforting, that friendly sort of teasing. It's almost as good as having Blaine around.

We celebrate the holiday over drinks. Isaac offers up a large jug of clear alcohol but refuses to join in the festivities.

"We mighta dodged that inspection back in town," he says, "but that don't mean the Order won't flag us down out here if they have a chance. Navigating this ship clear of their standard routes is like threading a needle. But don't let me stop your fun." He turns toward the wheel, looking somewhat disappointed.

We should probably be more worried by Isaac's words, but Xavier grabs the alcohol and we gather around the cramped table. I think we all just want to forget that there might still be a need to keep glancing over our shoulders.

"So anyone believe there's truth to this Expats nonsense?" Sammy says as the jug makes its way from person to person. "That they're AmWest citizens in opposition to Frank—sort of like the Rebels, only stuck on the other side of the border?"

Bo wrinkles his nose. "If they're gathering compromising Order information and helping out the average AmEast citizen in the process, they certainly don't sound like monsters."

I tell everyone about May's letter and the *Harbinger*. Isaac chimes in on the latter.

"That thing's written by a bunch of Bone Harbor locals practically asking to be arrested. They hate the Order, always looking for ways to one-up 'em. I bet they'd fit in well with your lot. That tip about trading with Badger has saved me a ton of money, though. I hear he's not even taking on new customers anymore; too busy."

"If AmWest isn't any different than the Rebels, why did they attack Taem last summer?" Emma says. I think back to the planes I saw from Union Central's roof. "They would have killed so many innocent people if they'd been successful."

"Maybe they thought it was a necessary sacrifice," my father offers. "I'm not saying I agree with it, just that if their goal was eliminating Frank they might have thought it was their only option."

"Questionable morals, if you ask me," Sammy says, and then, as if it makes up for it, he adds, "At least they've got a ballsy name."

"How's that?"

"Well, the East referred to everyone in the West as expatriates during the War because the West *wanted* to secede. They were happy to renounce their country. But now, it looks like they've taken what used to be an insult and embraced it. It's like a slap in Frank's face."

"It's ironic, too," Isaac says from the wheel. "Especially given their new slogan, how they're saying fighting Frank is the truly patriotic act."

The jug reaches me and I take a swig before passing it on to Bo.

"What about that virus they released at the start of the War?" he says. "Was that *patriotic*?"

Isaac shrugs. "My old man used to say revolutionaries and terrorists are one and the same. It ain't logical, that theory, and at the same time, it is. Makes my head hurt."

My father frowns, deep in thought. "That virus was released decades ago, so the people responsible are likely no longer the ones in charge. Maybe we don't know as much about AmWest—about the Expats—as we think we do."

Emma looks like she wants to bring up their air attack again, but Bree cuts in. "It just seems awfully suspicious to me. How these rumors and stories have started popping up all of a sudden."

"We *have* been heading west," Xavier points out.

Sammy taps the table livelily. "Yeah, maybe we're hearing all this because we're moving closer to the source. Maybe these stories die out before ever reaching Taem."

My father raises an eyebrow. "And maybe Frank makes sure they die out."

"Wait a minute!" I say, an idea slamming into me. "Remember when the Forgery laughed about our plans with Group A? He said Frank was giving us too much credit to assume we were extending our reach in the West. Well, maybe he meant the west-west. As in AmWest! Maybe Frank *knows* they'd make a good ally for us and that's why he's been so bent on stopping this mission."

Everyone twists to face Jackson, who is slumped against the glass windows, looking bored. "You think whatever you want. Unless we revisit our deal, the only thing I'm giving you is a way into the Outer Ring."

Owen stands. "I've got September scouring Bone Harbor over these Expat rumors, but maybe she should be trying to get in touch with Ryder instead. I'd love to know what he makes of all this."

He scrambles for the radio beside Isaac, desperate to make a call before we slip out of range. Our speculations continue until the alcohol starts warming us, convincing us to trade serious talk for something more relaxed. When Owen rejoins us at the table, Emma suggests a game of Little Lie, or, as the Rebels call it in Crevice Valley, Bullshit.

We play for what feels like hours, everyone telling five supposed facts and the group attempting to guess which one is a lie. Xavier lets slip that he hates cats, and everyone shoves Dixie at him for the rest of the evening. Clipper and my father both admit to fears of heights, which I may have guessed about the boy, but not Owen. The story of how Sammy's father was executed for forging water-ration cards in Taem somehow comes up, turning the mood sour, and Bree counters by sharing a handful of embarrassing things that have happened in her lifetime, many of which I wish I could unhear: rolling in poison ivy naked on a dare, wetting the bed once as a child, getting her first monthly bleeding while hunting and having to retreat home empty-handed for fear she was dying.

The team is laughing hysterically. Bree's cheeks are flushed, but I'm positive it's not from shame. She's just let the alcohol get the best of her. We all have. I've drunk so many times in defeat that my head has started spinning. The bridge is blurry—the faces around the table, too. It's all Bree's fault. She keeps spotting my lies without any real effort and it's driving me mad.

"I think that's enough," Isaac says, snatching the nearly empty jug back a while later. "I ain't got a need for hungover help come morning."

"Well, that's what you're gonna get," Sammy mumbles. "At least in me."

Owen hits him playfully behind the head and the group cracks up. I can't remember the last time we laughed this hard. It feels good. I catch Emma grinning at me from the other side of the table, her smile inviting.

"Isaac's right," my father says. "Let's call it a night."

But my head has suddenly staged a revolt. Everything is spinning.

"You okay?" Xavier asks when I refuse to stand with the others.

I rest my head in my hands. "I'm fine."

"Sure you are," Bree says, her voice laced with malice.

"I'm *fine*," I repeat. "I just . . . it's too loud."

Xavier's laughter hits me like a raging storm and I shoo them away. Sammy's hand goes to the small of Emma's back. He's been making a habit of that.

With the exception of Isaac at the wheel, I'm soon left alone. I thought the quiet would help, but it's somehow making my head spin even more.

I'm going to be sick. I am finally going to be sick.

I get up and stumble from the bridge. My legs betray me on the steps to the main deck and I end up on my hands and knees. A pair of boots enters my vision.

"Well, aren't you a sight." Bree. The last person I want to deal with right now.

"I needed fresh air," I manage as I climb to my feet. "It's the boat. It's making me sick."

"You sure it isn't the alcohol?" She's blurry, dancing before me, but I can see well enough to note her smug expression.

"You've picked a real convenient time to start talking to me again."

The *Catherine* lurches over a rough patch of water and I nearly fall. Bree grabs me at the elbow and helps me toward the railing.

"Just get it over with. You'll feel better after."

I grab the cool iron, hang my head over the edge. I need to throw up. I can feel it coming, but doing it in front of Bree seems like a terrible idea, like she'll win some game I didn't know we were playing.

I tighten my grip on the railing. "This is embarrassing."

"You're not the only one who drank too much," she says. "You only think I'm sober because you're too gone to know the difference."

"It's the boat," I argue again.

A tiny smile. "Keep telling yourself that."

I close my eyes, which only makes it worse. The deck seems to be moving beneath me, independent of the waves. I look out to sea and even the horizon appears to be bobbing around like a madman. The ship lurches again and finally, I am sick.

I do feel better when it's over, even if only minimally. I wipe my face on my sleeve and turn toward Bree. She's still a blurred version of herself, and she's smirking.

"What? You think this is funny?"

She smiles wider. "Absolutely."

"At least I didn't throw myself at you," I snap, thinking back to the last time Bree and I were drunk. I'd held things together while she begged me to kiss her and later got sick on my boots.

She scowls, vicious, furious. "I really hate you sometimes."

"Yeah? Well, the feeling's mutual."

She spins so quickly her braid fans out, but when her arm finds the railing of the stairwell, she pauses. "And for some reason, I still love you," she says, looking over her shoulder. "I hate you and I love you and I can't for the life of me figure out why."

My chest is pounding. From her, or that word, or the alcohol. I can't tell which.

Not that it matters.

She's already gone.

FOURTEEN

THE HEADACHE I HAVE WHEN I wake is sharp and merciless, a pressure behind my eyes that pierces clear through to my temples. Everything seems foggy: my head, the room, the events of last night. I remember only snippets—laughter around the table, Emma glancing my way, Bree's smug face when I got sick.

I'm lying in my bunk alone, my head pounding at the slightest of noises, when Emma walks in carrying a canteen. She glances at my bare chest, the floor, the wall, and finally sits near my knees.

"Water," she says, holding it out.

I take a few sips and the liquid sloshes in my stomach. I groan and pass it back.

"I promise it will help," she says. "You need to drink it."

"Can't you make me something for the nausea?"

"I don't have even a fraction of the ingredients. You're just going to have to fight it off with sleep and water."

I sling my forearm over my eyes. In the dark, the pressure in my head feels less intense.

"You'll be fine," Emma says, her voice so soft it is almost a whisper. "You always are." And then her fingers meet my skin, press against my forehead. I flinch, startled, and pull my arm back so that I can see her. She's looking at me the way she had from across the table last night: almost playfully.

"You're not warm," she says, which surprises me because I'm sticking to the sheets. She leaves her palm against my forehead, staring at me like I'm a stranger, her mouth slightly parted. What feels like ages later, she moves, bringing her hand to my chest. At her touch, I feel a familiar ache between my ribs—weaker than it used to be, but still there, just barely, desperate to reach for her, to fix things.

"Emma!" Sammy shouts from above deck. "The Forgery keeps complaining about his wrists. Wants you to look at them."

She twists to face the doorway, breaking contact with my skin. "I'll be right up!" When she turns back to me, the space between us seems incredibly vast.

"I should go see what he needs." She bites her lip, a small half smile sprouting, and hurries from the room.

Chest pounding, I climb out of bed, pull on fresh clothes. I should move, busy myself with something that will distract from my hangover. I don't know if Emma has intentions of coming back, but it's probably best that I'm not here waiting for her if she does. Especially when she didn't wait for me.

No wonder we haven't been able to move forward. I'm too busy basking in my grudge, dragging up things that have already happened and will never change despite how much I wish they could.

Jackson is tied to a railing, Emma's medic bag at his feet. She, however, is nowhere in sight. The rest of the group is mopping down the deck beneath the harsh glare of the afternoon sun. Bree notices me, and straightens up, scowling. I think I may have insulted her last night, but I can't remember. I'm never drinking again. Not only does it confuse your brain, muddy your senses, and encourage you to embarrass yourself, but it insists on making you feel like absolute trash the following day.

I head to the bridge in search of my father and find only Emma, bent over an assortment of Isaac's gear in the wheelhouse. The door closes loudly behind me and she jumps, dropping something on the table.

"Gray!" Her hand clutches at her chest. "Gosh, you scared me."

"Sorry. What are you doing up here? I thought you had to tend to the Forgery."

"Ran out of fresh bandages." She holds up a fistful of material and I spot Isaac's medical kit lying open behind her. "Well, I guess I should . . ." She glances out the glass windows at the deck and squeezes by me. My father enters with Bo and Isaac not a moment later.

"We'll stay west of this peninsula," Isaac says, spreading a map over the table. He taps at a protruding landmass between New Gulf's two northern bays. "Should reach it by nightfall. Then it's straight sailing up Border Bay 'til you depart."

"It'll be good to be off the open waters," my father says. "The fog offered some cover yesterday, but today I feel we could be spotted for miles."

"If the visibility's that great," Bo says, snatching up a pair of binoculars, "I can get my first glimpse of another domed city."

"Really?" I say.

"Haven." Bo turns the map toward me. The city is positioned at the tip of the more eastern bay, in a territory labeled Big Water. It's a fitting name, given the massive lakes nearby.

"Clear day like this, there's a chance you could spot the Compound, too," Isaac says.

"What's that? Another city?"

Isaac points at the map, noting an island in the middle of the Gulf, farther south. "Another area under Order control, and a water-treatment plant according to rumors. They take salt water and run it through a long desalination process so it's drinkable, I guess. I've wanted to check it out, see if I couldn't snag a little freshwater myself so I can stop relying on Badger, but the Order guards that island like a fortress. You ain't setting foot on it unless they bring you on themselves."

He straightens up. "Now if you're truly after some sightseeing, you better do it while you've got the chance. Weather can turn fast out here."

My father and Bo grab binoculars and skirt onto the small, exposed deck that circles the wheelhouse. I follow.

"You see that, Gray?" Bo hands me the binoculars and points north. I take a look, ready to shake my head, but then the sun breaks through the clouds and a beam of light reflects off something. A glinting dome on the horizon, no larger than my thumbnail.

"Haven?" I ask.

He nods. I admire the city for a moment longer, but the

gleam of the dome is making my headache worse. I pass the binoculars back to Bo.

It's cold again, given how we've been cutting northwest. The wind bites at my nose, my ears. Owen is still scanning the south, trying to locate the Compound, when I catch sight of Isaac through the glass windows. He looks panicked all of a sudden, tugging at the wheel, mumbling into his radio. He tosses it aside and yanks open the door to join us.

"You see anything to the south?" he shouts over the wind.

"Nothing but a few specks on the water; fishing boats, probably," my father says. "Why?"

"This ain't good, boys. This ain't good at all." Isaac rubs his forehead. "I just got a call from the Order. They're wanting me to drop anchor along the nearest shoreline and wait to be boarded. Said they found it suspicious I left port so early yesterday and so they're coming to me for an impromptu inspection. I told 'em I ain't up to nothing, just wanted to leave early and try my luck in the western portions of the Gulf, but they're sending a team our way regardless." He scans the horizon, rubs the back of his neck. "There ain't no one on our tail yet. We should make a run for it."

"No, it's too risky," Owen says. "Soon as we're along land, you should drop anchor like they say. We'll leave. It gives us more ground to cover on foot than we planned for, but at least your story will check out when they board. And by then, our team will be too far gone for them to track us."

"I wish that'd work," Isaac says, "but the nearest bit of shore? That peninsula we're approaching? It's a lookout point. The Order'd be all over you in a matter of minutes. We've gotta sail farther up Border Bay before it's safe to depart. Tomorrow morning, maybe. Tonight if we make great time."

My father frowns and glances to the south. "How'd they find us?"

"That's what worries me. We weren't the only boat getting an early start yesterday—I saw half a dozen docks already empty when we shoved off—and it was foggy as all can be until a few hours ago. I don't see how—or when—they could've identified us."

"Which means . . ." Bo looks down at the deck.

"The damn Forgery," my father says through clenched teeth. "I don't know how . . . but if he . . . I'm going to . . ." He shoves his binoculars into my chest and storms off.

By the time we sit down to eat dinner, I'm nervous. Everyone is. We've spotted a ship to the south with the binoculars that looks larger than the other fishing vessels. Jackson claims he has nothing to do with it, but the boat is clearly following us, a shadow in our wake. It gains. Isaac worries it will be far closer than comfortable come morning.

I've never felt so completely and utterly trapped. There is nowhere to run but as far as the *Catherine*'s deck allows. There are no trees to climb, no boulders to duck behind, no caves to burrow within.

I decide I hate the sea. It is an unforgiving place.

The team eats in silence, my father staring at me from across the table. He looks oddly distant. His mouth does this weird dance, attempting to pull into a smile behind his beard but always falling short. He drops his chin down, staring at his unfinished meal, and swallows, hard. Then, without warning, he grabs Jackson by the collar. Several mess kits are knocked to the floor as Owen tugs the Forgery to his feet and hauls him outside. We all watch through the glass windows, rigid with shock.

"Are you positive you don't recognize it?" Owen shouts. Jackson stands there, despondent, and my father brings a knee into his gut. "I asked you a question!"

Jackson looks to the south. "It's too dark to tell."

My father punches him and the crack of Jackson's nose breaking is so clear I hear it from where we sit. "Did you call them? Did you tell them somehow?"

Jackson is bent over, gasping for air. Owen grabs him by the shirt and throws him against the glass windows of the wheelhouse.

"My son is on this ship. My son and eight other lives, and

the only one I don't care about losing is yours. I will throw you overboard if I have to. You call them off. You do it now!"

"I can't. I don't know how."

Owen hits him again.

"I mean it," Jackson gasps, coughing. His bound arms are held before his face, frantically trying to shelter himself. "I don't. I can't."

But Owen is striking him again and again and finally I'm the one with enough sense to run outside and pull my father back. The Forgery's eyes are already swollen shut, his face a bloodied mess. My father is stronger than me and breaks free. He lunges at Jackson again, but stops midswing, turns to face me.

"I won't lose you because of him. I won't let this monster be our end."

He spits at the Forgery's feet and walks back inside.

"We're disembarking early," he says to the group. Everyone is silent, not a word exchanged. Even Sammy refrains from saying something clever. "I don't care if we're questionably close to the lookout point; we need to get off this boat before they overtake us. Tomorrow, the moment there's enough light in the sky to see the shoreline, we're gone."

Isaac nods and as Owen stalks off, Emma slips outside with her medic gear to tend to Jackson.

FIFTEEN

THE SUN IS BARELY UP. The clouds hang heavy and ominous.

"Snow," Xavier predicts.

But we all feel something far worse.

The boat on our tail is most certainly an Order vessel. It is gigantic, dwarfing our ship even at a distance. It is close enough that we can see the Franconian emblem on its side with binoculars—a red triangle with a cursive *f* in its center—but not near enough to make out anyone on board.

Isaac guides the *Catherine* toward what he's picked as our departure point. If the cold wasn't enough to remind us that we've been traveling north, the return of snow is. A thin layer covers what I assume is a sandy beach, and lines the branches of the few trees in the distance. A craggy outcrop of rocks to our left is clear of snow on account of the crashing waves. Isaac claims the rocks jutting from shore will offer us some protection; the *Catherine* will be able to maneuver into far shallower waters than the large Order vessel without hitting bottom.

It starts to flurry as Xavier loads the lifeboat. It is small, unable to support more than five in weight, which until now has never been a problem for Isaac. He claims he rarely fishes with a crew larger than four. Between our team and all the gear, it will take two trips to get everything to land.

We are on the deck, preparing to make the first run, when we hear a distant rumble. It is faint at first, like a rainstorm strengthening behind the shoreline trees, and then three cars break into view. I realize instantly what has happened. The Order boat has pushed us exactly where they want us.

We drop immediately, stomachs against the deck. I hear the vehicles come to a halt, followed by the opening and closing of doors.

"Isaac Murphy!" comes a man's voice from shore. He must be using something to amplify his words because he sounds as though he stands on deck. "Captain of the *Catherine*. Show yourself."

I hear the door of the wheelhouse slide open, and then Isaac's heavy footsteps on the bridge's exposed deck.

"Glad to see you're finally willing to cooperate, Mr.

Murphy. Now drop anchor."

"Afraid I can't do that," Isaac calls out. "Anchor chain rusted out a few weeks back and I ain't replaced it yet."

"We've got records from a week ago stating the *Catherine* was in perfect working order," the man continues. "Now, a person skipping inspection when they leave port makes me think they're hiding something. Water, for instance. Water they might have bought off AmWest scum and are now looking to make a profit on. If this is untrue—if you've done nothing wrong—then you have no reason to fear us."

"It's got nothing to do with fear," Isaac shouts, "and everything to do with how you ain't got proof I've done something wrong. This is *my* ship. You can come aboard when I invite you, which'll be never."

The Order member lets out an amplified sigh. "Drop anchor now. This is the last time I will ask."

"This is my property, bought with my own earnings, and you ain't got no right to board it whenever you damn well—"

A single shot is fired. Birds flee from the nearby trees and I hear Isaac collapse.

That didn't just happen. It couldn't have. But when I look up toward the bridge, Isaac is slumped against the walls of the wheelhouse, motionless. Blood trails the glass window above him.

I mutter a curse, hear my father do the same at my side.

From the shore there are shouts. "Get the raft. We're boarding and dropping anchor ourselves."

"Like hell you are," Sammy mutters.

Everyone looks at my father. He gives a single nod, and we scramble into position. Bree fires the first shots at the shore and my ears start ringing. There are no more than a dozen Order members on the beach and even though they fire back, we take out half of them easily. The rest crawl behind their vehicles for shelter. They shoot at us when they can, but the *Catherine* is a formidable piece of armor.

Sammy runs off, only to return with rags soaked in something that reeks.

"Diesel," he says. "From the engine room. Think you could get one of these inside a car?"

I nod, not sure how a smelly scrap of cloth will help us, but after he wraps one of my arrows with a rag and strikes a match against it, it goes up in flames. One of the cars is set far out of range, but with a good shot, I just might be able to reach the others. Bree and Sammy cover me as I stand and take aim, fire. The arrow goes clear through the closest car's window and buries itself into the seats, slowly burning the car from the inside out.

"Let's get another," Sammy says, and we repeat the process.

I send the second car up in flames and soon the Order

members are running into the open. Bree takes them down like it's target practice.

There's a blast on the beach, so intense it sends me to the floor, arms over my head. When I recover, I find the first car I fired at a mess of flames and smoke, its windows blown out. Sammy whoops triumphantly.

"Did you know that would happen?"

He winks and ducks to the deck as the second car explodes. He readies an arrow for the final car, despite the fact that I think it's beyond reach. Before I even can take aim, there is a monstrous noise from below. The *Catherine* lurches. We go sliding. I'm forced to let my flaming arrow drop into the ocean.

We are still in open water, far from the rocks that bordered the beach, but we must have run over something. The collision shifts the *Catherine* and she starts drifting into deeper waters, heading closer to the Order vessel at an awkward angle.

Just then, something strikes the walls of the wheelhouse, one of the few parts of the ship built with wood. It goes up in flames. I whip around. The Order vessel is nearly upon us, and apparently firing something as threatening as my burning arrows.

"Let's move!" my father shouts.

Xavier, Bo, Jackson, and Clipper climb into the lifeboat. I

grab Emma and shove her in as well. She barely fits, with all the gear already in the boat.

"What about you?" she asks, eyes wide.

"I'll come later."

Sammy and my father swing the boat over the water and start lowering it down by the pulley system. Emma refuses to let go of my hand.

An explosive noise erupts behind us. It is followed by a terrible screech as something fired by the Order vessel blows through one of the *Catherine*'s metal rigs used to haul fish from the ocean floor. The rig topples overboard, ripping itself free from the deck as it falls. The *Catherine* rocks violently and we lose our footing. Emma's hand is ripped from mine. The lifeboat drops nearly to the water and jams.

"Cut the ropes."

Xavier looks terrified by Owen's words. "But how will you—"

"Cut them now, Xavier. That's an order."

"What if I can't come back in time?"

"There's an inflatable raft below deck. Now go! We'll meet you on shore."

Xavier and Clipper cut the ropes in unison and the lifeboat drops the last several feet into the water. Emma is still staring at me as Xavier fires up the boat's small engine and pulls away.

"Bree!" Owen yells. "The raft!"

She races belowdecks to retrieve it while the rest of us return our attention to the last two Order members on shore. No sooner have we taken them out than the threat behind us gets worse. The Order ship is now close enough to fire bullets, and they ping against the *Catherine*'s deck. I can even make out the faces of the shooters. There is a man in the forefront, shouting savagely. He has a thick beard, a bald scalp, and livid eyes, one of which is as foggy as morning mist. Marco. Frank's go-to man. A man I eluded when I ran from Taem, and again when I returned for the vaccine. A man I'm terrified I may not elude a third time today.

He smiles, as if to say hello, and then aims his handgun directly at me.

He fires.

I don't know where my father comes from. I don't even remember him being near, but he is in front of me now, and then falling against my chest. His hand goes to his jacket and it comes away bloody, so bloody that I know even if I get him to shore there is nothing Emma can do to make this right.

Owen coughs out my name.

"Pa?" I shout, shaking him, but he can barely keep his eyes open. "No. No-no-no, don't do this, Pa!"

His bloody hand grabs at my jacket; his breathing grows ragged. I hear myself screaming, feel Sammy dragging me, his arms hooked at my elbows; but I see only my father, lying on the deck and gasping for air. I need to get him to shore. I need to put pressure on his bleeding chest. I need to send an arrow directly between Marco's eyes for taking him from me.

I struggle against Sammy, but somehow he is stronger. I'm lugged away from the bullets, away from a man I only met a few months ago, a father I've never been able to truly know. He is going to die alone on a sinking ship, end up at the bottom of a watery grave. I won't even get to bury him.

"We have to jump," Sammy shouts. He climbs the railing of the *Catherine* and I realize for the first time how unnatural its angle is. "Gray! Are you listening? Now!"

I glance away from my father, toward the stairwell. "Bree."

Sammy's face is blank and I know what he's thinking. But I'm not about to lose two people in a matter of minutes.

"I have to try." I tell him. "I can't *not* try."

His mouth hardens. He gives me a quick nod and jumps, plummeting into the icy water. I make for the stairs, sliding from the severe angle of the ship. I have only managed to descend half the flight when I am greeted by water.

The *Catherine* is flooding.

SIXTEEN

IT IS COLD.

Freezing.

I am shaking by the time the water crosses my ankles.

Every instinct tells me to turn around, but I force myself forward. My breath comes in short, panicked gulps as the water gets deeper, covering my knees, waist, now chest. I shout Bree's name but I hear only the sound of rushing water forcing its way into the ship, swallowing it whole.

I head for the storage closet, not knowing where else the raft could be kept. The heavy sliding door is still open on its tracks. I wade up to the frame and there's Bree against the far wall, the water creeping toward her chin. She's convulsing with cold and tugging at something beneath the surface. A half-submerged shelving unit has fallen right in front of her.

"The raft stuck on it?" I shout, heart sinking.

She looks up. "No, I g-got it already." She lifts a compact, yellow bag from the water, its shoulder strap already looped over her chest. "You p-pull the tab t-to inflate it."

"Whatever, let's get off this thing."

She tugs again at something beneath the water. "My leg. The shelves. Wh-when the ship went s-sideways."

I realize then how close the unit likely came to hitting her when it toppled. How its metal frame nearly has her pinned against the wall, and how beneath the water, where I can't see, it's somehow holding her in place like an anchor. I take a deep breath and dive. The water is so cold I can't control my exhale and I shoot back to the surface.

"Gray, just g-go," she says, teeth knocking. "T-take the raft and—"

I dive before she can finish. This time I make it to the floor, feel along the shelving unit's frame. It's lying right across her ankle—not crushing her foot, but pinning it so that she can't twist or rotate her leg enough to free herself. I grab the edge of the unit and pull upward. It's heavy. *Too* heavy. And I'm running out of air.

I resurface. The water level is at Bree's lips now, her head tilted back so she can breathe. "G-go," she says. "Before it's—"

"Pull with me this time."

Down again. I plant my feet against the floor, grab the edge of the shelving unit, and push off, like I'm trying to take it to the surface with me. The salt stings my eyes, and my lungs burn in my chest, but when Bree helps pull, we manage to raise the shelves a fraction of an inch. I can feel her twisting her leg beside me, trying to free her ankle. My lungs are screaming. Static darts into the corners of my vision. I pull harder, push off the floor with all my remaining strength, and the unit lifts a bit more. It's enough. I feel Bree slip free, let go of the shelves. I drop them as well and resurface, gasping.

With the raft still slung over her shoulder, Bree lunges at me, hugs me around the neck.

"Gray, I—"

"Come on."

I grab her hand and head for the hallway. I know what she wanted to say, and even if I didn't, we don't have the time to spare for thanks.

When we reach the main stairwell, the water is surging in so aggressively it feels like we're walking against a wall. I can barely move my legs. Bree can't take another step. I help her, but she's suddenly so heavy. I pull. And I pull. And we somehow make it onto the deck.

Here the flurries have become a full-blown blizzard. If the Order vessel is still nearby, it is impossible to tell. The world beyond our ship is a whirlwind of thick flakes, the sky now dark. We crawl against the awkward angle of the deck, climb over the railing of the *Catherine*, and after hooking our arms together, we jump.

My feet hit the water so hard I feel it in my back. We plummet as though we wear extra weight. The water is biting my lungs again. I can't tell which way is up. Bree has stopped kicking. She's become an anchor and she wants to bring me to the bottom.

I fumble with the raft on her shoulder, my eyes burning. I can't find the tab she mentioned. My boots are too heavy. My clothes tug me south.

We are trapped. Water is everywhere.

Ice.

Freezing.

Frozen.

We are going to die here. Drowned. The two of us. Going down with my father. With Isaac and his ship.

I find something protruding from the flattened raft—a loop large enough to hook my fingers through. I pull it.

The water around us fills with bubbles and we're jerked upward as the raft seeks out air. We break from the surface and I am gasping, shaking uncontrollably. Bree isn't breathing. I somehow manage to roll her into the raft, somehow manage to get myself into it as well.

I blow air into Bree's lungs. I push on her chest, which is pointless in the soft-bottomed raft. I try to revive her again, cursing her, shouting at her. She must hear me calling her a coward for dying because she coughs a mouthful of water onto me. Her eyes flutter open and she is shaking once more. She looks like she wants to say something but her lips are trembling too violently. I turn my back on her and begin paddling toward the sound of breaking waves because the snow is too thick to see land. By some miraculous stroke of luck, we wash ashore. The team is nowhere in sight.

"Bree, come on," I urge, my teeth knocking. "We have to move."

"C-cold," she stutters. "Too c-cold. Can barely move."

"That's why you have to."

She shakes, trembles.

"Dammit, Bree. Move your feet!"

And at the order, she does.

Flames still eat at the two destroyed cars. We stumble toward the undamaged one, which sits before a crop of trees. I pull the back open, my hands shaking against my will. The vehicle is loaded with gear: sleeping bags, blankets, Order packs, spare uniforms. These cars weren't planning on returning to the lookout point.

I go to the front. There are keys dangling near the wheel. I watched Bo drive before, and we don't have to go far now, just enough to be safe for the night. I'll have to manage. We'll freeze to death if we waste time looking for the others, and for all I know, the Order is already on our tail.

"Get in," I tell Bree. She does.

I turn the key as I saw Bo do in Taem. The car roars to life. I step on the pedal. The vehicle growls, but doesn't move. I press my foot down harder.

"Sh-shift," Bree says. "Shift it to *drive*."

I follow her eyes to a lever between our seats. I move it as she instructed, and this time, when I put pressure on the pedal, the car lunges forward.

We drive—no, lurch—following the Order's tire tracks from when they first ambushed us. I take a sharp turn, leaving their path, and head into a field of stiff, tall grass. Everything is gray and lifeless under the snowfall. I watch a compass mounted near the shift lever so I'll know how to find the beach again later. There is hot air blasting from vents behind the wheel, but it feels like the most feeble form of heat, too weak to penetrate the icy shell that is settling over my body.

I don't stop driving until the field dips low enough to keep us hidden from anyone passing by way of the Order's original tracks. The snow and wind should cover our own in time, making us invisible. I get out of the car, hands still shaking, and pull the gear from the back. My teeth chatter. My body wants to seize up, stop working, but some innate drive orders me to hurry, tells me what to do and in what order.

I blink, and I've lined the back of the car with sleeping bags. I blink again and I've turned the vehicle off, shut all the doors to lock the heat within. I blink a third time, and I'm stripping off my jacket.

"Take your clothes off," I order Bree.

She's just standing there shaking, her hair wet against her neck, her face so pale she already looks dead.

"Bree!"

"C-can't . . . I can't."

"You *can*. You can do anything I can do."

And something in those words wakes her. She pulls off her jacket and tugs her shirt overhead. And then another layer, and another. She fumbles with her pants but her trembling fingers can't manage the buttons. I help her out of them. I take her boots off, too. And her socks. I dry her hair as best I can with a blanket, help her into one of the spare Order uniforms, and send her into the warmth of the car.

My fists are cramping up. I can barely move, barely breathe. I'm so cold I think my lungs might freeze solid, shattering when I take my next breath. I pull off my shirt, my pants, everything. I force my cramping limbs into dry clothes and crawl back into the car.

I lie down alongside Bree. She is shaking uncontrollably. I'm shaking, too.

"Bree?"

There's something else I want to say, about body warmth, and staying near each other, but I can't form the words. I nudge closer to her, pull her into my chest, wrap us in the blankets. I hold her until our convulsions turn to trembles, which turn to shivers that finally fade.

It takes a very, very long time, but I finally feel warmth. It starts in my chest and spreads to my torso, then knees, then toes, and it is as I fall asleep that I no longer fear I won't wake up.

SEVENTEEN

WE RISE WITH THE SUN.

The storm has left no more than three inches of snow on the ground, meaning it must have arrived in a hurry and died out nearly as fast. Our clothes, which I draped over the front seats last night to dry, are still stiff and damp with salt water. We'll be wearing the Order uniforms for a while longer.

Bree nurses a fire to life, a blanket pulled tightly around her shoulders, while I dig through the car and assess supplies. Our personal gear—bags, tents, weapons, additional clothes, matches, flashlights, *everything*—was in the lifeboat that Xavier and the others escaped on. I find some wanted posters with my face on them in the car and pass them to

Bree. She adds them to the fire, which is smoking from the mostly green wood she's had to use for the base. Still, it's emitting warmth, and for that I'm grateful. A blanket, no matter how you wrap it, is not terribly warm. We need jackets. Underwear wouldn't hurt either, given how damn stiff the uniforms are.

"Do you think they made it?" Bree asks.

"They had to. If we don't believe they did, we're already doomed."

"And Sammy?"

"He jumped when I went back for you. If he got to shore and found the others, he might have had a chance. They had extra clothing, could have started a fire and made sure he was dry. If not, I don't see how he would have survived the night."

Bree bends to blow on the flames. I'm glad she hasn't asked about my father yet. I don't have the strength to even think about him. When she glances back at me, her face is softer than I've ever seen it. There is no scowl on her lips, no harsh angle to her brows.

"Last night," she says. "I was so cold my hands wouldn't work. And it hurt to breathe. I couldn't . . . I'm sorry I wasn't—"

"Stop it. You were fine. You were perfect." She messes with the fire a bit more, avoids my eyes. "I mean it, Bree. I wouldn't have made it through last night if it hadn't been for you."

"Me?" She straightens up, scoffing. "You were the one who did everything. You got me off the ship, you revived me on the raft, you set up the blankets—"

"And you kept me warm. All that stuff I did earlier? It would have been pointless if I'd frozen to death during the night. I kept you alive, and then you kept me alive. We kept each other warm. We got through it together."

She forces a smile, a tiny lopsided one. Her braided hair has dried in an odd manner, half of it clumped at the side of her neck in a mangled knot, but she somehow still manages to be stunning. It's her lips in that smile. Her chin, held defiantly high. It must require her to stifle every ounce of her pride, because she's frowning viciously when she adds, "I'm glad we're talking again."

"Yeah." I smile, unable to hide my amusement. "Me, too."

There aren't any jackets in the car, but I do find clean cotton shorts.

"Underwear?" I say, tossing the smallest pair to Bree. She turns her back to me, and shamelessly starts changing. I should really look away, but I can't help myself. When she's fully clothed, she goes back to poking at the fire, either unaware that I've been staring at her, or not concerned enough to care. I change, too, throw the blanket back over my shoulders, and return to assessing the gear.

There's not much else that will help us if we don't find the rest of the team in the next day or two. Some matches, dried fruit, a knife, binoculars, eyewear that I suspect to be night-vision goggles because they look similar to some Rebel gear I once saw Harvey working on. But no water: the one thing we can't go long without.

I scour the rest of the car, and find only a map and hand-gun in a compartment in the front. The weapon is fully loaded, so that gives us six precious shots between the two of us. I hope we don't need them.

I unfold the map. We may have wiped out the ground crew, but Marco and the rest of his men on the Order ship were unharmed. If we head south and return to the beach, we risk running into them. Unless they chose to stay on the water rather than pursue us.

Maybe Bree and I should just take the car and drive north-west, try to find Group A. Why had I never picked Bo's brain these past few weeks? He kept saying over and over that he practically had direct coordinates, and somehow I never managed to get them from him. That knowledge belongs only to him, Clipper, and my father.

No.

It *was* knowledge my father possessed. Just like that, he's become a piece of the past. Yesterday Owen stood beside me on the *Catherine* and today he's gone. Dead.

I ball up the map and slam my hands against the compartment where I found the gun. Hard. Then harder. Then again and again until my palms are throbbing.

"Are you okay?" Bree is standing outside the door.

I rub my forehead with the heel of my hand. "Yes. Why wouldn't I be?"

"You *are* crying."

I touch my cheeks and my fingers come away wet. I don't remember telling myself I could cry.

"I caught breakfast," she says, holding up a squirrel speared on a stick. "I'll cook it. You take as long as you need."

I flatten the map out, fold it up neatly, and immediately join Bree.

"That was fast," she says.

"I was wasting time."

"You lost someone you love. Not a single moment you spend in mourning is a waste." She skins the squirrel and sets the meat over our feeble fire.

"How did you know?"

"I saw him. When you pulled me up the stairwell and onto the deck. He was just lying there." She glances at me, her face somber. "I'm really sorry, Gray."

"Sorry doesn't change what happened."

"I know. But I still feel it."

When the food is cooked we sit on the rear of the vehicle—her feet dangling, mine planted in the snow—and pull apart the meat with our fingers. It is dark, but moist, and it fills us well enough. Bree tosses the spear into the fire when we're done.

"What now?" she asks.

"We should take the car, I think. Head west. Look for the team."

"I'll drive," she offers.

But I'm not ready. Because moving on means leaving this place and traveling farther from my father. Every moment from here on out will be a step away from him. I let a hand fall on Bree's thigh.

"I need a moment."

"Sure." Her fingers curl around mine.

We sit there, staring at the flames until I feel strong enough to continue.

Bree's driving is exceptionally better than mine.

Over the years, the Rebels managed to take a few abandoned Order vehicles into their custody and—with the help of workers in the technology wing—bring them back to life. Bree learned how to drive during her time at Crevice Valley before I arrived. She tells me that some cars run electrically while others require fuel. The differences mean nothing to me until Bree says we are in a fuel-powered model and that it is likely the best fit given our current situation.

"We've got about a half tank of gas left," she says, squinting at the markings behind the wheel. "Should get us another hundred fifty miles or so. Either way, we've got enough to track down the others."

"Assuming they want to be found." I'm fearful the team will be extra cautious from here on out, running for cover at the first sound of an approaching car.

"We'll find them," she says sternly. "And if we don't, we should be able to make it to Group A, and they'll catch up with us there."

I don't mention that I'm unsure how exactly to find Group A.

The car bounces over the uneven ground as Bree takes us out of the field. She slows as we reach the Order's tire tracks from yesterday. They are nearly invisible, almost completely filled in with fresh snow.

"What do you think?" she asks.

"We can't *not* check the beach. If they're not there, we may at least find their tracks. If there's no sign of them, we'll just keep driving."

She nods and fiddles with the dial controlling the heat. We may be miserable, but at least we're no longer cold.

Two skeletons of cars. Eleven dead Order members. One abandoned lifeboat.

This is what we find on the beach.

Our car is hidden back in the trees and the air feels frigid outside the warmth of the vehicle, but Bree and I scour the shore thoroughly. She carries the handgun because she's the better shot.

The dead Order members are covered in the snow that fell last night, and for this, I am glad. I don't want to see their faces, the look of shock in their eyes, the places where bullets met flesh. I feel like I've seen far too much these past few days.

We make our way down to the water, which is lapping peacefully against the wet earth. The rocky outcrop to our right is covered in the white froth of waves. Even when we climb out to the point, there's no sign of the Order. They could have gone to Haven, to gather another team so they could track us more efficiently. Or maybe they are still sailing, waiting to spot us from afar. Either way, they will find us. Marco will not let us slip away again. I'm sure of it.

A trio of crows soars by, circling over the dead bodies. I look out across the water, scanning for any sign of the *Catherine*, but the Gulf seems to have devoured her thoroughly. I wonder if Dixie made it off the boat or if she went down with her master. So much for cats being good luck.

Bree and I are carefully climbing back to the shore when I spot footprints heading toward the trees. They are mostly filled in by the snowfall, but one thing is clear: This person was walking with an uneven gait, almost as though he were shaking against his will.

"Sammy," I say, pointing.

We follow his trail into the trees. His prints meet another pair, where it appears that he was then dragged.

"Did the Order take him?" Bree asks.

I shake my head, uncertain, and we continue to follow the tracks until we stumble upon a particularly dense cluster of trees. Beneath them, kept mostly clear of snowfall, is a pile of dark coals. The Order wouldn't have stopped to make a fire. One of our team must have heard Sammy coming. He was not being dragged away against his will; he was being dragged because he couldn't continue without aid.

I put a hand over the coals, but they give off no heat.

"They're long gone. Doesn't even look like they made camp. There's no sign of tents being set up."

"But they're alive," Bree says, smiling.

"They are."

And when I say it, I feel the weight lift off my chest, a burden I didn't even know was there to begin with. The team is alive. *Emma* is alive. And right then I forgive her. For everything. I'm tired of living in the past and dwelling on things that have come and gone—especially when the people you care for can be taken from you in the time it takes to blink. I glance toward the shore, thinking of my father.

"They went this way," Bree says. She checks the sky. "North."

Our eyes meet and without exchanging another word, we hurry back to the car. The team has likely been hiking since yesterday, possibly traveling through the night to put extra distance between themselves and the Order. We have wheels and can travel quickly, but I worry about our chances. What are the odds our paths will intersect when this land seems to stretch on forever?

Bree drives. I watch the water disappear in the mirror that hangs between us. It fades into a blue sliver, dividing the snow-whitened beach from an overcast sky. In a matter of seconds, it is gone entirely.

It is only when it has slipped from view that the words escape me.

"'Bye, Pa."

I'm positive Bree hears, but she keeps her eyes on the horizon. I appreciate that small, private moment with my father more than she will ever know.

EIGHTEEN

WE FOLLOW THE TEAM'S TRACKS, but they are disguised by windblown snow, filled in, and often difficult to see. We end up having to obsessively right our course. The air in the car grows warm and thick. It's making me sleepy, but Bree's pace is so aggressive I keep getting jerked awake each time my eyelids drift shut.

It is midday when we spot dark silhouettes on the horizon.

"The Order?"

"Don't think so," Bree says, her lips pressing into a smile. "There're six of them. And look at that one on the end, being dragged. That has to be the Forgery. It's them, Gray!"

She throws a palm against the steering wheel, which makes the vehicle cry like a goose. As we slide over the snowy ground, I roll down the window and hang half my torso out. Bree is laughing and I'm shouting like an idiot at the ants on the horizon, one arm clinging to the inside of the car, the other waving frantically. The wind tears at my face. My eyes start streaming. Soon they are no longer minuscule shadows, but figures with recognizable features. They are all there: Xavier, Bo, Sammy, Clipper, the Forgery. And Emma. Emma with her hair whipping in the wind and sprinting toward the car to meet me. Emma who's dropping her bag so she can run faster.

Bree brakes and the car skids sideways in the shallow snow. I duck back inside, throw open the door. Emma's so close, and then she's in my arms, her body colliding with mine, and I'm hugging her, kissing the top of her head.

"I thought you . . ." She looks up at me, amazed, relieved. I hear the others arriving, their feet crunching in the snow. Someone is greeting Bree, hands are being clasped, but I can see only Emma, her eyes wide and cavernous, so large I lose myself in them.

"I'm sorry," she says. "About Craw, about everything. I'm so—"

"I know. And I'm over it."

She looks doubtful.

"I was furious, Emma," I admit. "Really, *really* furious. I felt so betrayed, so sick at the thought of you with him, and the anger was the only thing that helped me feel better. I *needed* the grudge. But then the Forged version of Blaine almost killed you, I nearly drowned on that ship, and now I just want to put it all behind us while we still have the chance. Please? Right now. Let's forget everything that happened before."

"But I don't want to forget it," she says. "Not the birds, or the day you taught me to shoot an arrow, or climbing the Wall, or how it felt to see your car crest that hill."

I can't help smiling, because I don't want to lose those memories either. "Fine. Only the bad moments. The mistakes. Let's forget the mistakes and move on."

She nods, buries her face in my chest. I hug her tighter. And then, in the back of my mind, a worry blooms. If Craw is the mistake Emma must forget, is Bree mine?

But Bree wasn't a mistake. Bree was *never* a mistake. I know it. I can feel it in my gut.

Which is why it is all so confusing. Because this, right here, is what I've wanted since I was a child: Emma. After so many missteps and grudges and errors, we might finally be able to set things right, and I'm happy at the prospect, so mind-numbingly happy, that I can't understand how it is possible to be simultaneously sad.

Bree and I ditch the Order uniforms and change into extra clothes from our gear bags, which the team thankfully chose to hold on to even when they assumed we were dead. Xavier explains how the lifeboat got them safely to shore, where they then headed into the trees for cover.

"We heard someone stumbling toward us. Thought it might be the Order, but it turned out to be Sammy. He was blue. Could barely walk. We started a fire but he was shaking so badly we practically had to undress him ourselves before we could get him warm again."

"Oh, I believe it," Bree says, and then she drops her head as if the memory of her own struggles last night embarrasses her. Sammy puts an arm protectively around Emma's shoulders and glares between me and Bree, eyes narrowed. I feel like he's hearing words that haven't been spoken.

It's quiet for a moment and when Bo speaks, my entire being tightens up.

"Owen?" he asks.

I swallow, look at my boots.

"He's not with us, and he's not with them, so where do you think that puts him?" the Forgery says.

My fist flies. I hear Jackson's nose crack, he falls into the snow, and then I'm grabbing the handgun from Bree. I point it at the Forgery, livid, possessed.

"My father is dead because of you!" I yell. The weapon quivers from how hard I'm squeezing it. "You called that Order ship and now he's dead!"

"Your ship was singled out because you left Bone Harbor suspiciously early," he responds. "You brought this upon yourself."

"You worthless, lying—"

"We had a deal! My safety for entry to the Outer Ring. If I'm going to betray you it will be after that deal is complete, not on a boat where I have nowhere to run."

I press the gun against his forehead and his face washes over with shock. "Tell me why I shouldn't do it. Give me one good reason."

Nothing. No pleading. No begging. No words of defense.

Almost as if he *wants* me to pull the trigger.

My finger moves for it, but it's like that time in Taem all over again, when I couldn't bring myself to shoot an Order member even though his bullet nearly killed Bree. My arm starts shaking. The outstretched gun grows heavy.

Killing Jackson won't bring back my father. And I don't want another face joining the one I already see in my nightmares: Forged Blaine, the arrow in his skull. No, if I have to meet the people I kill again in my dreams, I'm saving this bullet for Marco.

I lower the weapon, hand shaking, and pass it back to Bree. The team stands there in a ring around me and Jackson, speechless.

"Maybe we should talk about where to go from here," Bo says eventually. "Clipper, you want to share that theory of yours with Gray?"

The boy pulls out his location device. My pulse is still pounding from the confrontation with Jackson, but I take a deep breath and try to focus on what Clipper's showing me: the landlines running along the western edge of the water and continuing north once the bay ends, dividing AmEast from AmWest.

"Group A's around here." Clipper touches an area of land between the two ears of water. "As you pointed out on the *Catherine*, it seems like the Order is expecting us to enter AmWest. They'll probably sail up Border Bay and try to cut us off at the border."

"That theory assumes the Forgery didn't tell them *exactly* where we were going when he ratted us out," I say. Jackson glares at me.

"I think the Order would have followed us onto land if that were the case," Bo says. "And they didn't. That ship took back to sea."

"But aren't the borders highly patrolled?" Bree asks. "I can't believe they think we'd try to cross it on foot."

"Ignorant is what it is," Sammy says. "We should thank our lucky stars we're dealing with idiots."

"They're not so dumb if they tracked us and sank our ship!"

"I see the icy water didn't improve your spirits, Nox," he shoots back. "And here I was thinking you couldn't get any more frigid."

Bree shoves Sammy so hard he stumbles backward.

"Okay, okay!" Xavier says, stepping between them. "This is pointless. What's the plan?"

The group falls silent and everyone turns to look at me and Bo. I glance at him for help, but he just shrugs. "What do you think, Gray? This is your mission."

But it's not. It was my father's. I may have suggested the excursion, talked with Bo about getting Ryder to endorse it, but Owen was in charge. He was the leader. I'm just some guy whose father is dead, who climbed a Wall and got stuck in a mess far bigger than himself.

"How much longer until we get to the Outer Ring?" I ask Clipper.

"About three days on foot." He eyes the car behind me. "But we could be there tonight if we drove."

The car only has five seats, but the rear area is enclosed

and large enough to hold the other three in our group.

"We'll drive," I say. "It will be tight, especially with all the gear, but if the Order thinks we're walking, we should cover as much ground as possible."

"We'll run out of fuel soon," Bree warns. "We should be able to make it to Group A, but it will be a one-way trip."

"Good. Then it's settled."

The team starts loading up the gear and Emma brushes past me to examine Jackson. He's still sitting in the snow, touching his nose cautiously.

"Broken again. And I just set it on the boat." Emma twists to face me. "I know you're upset, Gray, but you can't go around attacking our team."

"He is *not* a part of our team."

She gives me a taxed look. "He's traveling with us and if he's hurt, I have to tend to him. That makes him part of the group."

"Maybe by your standards," I say. "But not mine."

Emma sighs, bandages in hand. "Can you please just think things through before you react? I know it's hard for you, but you have to try. You're better than this."

She sounds oddly like Blaine, disappointed, calling me out for my shortcomings. But in this moment I don't need to hear about my faults. My father is dead and I need to hear that there are situations where logic and reason don't apply, that sometimes an ugly action is a necessary one. I need to hear that I'm not a failure for being impulsive. Above all, I just need someone to say, "It's okay. I understand," and if they can't say that, I don't want them to say anything at all.

NINETEEN

CRAMMED BETWEEN EMMA AND BO in the backseat, Clipper calls out directions while Bree drives. Sammy and Xavier are in the rear with the Forgery and most of the gear. Each time we crest a new rise in the plain and see nothing but more land, Sammy asks for an updated estimate on our time of arrival. Bree's patience runs out quickly.

"Sammy, I don't see how you can spend weeks hiking and not once ask how much farther we have to go, but now, when we are in a car and you know perfectly well we'll arrive at Group A by dusk, you suddenly need a progress update every two minutes."

"Nox, if you had to sit back here, feeling carsick because

the person driving can't steer better than an uncoordinated toddler, you'd ask for updates, too."

Bree glares at him in the mirror. "You better watch your back when we make camp."

The team chuckles, but I'm staring out the window, watching the landscape fly by. Everything in the Western Territory is gray or white or dead. The snow accumulations seem to grow. The car slides now and again, but Bree makes no attempt to slow our pace. When the sky is just beginning to lose some of its light, a dull structure appears in the distance. The wall encircling Group A's Outer Ring.

"The nearest town is on the northern side," Clipper says, studying the location device resting in his lap. "Maybe a two-hour drive out. We should be fine approaching from any direction."

The car is silent except for the uneven rhythm of Bo's characteristic tapping as Bree brings us closer. Soon, the wall is towering above us. Imprinted on it is the same word, spaced out at even intervals: *QUARANTINE*. The letters are aggressive, each one blocklike and powerful despite its now-faded state. I know they are a lie, but I can see why people stayed clear when Frank set up these test groups to initiate the Laicos Project.

Bree takes us slowly around the structure. We're all

looking for an inconsistency in the facade, a place that might open wide enough for a car, when Jackson announces, "Right here. Stop."

Sammy and Xavier lug the Forgery outside on my instruction. From my seat, I watch as Jackson runs his hands along the wall, following a seam that is so subtle I'm amazed he spotted it from the moving car.

"You should have let me try first." Clipper sounds disappointed, like he's been told to sit out a thrilling game.

"We didn't even recognize this stretch of wall as the entrance," I say. "And besides, it's time we put all the Forgery's talk to the test."

Outside the car, Jackson brushes snow aside from the base of the wall and presses a palm against it. A panel the size of his hand pops open. He starts tapping at something I can't make out from where I sit.

"Say he enters the right access code," Bree says. "Will it even open? Frank cut off power for Group A ages ago."

"I talked about this with Ryder before we left," Clipper says. "There's likely a backup power source just for the entrance. One the Order can manually tap into if they ever chose to revisit the place."

Jackson rubs his forehead almost nervously, then stands. A moment later, the entrance is sliding open.

"Took him long enough," Emma says, which I find

amusing since it seemed rather quick to me and could have taken Clipper far longer.

Sammy shoves Jackson back in the car. "Can we off this maggot now?" he asks.

I almost say yes. The deal is complete and it's not worth keeping Jackson alive any longer. Not with the stunt he pulled on the *Catherine*. But my father is gone and he's never coming back and I want Jackson to suffer for it. I don't want it to be quick. I want him to feel pain and I want him to feel it for a long, long time. Maybe this makes me heartless, but I don't care.

"We're leaving him tied up to something in Group A," I say. "He can starve to death."

"You can't do that," Jackson says, voice panicked. "I held up my part of the deal."

"Well, Forgery, now you know what betrayal feels like."

"Dammit, put a bullet in me if you have to. But leaving me to freeze? To starve? No man should die that way."

I feel like countering with the fact that he's a Forgery, not a man, but I settle on an offer. A gracious one that he doesn't even deserve.

"Maybe if you tell us where Frank thought our mission team was originally headed, I'll reconsider. So how about it? Did he think we were trying to contact AmWest? Is there a reason we should stop thinking of them as our enemy?"

The Forgery doesn't respond.

"Fine," I say. "Starve to death."

He swears. I don't know what he expected. He made it clear that he'd try to complete his mission in the end, and our deal just prolonged the inevitable. If he has no information left to give me, I won't give him a chance to retrieve Crevice Valley's location. Especially when I know his methods of procuring it will include torture.

I tell Bree to drive into the Outer Ring. A shadow passes over the car, and we are inside.

It brings back a lot of memories. Running with Emma. The feeling of confusion and bewilderment at finding not only more land beyond Claysoot, but another wall still trapping us in place, not to mention the sprawling, unimaginable world outside it. I crack my window open, and the bite of cold air is a comfort.

We cut through the dead, snow-covered earth until Group A's Wall suddenly looms before us. I scramble from the car, walk up to the structure, and lay a palm against it. It is smooth and sleek, the facade like ice to the touch. It looks just like our Claysoot Wall.

"Now what?" Xavier asks.

The entire team is watching me, even Bo. I hate that I've somehow become the person in charge. I have no clue what I'm doing.

Bo seems frigid and miserable; Emma, anxious. Clipper looks . . . young. I don't know how my father handled having so many people under his command. I don't know how to lead them. I only know what I would do alone, so that's where I start.

"These people are cautious. When we saw them in the control room, they were barely visible—just a quick glimpse of a hand or leg. If we saunter in now, while there's still a bit of light, there's no way they'll show themselves. But at night, if we are quiet about our approach, we may be able to find them before they have the chance to hide. And we could use the cover of dark either way; I don't want to be spotted by the cameras."

Now that I've started talking, the plan is forming effortlessly. "We'll split up. Bo will man the camp here—with Xavier and Emma—so that we have ears on the outside. The rest of us are going in."

While Sammy warms canned beans over a fire for dinner, Xavier and I take an inventory of our weapons. What made it off the ship on the lifeboat is all we have left: Xavier's bow and arrows; two knives, carried by Bo and Clipper; two extra handguns stowed away in my father's pack. There's also the gun I found in the Order car that Bree's currently carrying.

When Sammy says dinner is ready, I bring a cup of beans to Jackson. He's locked in the car, staring at the towering

Wall through his window. Something in his eyes looks a bit too hopeful.

It should have been him, I decide—not Owen—that went down with the *Catherine*.

It is dark and once again snowing when we move the car alongside the Wall to make our crossing. Xavier lends me his bow—I've never favored firearms, especially if they don't have a lengthy barrel—and he takes one of my father's handguns so that the team staying behind isn't left unarmed. Sammy has the second of my father's guns, and Bree, the weapon that's been tucked in her waistband since I threatened Jackson with it.

There were only two pairs of night-vision goggles in the Order's car and I'm wearing one of them. Bree has the other. The rest of the team coming with us has flashlights stowed away, though the goal is to avoid using them unless absolutely necessary. We've also got a handheld radio so that we can communicate with the crew staying behind. Clipper double- and triple-checks the channels and reception before telling me we're ready.

As the team scrambles onto the car to make the climb, a hand grabs my elbow. Emma.

"I want to go with you," she says. "I could help if someone gets hurt." She puts her palms on the front of my jacket and

I feel a familiar ache in my chest.

"No one's getting hurt."

"But if they do, I should be there."

"Clipper knows enough first aid to handle anything minor."

She frowns. "If the worst injuries will be minor, I don't see why I can't come."

This debate could go in circles all night. I put my hands on her shoulders. "Emma." She looks up at me. "Please stay here, with Bo and Xavier. With people we trust. Where it's safe. I'll be back soon."

She glances at the Wall. "Just be careful?"

"I'll try my hardest not to do anything stupid."

"I'm not sure that makes me feel better. I know how you are."

I laugh, then freeze as she hooks her hands behind my neck. She raises herself up onto her toes and plants a kiss on my lips. Quick and friendly, but there are a million memories attached to it.

"I have a good feeling about this," she says, stepping back. "Group A. The mission. A real good feeling."

"Me, too," I say, overwhelmed with newfound confidence. "I'll see you soon. Promise."

She gives me her typical half smile. "I'll be waiting."

I head for the car, climb onto the roof where the team waits impatiently. Especially Bree. She's scowling at me, arms folded against her chest, pointer fingers tapping her biceps. There's something else to the expression, an emotion I can't place. Fear, maybe? Anxiety?

"You okay?" I ask.

"I'm a big girl, Gray. I don't care who you kiss."

"I meant about the Wall," I say, taken aback. "Are you ready?"

"Oh." Now she looks insulted, almost as if she wanted me to ask about a kiss I didn't initiate or plan for. "Of course." She pauses and frowns. "Unless they're crazy like Fallyn predicted—a bunch of savages. That would complicate things."

Fallyn, a Rebel captain and the main representative of Bree's people from Saltwater, never supported our mission. She swore we'd trek halfway across the country and find nothing but wild animals living behind the Wall, but I always thought the clips we saw in the control room suggested otherwise.

"We'll be fine," I say. "Especially together. I'm never more confident than when you have my back."

"Stop it," she snaps. "Don't say stuff like that."

"Like what?"

"Stuff about me and you and *us*. It only makes it harder."

"So I can't speak my mind? Even if it's true?"

She scowls so intently the look turns into something more sad than fierce. "Especially if it's true."

"You want me to lie to you?"

"I don't care what you do so long as it doesn't feel like you're standing on my chest and breaking my rib cage."

And so we are back to this—comfortable one moment, at arms with each other the next—and that's just fine. I can play this game with her. Push her, taunt her, egg her on, be consistently sarcastic. I can be all the reasons I told her we'd never work to begin with. It's not even a struggle; it's second nature, us at each other's throats. As easy as breathing.

"If you get spotted by a camera on the other side, don't expect me to save your ass when the Order swoops in to investigate."

She smirks, and it makes her look a bit more like herself. "Likewise."

"Also, your boots are untied."

Bree looks down and finds her laces tightly bound. She shoves me, her lips pinched together like she's holding in a combination of laughter and fury.

Sammy clears his throat. "Are we doing this or are we going to stand around all night?"

"No, we're going," I say, and at my words, Xavier is beside me, offering interwoven fingers to use as a stepping stool.

"I'll see you on the other side," I say to Bree. Her face

hardens and she nods: one small, curt movement of her chin.

I put my boot into Xavier's palms and he heaves me upward. My hands find the top of the Wall and I pull.

PART THREE

OF SURVIVORS

TWENTY

I HANG FROM THE STRUCTURE, dangling a moment before finally letting go.

For the brief slice of time that I'm in free fall, I imagine I'm returning to Claysoot, that when my feet hit the ground I'll find clay earth beneath them and a familiar hunting trailhead nearby. But inside this Wall, the land is as barren as its Outer Ring. Any trees that grow are saplings, rare and spread out over the snow-covered ground. I think I can make out the silhouettes of buildings in the distance, but the steady snowfall prevents me from being certain.

There is a soft thud and Bree is beside me. Clipper comes next, followed by Jackson and finally, Sammy. I move to rebind Jackson's arms, and he stumbles away from me, resting a hand on the Wall for support.

"I feel sick," he says.

I'm positive it's part of an act so that he can run for it, escape the fate we have planned for him, but then he loses his dinner in the snow.

"Come on," I say, tugging him.

He looks at the Wall and jerks his head to the side as though dodging a punch, then pinches the bridge of his nose and starts muttering.

"What's with him?" Bree hisses.

"Hey, pull it together." I shake Jackson and his eyes fly open.

"We can't go in," he says. "It's bad. This place is bad."

He keeps muttering, twitching. Clipper looks absolutely terrified, and I can't have the Forgery putting on a show over nothing, scaring the wits out of my team.

"Hey!" I slap at his shoulder. "Jackson!"

He freezes. "You said my name."

"If I knew it would make you easier to control, I would have stopped calling you Forgery a long time ago. I'm retying your arms and if you can't stay quiet, I have no problem breaking your nose again before we find a place to strand you. You want to starve to death with a broken nose, or just starve?"

He offers me his wrists. "I think . . . I need . . ." His head falls into his chest and he cringes again, like he's experiencing a jolt of pain. "I don't know anymore. I don't know anything."

"Let's go," I say to the others, startled at what a good actor Jackson's becoming. "He'll be fine."

Sammy grabs Jackson by the elbow to escort him. "A Forgery wasn't enough. We had to land one having a nervous breakdown."

Bree snaps at him to be quiet and we fall into a steady march. It's difficult to see through the flurrying snow, but I can make out barren crop fields and livestock corrals as we head into town.

Group A was the most well stocked of the test groups, supplied with electricity and running water until Frank cut them off. I've known this since the day I read his documentation of the project, but I never truly comprehended those living conditions until now, as we step into the town itself. How this group managed to revolt and attack one another, nearly dying out when they had so many resources at their disposal, is beyond me. Building after building stand pressed together, rooflines caved in. Some are mere skeletons, their frames exposed. Others have intact walls but look moments away from collapsing. Even given the deterioration, it is obvious they were once immaculate. And modern.

I squint, peering through the shattered windows of a structure to my right. School desks sit inside, some tipped over. The next building is a hospital, far more advanced than the Clinic Emma and her mother manned. Here, the beds are on wheels and the cabinets lining the walls are heavy-duty encasements with locks. Contents have been pulled from them and left scattered about the floor: rusted scissors, broken equipment, small bottles of medicine that rock in the wind.

Jackson is still muttering as we approach a wooden platform. A T-shaped formation rises from its base, and a looped rope dangles from the highest point. I think it must be like our Council Bell—a device somehow used to call meetings to order—until Sammy whispers, "Gallows." Then he reenacts pulling one of the ropes over his head and tightening it about his neck. He cocks his head to the side, lets his tongue hang out of his mouth, and I understand. We give the platform a wide berth as we pass.

"Remember when you said you'd prove me wrong?" Bree whispers to me. "Well, this place doesn't look very populated."

"They have to be here. We saw them."

What I don't say is that I'm growing as worried as she is that we hiked across all of AmEast for nothing. I didn't expect survivors to come pouring into the streets to greet us, but we haven't seen a single sign of life. The possibility that Group A killed one another off is seeming more and more probable.

But then . . .

"There!"

A streak of light moves through one of the buildings ahead. It is faint, blotted out by the snowfall. Bree and I break into a run. Sammy shouts something about staying with the Forgery, and we don't slow. I burst into the building, Bree on my heels. Two deer carcasses hang from the ceiling and the air is metallic with the scent of blood. The first sign of people. Of survivors.

"Hello?" Bree calls out.

We move around a table laden with cleavers and mallets. Floorboards creak on the other side of the room. I have an arrow ready and Bree's got the handgun pointed into the darkness. I hope whoever is in here can't see as well as we can with our night vision. I doubt we look very approachable.

"Hello?" Bree tries again.

Footsteps, and then a figure carrying a torch, rendered white by my goggles.

It sprints between the two carcasses and out a side door. Bree and I follow, darting across an alley and into another building. We enter a wide room—a barn, maybe—empty except for wooden crates and a couple of shovels.

Weapons ready, Bree and I move into the center of the room. The torch, and the figure carrying it, have disappeared.

An outburst from the streets reaches us: Clipper scream-ing for help; Sammy shouting.

Jackson. We never should have left the others alone with him. The Forgery's hysterics were an act, just as I suspected. He's probably making a run for it right now.

But before I can move, the floor comes to life beneath me, folding in on itself. Bree and I glance at each other and then we are falling.

I hit bottom and see white. Heat shoots through my back. I gasp for air, over and over, and finally it returns to my lungs. A stranger leaps from above and the trapdoor through which Bree and I fell is pulled shut.

The stranger holds the torch at arm's length, blinking rapidly, as though its brilliance hurts his eyes. I pull off the night-vision goggles to see him properly. He's not much older than I am, with wild hair that clumps together in matted, shoulder-length sections, and pale—almost trans-lucent—skin. Something dark and tarlike is smeared across most of his face as a sort of nighttime camouflage. He leans forward and flashes a blade before me.

"It 'pears we have guests," he says.

It is only then, as additional torches are lit, that I notice the half dozen bodies waiting along the edges of the room. The group is entirely male, their clothing a haphazard blend of materials—furs patched with cotton and wool and leather.

They crouch like animals near the walls—knees bony, palms against the floor—and blink their bloodshot eyes.

A single word comes to mind, a word Fallyn spoke when she laughed at our mission plans.

Savages.

And they have us surrounded.

TWENTY-ONE

I SCRAMBLE BACKWARD, MY SHOULDERS pressing into Bree's. The boy lays the flat edge of his blade beneath my chin and presses upward, forcing me to look at him.

"I wouldn't be makin' fast moves." His words come out strung together, bleeding into one another as he disregards consonants. "I might think yer comin' after me. Be forced to slit yer throat."

A door behind him bursts open and two males enter, dragging Clipper, Sammy, and Jackson. All three are bound and gagged. The team's earlier shouts had nothing to do with the Forgery after all.

"We got the others, Titus," one of the escorts says.

Titus lowers his knife from my chin and turns toward

them. Bree and I sense our chance and act at the same moment. She scrambles to her feet and I grab the radio from my hip.

"Xavier. We're—"

Titus's fist comes out of nowhere. I taste blood, drop the radio. The world goes momentarily blurry. When my vision steadies, Titus is standing before me, unwrapping a metal chain from his palm. He stomps on the radio, crushing it beneath his heel.

"That's enough!" Bree shouts, the handgun trained on him. "Untie them." She motions toward the rest of our team with the barrel. "Do it now or I swear I will fire."

Titus slashes his knife so quickly I don't see it coming. One moment he's still and the next my chest is on fire. I gasp, press a palm against my shirt. The material grows damp, and my fingers sticky.

"Put it down, girlie," Titus says to Bree, "or next time he's gettin' worse."

"We came to help you," she says, refusing to lower the gun. "We came—"

"And we ain't askin' for yer help! But that's the thing with yer people. Ya think ya know what's best for e'erybody. Ya think so much ya don't think at all."

I blink, and his blade is against my neck for a second time. The two men behind Titus have brought knives to Sammy's and Clipper's throats as well. Only Jackson is left unthreatened, but seeing as we had him bound from the beginning, it was probably clear we never cared much for his safety. For a split second I hope that he will take advantage of this and somehow free us all. A foolish, desperate thought.

"Put down yer weapon and we'll have a nice talk," Titus says to Bree.

"How do I know you won't slit his throat when I lower my gun?"

"Yer just gonna have to trust me."

"Why would I do that?"

"Cus if ya don't, I'll kill yer whole team instead."

Bree shifts her footing. "You're bluffing."

But I know he's not. I can see it in his bloodshot eyes. We were wrong to think these people wanted our help, that we could convince them to join our cause, turn their prison into our hideout. So wrong.

"Bree," I say. Titus's knife grates against my throat. "It's not worth it."

"I can do this," she says.

They are too spaced out. She'll only get a shot off, two at best, before one of us is dead.

"You're good, but you're not this good. No one is. If you're smart, you'll acknowledge that."

Her grip is shaking now, the gun quivering as it darts between Titus and his men. Bree swallows and lowers the weapon. Titus snatches it from her. He turns to face a vacant wall, and pulls the trigger six times. My ears ring, pound, throb from the shots being fired in enclosed quarters.

Titus hands the gun back to Bree, smiling. "So powerful 'til it ain't, eh?"

She looks at the weapon, now an empty piece of metal. Her jaw clenches. She lunges at him, but someone along the wall jumps to restrain her.

Titus wraps the chain back around his palm.

He's struck Bree all of three times when I'm blindfolded and dragged from the room.

I'm shoved to a sitting position, the ground beneath me cold. Pain flares through my shoulders as my hands are pulled behind me and bound. Then my shirt's being torn open. A moment later comes the sting of a needle, stitching the cut on my chest but not bothering to be gentle about it. A gag ends up in my mouth when I won't stop yelling for Bree and the others.

When the wound is dressed and the blindfold finally pulled off, I find I'm in a dingy room filled with pipes and poles and oddly sized metal containers. The view is engulfed by darkness as the healer leaves, pulling the door shut behind him. My only company now is a flickering candle set far out of reach.

"Hey!" I shout through my gag. My voice echoes through the dark room. I scramble to stand up and find my arms are not only tied behind my back, but around a pole as well. I twist, attempting to free myself, and feel the stitches strain from the motion.

"Hey!" I shout again. "Untie me!"

"They're not coming," someone says. Jackson.

I flatten myself to the floor and peer beneath a metal vat behind the pole I'm tethered to. I can just barely make him out on the other side, sitting with his back to me.

"Jackson. Can you untie me?" The gag is muddling my words, but he seems to understand me well enough because he laughs.

"Why would I help you? And besides, I can't. I'm tied up, too."

"Where are the others?"

"Sammy and Clipper were dragged off somewhere. I don't know where they took them."

"And Bree?" I ask, my voice catching. "What about Bree?"

"Titus beat her until she passed out. Then I was dragged here, but you were too busy screaming to hear them bring me in. I don't know anything else."

My mouth goes dry. How did this happen? How did I manage to botch our mission, get my entire team caught? And Bree. It's completely my fault. I told her to put the gun down. I told her to surrender her only way of protecting herself.

A loud screech echoes through the room and torchlight floods in. I shrink away from it. A man dressed in furs and leather enters, dragging Sammy and Clipper behind him. Sammy's blond bangs are slick with blood and his nose is swollen to double its normal size. It's broken for sure. I feel a small surge of relief when I see Clipper unharmed.

The man binds Sammy to the pole in front of me, and Clipper to the one behind Sammy. Then he notices me watching and shouts back toward the doorway.

"Did he wanna see the leader next?"

"Bring him," comes the reply.

I'm promptly untied and dragged from the room. We go up a flight of stairs and through a series of hallways. Some have cold, concrete walls; others are nothing but frozen dirt tunnels. Not once do I see a window. We are still underground. Even stranger, I don't see a single person. There have to be more than the handful Bree and I saw after falling through the trapdoor.

We make a quick turn, and I'm shoved into a room. A hammock hangs between two poles. A bedpan rests on the floor. Several candles sit on the surface of a crudely fashioned table. Titus steps from a corner and into their glow.

I'm pushed onto a crate serving as a chair, and while my arms remain tethered behind my back, at least the gag is removed.

Titus waves at my escort dismissively. "Put the damn torch out or get gone, Bruno. It's hurtin' my eyes."

Bruno grunts and leaves. As soon as I'm alone with Titus, I spit out the first thought that comes into my head.

"Where's Bree?"

His lips spread into a thin smile, which looks wicked in the candlelight. "You ain't here to talk about yer woman."

"Where is she?"

"Tell me yer name, and maybe I'll tell where she's at."

"Gray," I say immediately. "Gray Weathersby."

He says the name back to me, like he's trying it on. Then he runs his fingers absentmindedly through a candle's flame.

"I gave you my name. Now where is she?"

"I've changed my mind."

I writhe against my bindings. "You said—"

Titus picks up his knife and drives it into the table. It stands, wobbling upright, light bouncing off the blade. "What's it this time?" His lips are pulled back in a snarl, his chest heaving. "What do ya want?"

"This time? We came to help you."

He folds his arms across his chest and laughs. "That's what yer people said last visit, and 'member how that went?"

I'm trying to make sense of his words, but they don't add up. I run through everything I know about Group A.

The test subjects became uncivilized. They were fighting, killing one another off, completely out of control. Frank turned off their electricity, hoping they would perish. They did; Bo overheard the confirmation years ago, a report from one Order member to Frank. But then we saw survivors, just months ago, darting in and out of the Group A screens in Union Central's control room. I must be missing a detail—a crucial detail—because nothing Titus is saying makes sense.

"Yer men gave me the same lie when we questioned 'em," Titus says. "*We're here to help.* The blond was partic'ly useless. Refused to say a damn thing. Claimed ya wouldn't want him to."

I feel a surge of gratitude at Sammy's loyalty.

Titus sits on the crate opposite me and pulls his knife from the table. He points it at me.

"Now ya listen, and ya listen careful. Yer not wearin' those black uniforms, but I know what yer plannin'. And even if I weren't alive the first time Reapers crossed our Wall, I know the stories well 'nuff. I know the sufferin' ya sow."

The truth hits me like a blow to the gut. Bo interpreted

the report about Group A dying off the way the way anyone would. But now, I think I know. I don't want to believe it, but I think . . .

"Titus, what happened the last time someone visited?"

"Ya know perfectly well what happened," he spits. "It was yer people, and it was a massacre. E'erybody livin' above was slaughtered."

TWENTY-TWO

MY MOUTH FALLS OPEN. IT'S impossibly cruel, but it makes sense. It explains how so many of them survived, why they stay so cautiously hidden even now.

"Your people had been fighting back then," I say. "It was a war. Those who didn't want any part in the bloodshed must have gone underground. The others continued to battle above, in the open, for months. And then . . ." I think back to the word Titus used to describe what must be the Order. "And then the Reapers arrived."

"I see yer finally 'memberin'. So I'm askin' again: What do ya want this time?"

"We aren't with them," I say. "Those men . . . the Reapers. They're part of the Franconian Order, a group that serves

Dimitri Octavius Frank. *He* is your enemy—not my team. He put you inside this Wall and when things got too out of hand for his liking, he decided to clean up the mess he started by slaughtering your people."

"Ya know an awful lot 'bout our history." Titus's eyes narrow in thought. "Too much."

"We are like you, Titus. I grew up inside a Wall, too."

He grunts doubtfully. "Yer lyin'."

"Why? Because anyone that climbs the Wall ends up burned to death? Because it would be impossible for me to be here if I climbed?"

He looks up. "Course ya know that detail. Any Reaper would."

"I am *not* a Reaper. My team has nothing to do with the Order."

He cocks his head at me and blinks those bloodshot eyes. I get a sickening feeling he's deciding how to dispose of me when our meeting is complete. He doesn't believe a word I've spoken.

"You said you want answers and I have them," I say desperately. "I'll explain why my team is truly here, but only if I can see Bree afterward, confirm she's okay."

He considers this, and eventually nods for me to continue. I start the way the truth was once told to me.

"This place, your home. It's part of a project. The Laicos Project."

I tell him everything.

I explain how Frank set up five test groups across AmEast. How he forced societies under various living conditions to create his own brand of soldiers. How he Heisted boys at eighteen, and in the case of Saltwater, the occasional girl at sixteen. I tell him about the Forgeries, Frank's plan to replicate each Heisted subject for his ongoing battle with AmWest, and his end goal of limitless replicas, an expendable army of soldiers, which I fear he's finally accomplished. I end with how the Rebels spotted Group A's people on the screens in Frank's control room and decided to investigate.

"We want your help rebooting the power here. Then we could get in touch with our people back east, fight Frank from two directions. You can help us. Or you could leave, climb the Wall, and start a life somewhere else. Whatever your people want. The point is that you don't have to live like this anymore. The Rebels are willing to help you."

"Anybody climbin' over that Wall ends up dead," Titus says firmly.

"I just told you: Frank doesn't even know you are here. He thinks he killed everyone. Nothing will happen if you climb."

"Lies! We all 'member the tales of our grandparents, stories 'bout Reapers dressed in black, whose sole purpose was gatherin' the dead. Death claims all climbers."

"Oh, really? When was the last time anyone tried to cross the Wall?"

"They ain't climbed in decades, and there ain't gonna be climbin' anytime soon. We go above only at night; dark is safe, day is danger. Nothin' good comes from up there."

"No, plenty of good exists. There is bad, too, but I'm offering you help. Hundreds of us, *thousands* of us, are on your side. We want to make it right. We want to overthrow Frank so no one fears him anymore, including your people."

He twists his knife on the table, the point carving out a tiny divot. "This is a complicated lie yer weavin', Reaper. Do ya think I'll fall for it cus it's so layered?"

"I'm telling you the truth!"

"The Heists ya mentioned, the whole point of this s'posed Project. They ain't happenin' here. They *ne'er* happened here. Yer story is full of contradictions and I ain't buyin' it."

"Of course they don't happen here! Frank thought your people were unstable. He didn't want to use them as a base for Forgeries. He thought you were so wild, he came in and murdered everyone aboveground just to put an end to his own mess. And now, even if he *did* want to Heist from your pool, he couldn't because he doesn't know you exist. You've been hiding down here for years, terrified to show your faces."

Titus slams his palms on the table. "Ya weren't here to

witness the slaughter. Ya didn't hear the screamin', the pleas for mercy, the Reapers tearin' our people apart."

"Neither did you! This happened years ago."

"I don't have to live somethin' to know it!" he shouts. "We've ne'er forgotten the dangers that live above, and I ain't walkin' outside with ya. I ain't helping ya power nothin' neither."

"I want to talk to the person in charge."

He smiles. "Yer looking at him."

"There's no one older?"

"There're many, but we ain't got much use fer a person can't no longer hunt, or scavenge, or make new life. The elderly got no power in Burg."

"Burg?"

"Don't act like ya don't know where yer at, Reaper."

So Group A finally has a name. "How many of you are there? In total?"

"I ain't giving my enemy more information," he says, standing.

"We have the *same* enemy! How many times do I have to say it?"

But he's beyond listening. "Bruno! Kaz!"

Bruno reenters the room. In the candlelight, I can see him clearly for the first time. He has a patchy beard and beady eyes and he can't be much older than Sammy. The second man looks the same age and wears a wool sweater reinforced across the elbows and shoulders with leather.

"Take him to the holdin' cell," Titus says. "Give him five, then put him back with the others."

"Wait!" I shout. "You have to listen to me. You have to—"

But Bruno and Kaz are already dragging me from the room. I lose track of where we are going because I'm struggling so much. We take a sharp turn and stop before a solid, ominous-looking door. One of them opens it as the other unties my hands. Then I'm shoved inside, bolted in with the darkness. There is a lone candle on the floor. It takes a minute for my eyes to adjust, but when they do, I realize Titus has kept his word about one thing.

He's let me see Bree.

She's lying facedown on the hard floor, head resting against her forearm. A small bowl of water, practically empty, sits nearby.

I crawl to Bree's side, put my ear near her face. A warm exhale hits my cheek.

I roll her over and cringe. I don't think I've ever seen her in worse shape. Her lip is split in two places, and her nose, like Sammy's, is far larger than it should be. A gash on her forehead from Titus's metal-laced punching has left her hair traced with blood. There's an even nastier gash above her left eye. It needs stitches. Badly.

"Bree?" I shake her shoulder gently.

She moans, forces her eyes open. They go wide when she sees me, and my name is laced with pain when it falls from her lips.

I rip a section of cloth from my shirt and dip it in the water bowl so I can attempt to clean some of the blood from her face.

"I'm gonna kill him for this. He thinks this proves something—beating someone whose hands are held."

"Don't waste . . . your energy," she says between sharp inhales.

I raise an eyebrow.

"I'll kill him myself," she clarifies. "I don't need anyone fighting"—she winces as I press the cloth to the gash above her eye—"my battles."

I grin at her stubbornness. "It's good to know he didn't break your spirit."

"And that surprises you? You thought I'd break from a few punches?"

"No. Definitely not. I just—"

I suddenly want to touch her with my hands and not the damp cloth. I want to feel her skin and pull her into my chest and tell her it's okay to let her guard down. Just once, she doesn't have to be so tough. I understand, and I won't judge. She could even cry for all I care, because it won't change how strong she is. Not to me.

"What is it?" she asks.

Her eyes are searching mine, clear and blue and hopeful, but I don't know how to answer her. There are not enough words in the world to even begin to explain how I feel. Without thinking, I put a palm to her cheek.

She goes rigid. "Gray?"

I reach for her, and suddenly her face is cupped in my hands and I'm staring right at her, dumbstruck by the simple fact that I want to kiss her. Softly, so as not to cause her more pain. Passionately, because the pain will be worth it.

But then she says, "Don't do it unless you mean it," and I realize my life is one impulsive reaction after another. That what I want in this moment might not be what I want tomorrow, or the day after; and that kissing her now could turn out to be as good as stomping on her heart, just like she warned that night with the loons.

So I say, "Do what? I'm resetting your nose."

Even when I reposition my thumbs, I can tell she doesn't believe me. I push her bones back in place and she yelps.

The door is yanked open behind us.

"Time's up," Bruno barks, and then he is dragging me from the room. This time, I don't struggle as he leads me.

I count steps and turns and stairwells. I memorize the way back to Bree.

"I saw her," I tell the team after Bruno reties me to my pole and wishes us sweet dreams with a ruthless smile. "She's alive."

"And?" Sammy asks through the dark. "What'd she say? Any ideas for getting out of this?"

It's not until he says this that I realize I squandered my time with Bree. Instead of trying to devise a plan, I spent those five precious minutes focusing on all the wrong things. This is why I will never be half the leader my father was. I am selfish and careless and irresponsible. I am in over my head.

I roll onto my side without answering Sammy.

"Sure, take your time, Gray. It's not like we're being held against our will or anything."

Moments later he's snoring, as though a hostile argument is the best recipe for a good night's sleep. And maybe for him, it is; he spoke his piece. But I dream up an unsettling sort of nightmare.

The sky is black with crows, their wings beating against the clouds, blotting out the sun. A red-tailed hawk tries to pass through, but he is no match for their numbers. Ebony beaks descend, and then there is blood. Everywhere. The sky ripples and suddenly it is the surface of a lake, dark beneath a sliver of moon, a single loon on its center. He's bleeding, too. And crying. A sorrowful, lonely song.

He calls again and again and again.

The night passes.

And he remains alone.

TWENTY-THREE

WE ARE UNTIED AND LED to a shared washroom by Bruno and
Kaz many hours later. I assume it's morning, but it's impossible to tell in Burg's windowless tunnels.

The men leave us with two lit candles before they step into
the hall, bolting the door behind them. There is little water,
just a bucket for the four of us, and we wash as well as we can.
I clean the dried blood from my face and chest. I have a black
eye from Titus, but I look phenomenal compared to Sammy.
Bruises surround both his eyes, and his broken nose looks
worse than ever.

"How are you feeling?"

"Like hell." He turns toward a sliver of mirror on the wall
and examines his nose.

"You want me to reset it?"

Sammy ignores me; just takes a deep breath, positions his fingers accordingly, and presses the bones back into place. His eyes are streaming by the time he's finished.

"That seem straight to you?"

I nod, and he gives me a cocky grin.

"So what are we going to do?" Clipper asks. His eyes are heavy, like he didn't get more than an hour or two of sleep, which could very well be true. I fill them in on the horrific slaughter of Group A's people years ago and how Titus believes we are with the Order, or, as he likes to refer to them, the Reapers.

"I think the only way to move forward is if Titus truly believes we are on his side," I say. "We have to earn their trust."

Sammy sighs dramatically. "This means I can't break his nose and even the score, then, huh?"

I shoot him a look. "Definitely not."

"What about Bo and the others?" Clipper asks. "They'll come for us, right?"

"I don't think so. The plan was for them to give us a few days to warm up any survivors. Get them on our side. Find out how to restore power. Until you saw to the cameras and got the feeds looped, Bo and Xavier were going to stand watch."

"But you radioed them," Clipper says. "You only managed to say Xavier's name before Titus smashed the thing, but if he heard it, he'd know how panicked you sounded. They'll suspect something is wrong. Try to break us out."

"They're smarter than that," Jackson says. I'm surprised not only to hear him chime in, but to have him share my point of view.

"Exactly," I say. "They won't come barging into Group A blindly. Not when they don't know what they're up against. We need to be patient. Make Titus see that we really do want to help his people, that we're not here to ruin them the way the Order did years ago."

"You know, *Reapers* has a better ring to it," Sammy says. "Much more threatening and ominous. Frank really missed the mark naming his army."

For some reason, this is the comment that sets me off. "Is it impossible for you to be serious? Ever?"

"Me?" he says, looking both innocent and furious at once. "You're the one who got us into this mess."

"This is *not* my fault."

"Oh, really? Funny, seeing as you're the one in charge."

"I didn't ask to be!" I snap back.

"So man up or let someone else take over!"

"Fine! You want me to start dishing out orders? Here's one: Quit it with the endless sarcasm!"

We have gotten very close in the shouting. I realize for the first time that Sammy is slightly taller and I have to look up at him. I don't like it.

"I'll be serious, Gray," he says slowly, "soon as you stop dragging Emma around like a rag doll."

"What, exactly, does that mean?"

"It means all she does is talk about you. That she's torn up about everything and yet you're still stringing her on, acting like she has a chance when it's perfectly obvious where your mind's at. Why don't you sleep with Nox and get it over with? Break Emma's heart so she can move on already!"

I shove him as hard as I can. He throws a punch that I barely manage to dodge and before I get a chance to throw one back, Jackson launches himself between us.

"God, you and Nox deserve each other," Sammy spits over the Forgery's shoulder. "You're both selfish, bitter, and completely crazy."

I lunge at him, but Jackson holds me at bay.

"Are we actually doing this?" Clipper says. "This is a really dumb thing to be fighting about right now."

I quit straining against Jackson, drop my arms to my side. Clipper is right. We can't be fighting now. Not about this, not about anything. If we are not united, there is no way we will get out of this mess.

I wipe my palm on my shirt and offer it to Sammy even though I still feel like clocking him. "Same team?"

He stares at my outstretched hand, and finally takes it. "For now."

Clipper looks nervously at the door and all I want is for him to trust me, but I don't know how to do this *leader* thing. I need my father here. Or Blaine. They'd probably say something inspirational, or at the very least, reassuring.

"I'll crack Titus," I announce, trying to sound sure of myself. "I don't know how, but I'll get him to believe our story. I just need a few days."

"What if he decides something else first?" Clipper asks, his face pale with worry.

"Like what?"

"He thinks we're with the Order, that we are the same murderers that killed his people. You really think he's going to keep us alive long enough to come around? Untie us? Let us start searching this place for its power source?"

I knock on the door, letting Bruno and Kaz know we are done.

"Well?" Clipper says, but I don't answer him.

There are hundreds of survivors in Burg after all. We're standing in a hallway with them, waiting in a line that twists out of view beyond a corner.

A girl who can't be much older than I am is just ahead of us. She has her hand on the shoulder of a small boy of three or four. Resting on her hip is an infant and, by the looks of her bulging stomach, she has another on the way. Her skin is dark—not as dark as Aiden's, but it has an almost tanned quality to it, as though she spends her days in the sun. It's her eyes that give away the truth, though: bloodshot and squinting, downturned to avoid the glare of torches that line the hallway. Her hair hangs in clumps like Titus's.

"What are we waiting for?" I ask her.

She pulls her son to her side, as if I might harm him by breathing on him. "Yer the Reapers that came durin' the night," she says. "The ones they're keepin' in the boiler room."

Bruno shoves the girl's shoulder. "They ain't got no need to know where we're keepin' 'em."

"What's a boiler room?" I ask, but the girl is already turning away from me. I know it's not even worth trying Bruno.

"It's a mechanical room," Sammy explains. "Full of water heaters, pumps, generators. It probably powered this place once."

There is a shift in the hallway before I can thank him. The line quiets, and then: a humming. Deep and cavernous. Unearthly. There's no variation to the drone, no change in pitch, but I *feel* it. In my bones, on my skin. It's like the world vibrates slightly under its power.

The line starts to move, shuffling forward.

"That almost sounded like a furnace kicking on," Clipper says. "A big one."

The young boy ahead, who still stands with his mother's hand on his shoulders, twists toward us. "It's the Tollin'," he says.

Sammy looks baffled. "Tolling?"

"E'ery mornin', e'ery night," Bruno explains. "It means food."

When I was younger, Ma sometimes rang a bell to tell Blaine and me that it was dinnertime. We'd be off in the livestock fields, or goofing around on the Council stairs, and we could always hear it ringing. It had an unmistakable tone, and carried more clearly than her voice ever could. We'd come running home, feet flying and bellies growling.

But this noise is not a bell. It sounds unnatural, like an endless exhale from a sleeping giant.

"Where's it coming from?" I ask.

"The Room of Whistles and Whirs," the young boy says.

I laugh lightly, expecting the mother to acknowledge her son's creativity, but she only turns and says, "It's true. That room ne'er sleeps. There're always noises behind the door. Soft whirring noises, the purr of a monster." Her baby starts to cry and she bounces him on her hip. "Who knows what's in there, though. It can't be opened, that door. Ne'er has."

"You base your entire eating schedule around a noise that comes from a room you've never actually entered?"

The girl's eyes bulge. "Don't go insultin' the Room of Whistles and Whirs. It'll hear. It'll know."

Sammy rolls his eyes. As the line starts moving he leans toward me and whispers, "We are so screwed."

I cringe, knowing he's right—that Fallyn's original assumptions were right, too. We have hiked across all of AmEast for a mission that may be doomed. Even if we do manage to escape our bindings long enough to find a way to repower the town and see to the cameras, the survivors here won't join our fight. They won't leave, either, so long as Titus is in charge, and there is no way Burg can become a secondary Rebel base without their cooperation.

Coming here was always a risk, but I never expected to be in this deep, this trapped. I get a sinking feeling in my stomach when I realize that in the course of one day, our mission has completely changed.

It is no longer a rescue mission; it is a breakout. For us.

We need to escape Burg.

TWENTY-FOUR

BREAKFAST IS TWO STRIPS OF dried meat and a small crust of bread, and it is not enough to quiet my grumbling stomach. We are brought back to the boiler room as the line disbands, Burg citizens scattering as soon as they retrieve their food. Bruno has nearly finished securing us when Kaz calls in.

"Titus wants to see the young one again."

"If he hurts him—"

"Ya'll what?" Bruno snaps at me. "Hit him? Kill him? Spit in his eye? Yer threats don't mean nothin' unless ya can free yerself from those ropes, Reaper."

He yanks Clipper to his feet and leaves, shutting us in with the darkness.

When I close my eyes, I see Titus with chains on his fists,

and Clipper trying to shield himself with lanky hands. I work over escape possibilities to distract my thoughts, but I need to win over Titus first and foremost, which will be impossible if he refuses to see me. I start worrying that Clipper's concerns could come to fruition: Titus may dispose of us.

"Sammy?" I call, hoping he can help me brainstorm. "Sammy!"

But he's snoring ever so lightly.

"Funny, isn't it?" Jackson says behind me. "We'll soon be sleeping forever and he felt the need to get one more nap in."

"Sure, Jackson. It's downright hilarious."

"My name. You're still calling me by my name."

"We're on the same team now."

"Amazing how that happens." Only he doesn't sound amazed. He sounds smug, like he knew it would come to this all along.

"Did you know about these people? That they'd be crazy?"

"How could I have known?"

"We climbed the Wall and you said we shouldn't go into the town. You said it was bad."

"I knew nothing. I still know nothing."

I wish I could read his face for lies, but I can only stare ahead from where I sit, in the direction of Sammy's snores. I wonder how bad Clipper will look when he comes back. I wonder *if* he'll come back.

"I have to tell you something," the Forgery says. "I tried the night we climbed the Wall, but you wouldn't listen."

He pauses, like he's waiting for permission to continue. "Well? What is it?"

"I remember."

"Remember what?"

"The pieces of my life that have always been foggy, what happened when I turned eighteen. It came back when I saw the Wall. It felt like a dream at first, like something my brain must have conjured up to amuse me, but then we climbed and the truth hit me so hard it was like getting my wind knocked out."

He takes a deep breath and I'm worried that if I say anything he won't continue, so I sit in silence, afraid to break the spell.

"There are things I've always known, like how hot it was where I grew up. We didn't have winters like this, but we did have a Wall. And you couldn't cross it. If you did, you died. Dextern. That was my home. It was named after someone important before my time, but he went missing. They all went missing at eighteen, the boys. I had two brothers: one older, one younger. The first one left me and then I left the youngest. Something took me." A short pause. "And here's what I never used to be able to remember but now can:

lights. Blinding lights. And wind, raging, like I was caught in a storm. Then a room and a cold slab of metal beneath my back and faces overhead that wore white masks covering their mouths and noses. I fell asleep and almost immediately I was waking up again, only it felt like I was waking up for the very first time, like every moment beforehand had been a dream.

"It makes sense now, the way it's all coming together. It's like I was trying to braid with two strands and only just found the third. I think I know what it means, but I want to hear you say it." He's quiet for a moment and then asks, "What happened to me, Gray?"

"Nothing happened to *you*. It happened to Jackson."

"But I'm Jackson."

"You're a Forgery named Jackson. There's a difference."

Harvey once explained that a Forgery is a perfect replica of a Heisted boy. They have all the same appearances and mannerisms and even memories. It's the software integrated with their minds that keeps them acting on Frank's orders despite what he's done to them. The code Harvey wrote is so powerful, it can override free will, convince a Forgery to block out certain thoughts and act in a way they wouldn't if their minds were unburdened. It could make them forget their Heist, for instance, as well as the moments following it.

But Jackson . . .

Maybe the Wall triggered something. Seeing it could have been too personal. Climbing it might have pushed him over the edge, caused some glitch in his internal software. His mind could now be processing things beyond what his programming intended. Or maybe he's making it all up. I worry I'll never be able to figure him out, separate his truths from his lies.

"Frank—the person who sent me to tail your group," Jackson says. "He is the person who put me behind the Wall in Dextern. He's the Order and the Reaper. That's what I can see now. They are one and the same."

"Yes," I say, even though he didn't ask for confirmation. There is a mangled noise, like Jackson is sobbing into the folds of his shirt. "Are you crying?" I ask. The act should be impossible for a Forgery.

"No," he says. "But it hurts."

"Welcome to the Laicos Project, Jackson. He hurt a lot of people: me, Bree, Xavier, my father. He hurt them all to build people like you."

"It's not the truth that hurts," he says. "It's a question I have. I only recently started thinking it, but every time it wanders into my head I feel like my skull is about to crack under the weight of it all. It is the worst headache I've ever had. It makes me want to die."

"Must be one heck of a question."

He exhales quickly, like breathing hurts. "I keep . . . I keep asking myself if you're really the enemy. I wonder if maybe . . ." He pauses, choking on his own words. "I keep asking myself if I should help you."

The metal vat between us vibrates as Jackson collapses against it. I listen to him shudder, wheeze, cough in pain.

I wonder what it means.

And then, I wonder if it's all a lie.

When Clipper returns, he looks fine. Shaken, but fine.

"What did Titus want?"

"He wanted to know why I'm here," the boy says. "Because I'm so much younger than the rest of you."

"What did you tell him?"

"The truth. That I'm the technical lead. That I was supposed to get this place up and running again, fix the cameras with looped footage. He seemed interested in that. Brought me to the Room of Whistles and Whirs and made me put my ear against the doorway. Asked me what was on the other side."

"And?"

"It could be exactly what we're looking for: a control room with access to the camera feeds. I'm actually wondering if there are generators in there, too, and if that's all the Tolling is—the people of Burg hearing them kick on and off."

"But why would they need generators?" Sammy asks, finally awake. "There's nothing powered here."

"Except the cameras," I say.

"Titus wants me to open it," Clipper says after a brief pause. "The door."

"Maybe I can strike a deal with him. Our freedom for the door. If I can arrange that, can you open it, Clipper?"

"I have to try. If that room's holding what I think it is, getting inside means we might be able to salvage the mission after all. Might even be able to get Titus on our side, too."

"What will you need?"

"There was a panel near the door, probably for an access code. I need my gear, but tell Titus I'm after tools."

"What kind of tools?" I ask.

"Make something up. Copper wiring. Alcohol from the hospital. I don't care. Anything that will get you aboveground to search for it."

"And why do I want to go aboveground?"

"Because I stashed my pack before they grabbed us the other night. It's under the gallows. There's a loose board at the base. You get the pack and I can put us in touch with Xavier again. Just as a backup. In case this door thing doesn't work out."

"Clipper, you're a genius."

I wish he could see me in the darkness, because I'm smiling. For the first time in days.

When the Tolling strikes again that evening, Bruno escorts our team to the food line. Again we watch the people ahead of us collect their strips of dry meat before dispersing. But rather than scattering as they had earlier, many head for the stairs. Half of them are extremely young, and small, and they wear cloth bags over their shoulders. The older portion of the group, made up mainly of males, clutch knives and spears. Most have tar smeared across their faces the way Titus did when we first met, darkening their skin to blend with the night.

"Where are they going?" I ask Bruno.

"To work," he answers without looking at me. "Scavengers and Hunters work nights. E'eryone else, days."

"Unless yer unlucky and get saddled with two jobs," a boy grumbles as he brushes by.

"Yeah, bein' a Breeder's a real chore," Bruno snaps after him.

The boy tightens his grip on his knife. His skin is so dark he's forgone camouflage. He looks about my age, but it's hard to be certain because he has a hood pulled up and it casts most of his face in shadow. I think of the girl I saw at the morning Tolling, children in her care spaced out like clockwork, and think I may know what a Breeder's job is in Burg. Even though the concept is the same, something about it seems far worse than Claysoot's slatings.

"Take me to see Titus," I say to Bruno. "I have a proposition."

"He don't make deals with Reapers."

"Even if they know how to open the Room of Whistles and Whirs?"

Bruno's lips pinch and he tugs me out of line. I look over my shoulder at the team and Sammy winks at me as I'm led away. We may have an unfinished argument lingering between us, but I know he sees the same opportunity I do, and for once, it's nice to be supported.

TWENTY-FIVE

"MY DOOR FER YER FREEDOM?" Titus repeats after I've made my proposal.

"That's the plan."

"How do I know yer not gonna send more Reapers in yer place?"

I give him the same answer he gave Bree when she was in a standoff with his men: "You're just going to have to trust me."

Titus rubs the back of his neck. "Ain't sure I can do that."

"We are not with them, and I can prove it to you when we open the door. We think the Room of Whistles and Whirs might be a control room."

He tosses his knife from hand to hand.

"If I'm right, we can alter the cameras. Make it safe for your people to walk aboveground. You could even leave if you wanted."

"Course we can leave. That's why we're openin' it. It's the only way out."

I almost laugh, but the look on his face remains stern. "Titus, whatever lies behind that door is *not* going to lead you out of Burg."

"Our tales say it Tolled the day the Reapers came," he says. "Just moments before they arrived. Like a warnin'. Like it *knew*."

"Coincidence."

"It'll lead us to safety."

"It's just a room."

"And the Wall ya want us climbin' is just stairs to a fiery death," he snaps.

There is no point arguing. I will not change his mind— at least not until the door is open. Maybe then I'll be able to convince him I'm not with the Order. Maybe he'll even join our side, make this trip not an entire waste. But until then . . .

"Fine. The deal stands. The door for our freedom, nothing more. I'll need to go aboveground to gather supplies for Clipper."

"Why can't the boy get 'em himself?" Titus asks.

I lean back on my crate, attempting to appear indifferent. "He could. But they'll spot him, the Reapers. They watch this place. You know it. It's why you only go out at night. And Clipper doesn't stick to the shadows the way I do. If you want someone invisible, like your Scavengers and Hunters, you'll send me."

"Tell me what ya need and my people'll get it."

"I won't know it until I see it."

Titus rolls the knife over in his palm. "Ya see this here blade, Reaper? I love it more than anythin'. I hone it e'ery day. I polish the handle. I wipe it clean when it gets bloody and then I polish it some more. It's an extension of my hand." He holds it out in demonstration, jabbing the air.

"What's your point?"

His eyes narrow. "My point is I ain't got no problem usin' this knife and usin' it well. If yer not back within a timely fashion, that girl of yers will be dead."

I don't like it, but I don't have another choice.

"We shake on it," he says. "In blood. Yer back quickly, or her life is mine to take. Then, if ya get that door open and promise no Reapers will enter in yer place, I'll let yer men walk."

He makes a fist around the blade and draws back quickly, splitting open his palm. Bruno takes the knife from him and does the same to my hand. The weapon is so sharp I barely feel its slice, until suddenly my palm is white-hot.

"Do we got a deal?" Titus says, his hand outstretched.

I can agree to it all but the promise at the end. I have no true control over the Order, no ability to swear they won't ever set foot here. But why would they? They no longer think twice about this place. And I need that gear bag waiting under the gallows. I need to speak with Xavier and Bo, arrange alternate escape plans in case Clipper has issues with the door.

So I reach out. I press my palm into Titus's. We shake.

Bruno hands me a rag to wrap around my bleeding palm, and a cloth bag like the ones I saw the Scavengers carrying earlier. Then he leads me to a lone stairwell just beyond Titus's room.

"Don't linger. He really will spill her blood without hesitatin'."

But I already know this, and I ascend the stairs without another word.

I push open a set of cellar doors and step into a dingy alley. The moon is lighting up the snow like sun on a body of water. I blink, temporarily blinded after a full day in the dimly lit tunnels.

The smell of life is exhilarating. Dirt, frozen beneath my

feet. Bark and pine of trees that are not visible from where I stand. Even the snow seems rich with sensation. It's like I've awoken from a bad dream and am living once more. I don't know how Titus is content to keep his people trapped beneath this town, living like moles, when he could be out here.

I take a deep breath and it burns. How quickly I forgot the sting of cold.

The moon is much brighter than when we infiltrated Burg, and without snowfall to obscure it, I can see easily. Which means the cameras can, too. I zip my jacket up as tightly as it will go, pull my hat as low as possible, and slink down the alley.

Ahead, two figures dart between buildings. Scavengers. I wait for a large cloud to pass over the moon, and then I sprint toward the gallows. It takes me a moment to find the loose board. I kick it in and sure enough, Clipper's pack is there, cold to the touch.

For a split second I contemplate sprinting for the Wall. I could make it there and back quickly, alert the others of our situation in person. But my idea of quickly might be different than Titus's, and I can't take chances with Bree's life on the line.

A cloud shifts overhead and as the moon casts its glow

back on the land, I snatch up the pack and duck into the nearby schoolhouse. Worried there may be cameras inside the room, I wedge myself between two overturned desks so that I'm mostly hidden from view, and start rooting through the bag.

I set aside anything I think Titus may confiscate—a small pocketknife that folds down compactly, a flashlight that could be used to strike someone, the clipping device, which is menacing just to look at—but the rest of the gear is harmless. The location device. Food and water. Wires and computer chips and batteries and all sorts of technological gear I can say Clipper needs to break open the Room of Whistles and Whirs. I transfer everything from Clipper's bag into the cloth one Bruno provided. Then I pull off my boot and use the knife to cut out a piece of the insole. I collapse the weapon, tuck it in place, and pull my boot back on. When I stand, I can feel it beneath my heel. I wouldn't want to walk any distance on it, but if I'm going to get free of my ropes tonight, I'll need it.

I peer out the window, gazing in the direction of the Wall. I imagine Emma twisting a bit of hair around her finger—she always does that when she's anxious. I wonder for a split second if Sammy is thinking about her too, and the idea makes my stomach tighten.

"What are ya doin' in here?"

There's a figure in the doorway. I squint and recognize him as the boy who brushed by Bruno earlier, complaining about working two jobs. His hands are stained with blood.

"I could ask you the same. Aren't you supposed to be hunting?"

He snorts. "Puck and I already took down a deer. I gutted it. He went back fer smaller game."

"But not you?"

The boy shrugs and moves silently past me, procuring a small book from a gap between the windowsill and wall.

"It's a little dark for reading, don't you think?"

"I'll read when I can, and now is the only time I get. It ain't like it's allowed below."

"Titus doesn't—"

"No. My ma taught me, cus her ma taught her, and on and on cus someone once knew how, only that person is long gone." He runs a hand over the cover. "I don't really need to read it anymore—I got the whole thing mem'rized—but I like comin' here on nights I catch game early just to hold it. So I don't forget."

"How to read?" I ask, because I don't think it's a skill a person can lose when they fail to exercise it.

"No," he says, glancing up at me. "I don't want to forget what it says. It's a journal. Some girl's. She talks 'bout what she sees each night when she's dreamin': a world bigger than Burg, with mountains and oceans and peace. Where there ain't no fightin'. Where the sleepin' are buried in grave-yards and the livin' walk together and their children chase their heels. She sees this all when she climbs the Wall. She dreams it e'ery night." He looks down at the journal in his hands. "I wish I could thank her. She keeps me sane. E'ery time I have to go back under I 'member that this journal is here, that I can return and relive her dream."

"Why are you telling me all this?"

He screws his face up for a moment. "Reaper or not, yer from out there. Her dreams are real in a way, ain't they? Ya've seen 'em."

"Yes," I say, even though the world beyond Burg's Wall is nowhere near as peaceful as the one in the dream journal. "You can see it, too. If you climb."

"I tried makin' a ladder once," he says, shaking his head, "but Titus caught wind of it and beat my ma senseless. So I made somethin' smaller, easier to hide. Sawed off the handle to a busted hayfork—its prongs are bent so badly they'd be more useful fer hookin' somethin' than movin' hay—and I tied a rope to it. With a good throw I could pro'ly hook the top of the Wall and scale the thing, but I . . . I keep losin' my nerve."

"We might be leaving soon," I tell him. "You could come with us."

"Yeah. Maybe." But he doesn't sound convinced.

"We also might be staying, depending on what we find in the Room of Whistles and Whirs. I guess what I'm saying is either way, you could stick by our side. You don't owe Titus anything."

He runs a hand over the spine of the journal absentmindedly. Sighing, I grab the cloth bag at my feet and move for the door. I've wasted too much time.

"What's yer name?" he calls after me.

"Gray."

"I'm Blake, but e'erybody calls me Bleak."

"Why's that?"

"Cus I'm so negative all the time. Cus I hate Burg and those tunnels and our jobs and my life." I'm thinking how the name does indeed fit him when he adds, "But I don't see what's so bleak 'bout wantin' something better. 'Bout hopin' for more."

I shoot him a quick smile and duck outside, then skirt back up the alley. Before pulling the cellar door open, I take a deep breath. The wind is whipping over the ground, picking up the snow, twisting it, throwing it. It dances until the wind tires and then the town is as still as a tombstone. Just moonlight and clouds and skeleton buildings.

I think about Bleak and his journal, how those small words recorded by a complete stranger are the things that have kept him hopeful when everyone else sees nothing but his negativity. So much power in those words. So much in dreams.

I drop down the stairwell, shutting out the world.

TWENTY-SIX

BRUNO AND KAZ EMPTY THE cloth bag onto Titus's table to root through my supplies. They grunt and point and mumble questions to each other. Titus eventually nods at his men and they stuff the contents back into the bag. Bruno turns to me and starts patting at my shirt, my pants. He checks each and every pocket, but never removes my boots.

"The boy starts workin' on the door first thing tomorrow," Titus says. "Now, Bruno, get this Reaper outta my sight."

"Hang on. I want to see Bree first."

"Yer here, and ya weren't slow. She ain't been touched."

"I'd still like to confirm that."

"Ah," Titus says, his lips curling playfully. "So that ya can touch her *yerself*, maybe?"

My jaw tightens. "Bring me to her or Clipper doesn't open the door."

"Perhaps I should give ya some blankets, too," Titus jeers. "So ya can have yer moment in luxury."

"Now!"

He bursts out laughing. "Yer so easy to rile, Reaper."

I hate being called that, being associated with Frank and his Order, with the people who have ruined my entire life. I wonder if this is what Jackson felt like when we called him Forgery.

"Give him another five with the girl," Titus says to Bruno. Fingers clamp down on my elbow and I'm tugged from the room. When we arrive at Bree's door, Bruno smiles. "Have fun. I'll try not to listen."

I shoulder past him. Bree is sitting in the far corner but the door is slammed behind me and she is immediately swallowed by darkness. I might as well be blind for how much I can see.

"Bree?"

"Here," she says. "I'm here." And she repeats herself, calling out to me as I crawl through the darkness toward her voice. My hands find her knees and I sit next to her, back against the wall. She is right beside me, and I still can't see her. We are lost in a sea of black, floating.

"Why don't you have the candle lit?" I ask.

"It burned out. They haven't brought another."

"Have they been feeding you?"

"Yes."

"And the washroom. They let you out to visit it?"

"Twice a day, after meals."

A pause. Silence except for my pulse beating in my ears.

"And a few nurses visited once," she adds. "Stripped me of my clothes and examined me."

"Did they hurt you?"

Another pause.

"Bree, did they hurt you?"

"No," she snaps. "They just prodded me like livestock and left."

"And now?"

"And now nothing, Gray. This is it. Me and these walls. The darkness. My eyes burn every time they open that door. How did this happen? How did we get stuck down here?"

"I'm fixing it."

I tell her about the Room of Whistles and Whirs, and Titus's belief that his people can escape Burg through it. About the deal I struck and how Titus agreed to free us so long as Clipper opens the door.

"That sounds too easy," she says. I can't see her face but I'm positive it's dressed in doubt and furrowed eyebrows and the most stubborn sort of scowl.

"Why are they keeping you separate from us?"

She snorts. "If I knew, I'd do something about it."

The darkness is so thick I'm starting to grow dizzy. If it weren't for the floor beneath me, I might not know which way is up.

"Gray?" she says, and her voice has this quaver to it I've never heard before. "What if we actually can't get out of this one? What if Titus doesn't honor the deal and what if this is it, us stuck down here? I mean, I don't want to think that way. I keep telling myself not to. But I have this terrible feeling that—" I feel her shoulders shake next to me. She takes a deep breath. Another. "I'm scared we're actually in over our heads this time. I've never felt that sort of doubt before. Not once. But then they close me in without you guys, and I've got nothing but walls and darkness and all these hopeless thoughts that won't stop rocketing around my head. No matter how damn hard I try to silence them, they just get louder and louder and—"

I reach for her. Her hands are rough like mine, calloused from working a knife and throwing spears, but still so delicate. Thin. Small. I squeeze her palm and she lets out a sob.

"Bree?"

But her head is already against my chest. She's crying, letting these giant, shameless sobs escape her. I don't say anything because I somehow know she doesn't need words.

She's not looking for reassurance, or for me to promise her everything will be okay. She just needs me to be here. With her. Sitting. One hand in hers, the other on her back. That's all she needs and all she wants.

So that's all I do.

A moment later she pulls away from me. "If you tell anyone about this, I swear I will kick the crap out of you."

"Like you could."

"I mean it, Gray. Don't tell them I broke. I couldn't bear it."

"Who broke? I don't know what you're talking about."

I would give anything to see her face right now. In my mind, I picture her smiling.

But she's not, because right then the door is yanked open and as light floods the cell, I can see her. Bruises paint her skin in angry shades of purple and yellow. Most of her minor cuts have closed to dry, ragged scabs, and the bad gash above her eyebrow is now held together by stitches someone was kind enough to administer. Her eyes are puffy from crying and the blue of her irises is brighter than I remember. She looks scared. I've never seen fear on her face before and it freezes my heart.

Bree's grip tightens on my hand. Her eyes glisten. Bruno drags us apart before any more tears can fall.

We're locked in just as we were the previous night, with a lone candle that will burn through its wick long before morning. The gear I gathered sits near it, far out of reach.

Once Bruno's and Kaz's footsteps fade down the hall, I kick off my boot. I feel my way in the dark, peeling back the insole, finding the knife, flicking it open. It takes forever to saw through my ropes, but I manage. I grab the candle and gear bag, and untie Clipper. He digs through the supplies until he finds a spare radio. Leave it to Clipper to have extras of everything, even if it did make his pack heavier during our travels.

He fiddles with the thing for a few minutes and then hands it to me. "That should be the right channel. Reception could be poor—I'm not sure how far underground we are."

"Xavier? Bo?" I ask hesitantly.

There is a crackle from the unit and then Xavier's voice, slightly choppy. "Gray? Thank goodness. Bo was just about to head in after you—it's been silent for way too long. What happened?" There is a muffled noise in the background. "Yeah, he's fine, Emma."

I give Xavier a quick rundown of our predicament, explaining how Clipper needs to open the Room of Whistles and Whirs to secure our freedom.

"If it's not a control room like we suspect, we probably

won't be able to convince Titus to join our cause," I explain. "But we'll be able to leave so long as we get the door open. And that's why I wanted to talk to you. If you don't hear from us by nightfall tomorrow, something went wrong."

"Wrong how?" he asks. "Like being held against your will wrong?"

"Probably."

The unit crackles a few times and I can't hear all of what he's saying.

". . . found more fuel in the back of the car, stored under the seats. Must have been why those other two exploded so easily when you shot them from the *Catherine*. Point is, we'll have the means to run for a while if it comes to that." Another crackle, muffled voices. "Emma, he's okay. We're speaking right now . . . No, you can't talk to . . . Fine."

"Gray?" Emma's voice is so soft and delicate it is as if she stands beside me. "What happened?"

"It's a long story."

"I should have been there."

"No, I'm glad you weren't. Trust me."

A pause. "Are you going to be okay?"

"Yes," I say firmly. "We'll be in touch tomorrow, and everything is going to be fine. I swear it."

She lets out a tiny laugh. "You shouldn't make such lofty promises, Gray. You might not be able to keep them." It's quiet for a moment and then her voice reaches me as a whisper. "I love you, Gray."

That word. I would have given anything to hear her say it over the summer, to have had the chance to say it back, but now, more than ever, I understand its true power. How it can make you ache as much as it can make you soar. How it shouldn't be said in return unless you mean it as deeply as the speaker. And that's not something you can ever know. Not truly. There's too much blind faith involved and that word is always, *always* a risk. You'll get hurt. Or the other person will. You'll stomp on someone's heart without meaning to. Loving is foolish and risky, like trying to raise a building in a bog. Emotions don't make strong foundations.

So when Emma says my name, repeats that word, asks me if I'm still here, I only tell her she's breaking up, that she should put Xavier back on before the connection dies.

I end up getting Bo instead.

"There's something else," he says. "I was switching radio channels last night, wondering if you were trying to reach us on the wrong one, and overheard a staticky message: *Friends of the Resistance, please repeat: The phoenix thinks you should engage the enemy.* Then today, I came across it again. Different voice, different channel, same message. Clearer this time, too, like the source was closer."

"The phoenix," I say, puzzled, and I can feel my face screw up in concentration.

"Come on, Gray. Don't you see? I thought that Ryder . . . maybe . . . because Owen said he was going to radio September when we were on the boat."

And suddenly it is obvious.

"She got through to him! September somehow reached Ryder from Bone Harbor, told him all of our suspicions about AmWest, and this is his response, being passed on by Rebel supporters who stumble upon it. Ryder *Phoenix* thinks we should reach out to the Expats! Unless . . . Couldn't *engage* mean battle as much as conversation?"

"We've always seen them as the enemy," Bo answers. "And I know Ryder. He wouldn't go through all the trouble of sending this message back if it only meant to keep viewing AmWest exactly as we always have."

"So you think it means . . . ?"

"I do, yes. We were right to wonder if the Expats were another group of Rebels, not unlike us."

I glance toward Clipper and Sammy. They both look like they're not sure what to make of this news.

"Little help this does us now," I say to Bo.

"Are you entering a control room tomorrow or not?" he responds. "Get Titus on your side; then Clipper can go to work. We could have both Burg and a few Expats manning the Rebels' newest base by nightfall."

I promise Bo updates as soon as possible, and Clipper stows the radio away. After retying him to his pole, I put the gear and candle back near the doorway and return the small knife to its hiding place within my boot. I manage to secure my arms behind my back and kick the excess rope I cut when freeing myself aside, hoping Bruno won't notice the difference come morning. The candle hisses out moments later, and I realize, despite everything, that I am hopeful.

I listen to the others, their breathing slow as they sleep. My eyelids are finally growing heavy when Jackson whispers through the dark.

"I guess Frank didn't overestimate you after all."

"What are you talking about?"

"AmWest. He feared you were going to join forces with them from the beginning. Naturally, they'd be your best ally."

Of course he would admit this to me now, when we've finally worked it out ourselves. Not earlier when we could have more effectively used the information. Not when we asked him for it. And he claims he wants to help us.

"Are you still planning on stranding me here when you're released?" he asks.

"Are you still planning on torturing us for headquarters' location?"

"I know I should. And it wouldn't even be that hard. You, Gray, would tell me what I want to know in an instant."

I think of all those people still holed up in Crevice Valley. Ryder, the captains, families, and children. *Blaine.*

"I'd die first."

Jackson laughs. "Oh, I wouldn't touch you. I'd start by cutting up one of the girls and you'd give me the location before I could even get creative with my blade."

"And you still have the nerve to ask if I'd spare you?"

"Caring for people is a weakness, Gray," he says. "Let your enemy know what's closest to your heart and you're as good as beaten before the fight even begins. But the thing is, I don't—" He coughs, and when he speaks again, it sounds as though he is forcing out the words. "I don't think I *want* to be your enemy." A few rapidly drawn breaths. "And I don't want to hurt Emma or Bree either."

"Then don't."

"It's not that simple."

"Yes, Jackson. It really is. If you don't want to do something, *don't*."

I am so sick of his games, the lies.

"Did I ever tell you about Kay?" he asks. "He's my youngest brother, and was right around Aiden's age when I was taken from Dextern. Aiden reminded me of him. The way he wasn't afraid to smile, how he didn't let the cruelness of life turn him bitter. I played hand games with Kay, too. They always made him laugh and that sound could brighten any day." He chuckles at his own memories. "I loved him so much."

These words aren't right. They are impossible. Harvey claimed as much the day I arrived in Crevice Valley. I spoke of Emma and how much I loved her during a series of Harvey's tests, and he immediately said I couldn't be a Forgery because they were incapable of the feeling. But if Jackson still loves his brother now, in his Forged state, what else is he capable of? Remorse? Pity? Can he feel emotions as strongly as I do? Maybe the Wall really did cause something to break down in his programming after all. Maybe he truly is a Forgery with a heart.

I must be crazy to think this. Jackson is a machine. He doesn't have a conscience, and even though he's musing about right and wrong now, the mere thoughts hurt him. I doubt he could truly lift a finger in a manner that goes against his commands.

"I wonder if Kay misses me," he says.

"Kay doesn't know you exist. He only knows that his *real* brother was Heisted on his eighteenth birthday. I'm sure he misses the *real* Jackson."

"What makes me less real?"

"If you choose to act the way Jackson would, maybe nothing."

"The real Jackson would help you. I—" He coughs once, twice. Gasps in pain. "*I* want to help you."

"Then when the time comes, you should."

"Al—" He cuts off, cursing. I listen to him groan. "Allies," the Forgery says, panting as though he's just sprinted a long distance.

"Allies."

I'm surprised to discover that I want to trust him, that I'm hoping with every fiber of my being that the pain in his voice is real. If a Forgery can become a Rebel's ally . . .

"I know you won't believe me," he says, "but I *am* sorry about your father. It was a horrible thing."

A shred of humanity. A declaration of remorse. I should be happy, but the possibility that Jackson is now on our side is so promising, so huge, so unprecedented, that it also makes me doubtful. My muscles tense, like I'm already bracing for the letdown.

TWENTY-SEVEN

I AM WITH MY BROTHER in Claysoot, tracking a deer by the light of a full moon. Blaine startles it purposely, and then it's fleeing, away from him and along the Wall, directly toward me, just as we planned. When it appears, white tail upright, eyes wide, I take it down with a single arrow.

"We should make stew," Blaine says when he catches up to me. "The way Ma used to."

"I'll go to the market in the morning. Trade for some vegetables." I stoop to retrieve the carcass.

"Let me help." But despite the long haul back to town, I want to do it alone. He grabs my shoulder when I ignore him. "I want to help you, Gray."

A series of clouds swallows the moon and as I glare at

Blaine, annoyed he's pressing this, I catch something unnatural in his eyes. They are lifeless, inanimate, his pupils barely growing as the world darkens. I realize that this is a sign. A terrible sign that up until now I've never been able to identify. A girl warned me about it once. I can't remember who she is or what the sign even means, only that I can't trust Blaine—not after I've seen this. I step away from him, heart hammering.

"Where are you going, little brother? We are allies, a team, twins." He pulls a knife from his waistband. "I want to help you." He turns the blade over. "Let me help you."

I run. The wind is howling and his footsteps pound after me. I trip on a tree root and tumble forward. When I roll over he is above me, diving, pinning me to the earth. I barely get my arms up in time. The knife glints, held at bay inches from my neck.

I throw an elbow into his face and he flinches enough for me to free myself. He slashes with the blade as we scramble to our feet. My shirt tears open, but not my skin. Grabbing Blaine's forearm, I bring it against my knee—once, twice, again—until he drops the knife. I grab it and then I'm backing away, panting, the weapon out-held.

Blaine watches me for a moment, head tilted in amusement. And then he charges. He's running full-out, a sprint, no sign that he might slow. He is going to crush me, tackle me, strangle me with his bare hands. I jump aside at the last moment, swinging the weapon in defense.

Blaine staggers to a standstill, arms on his stomach. When he moves them, his palms are wet with blood.

"Gray?"

His voice has changed somehow, grown softer. He drops to his knees and stares up at me. The moon reappears, lighting Claysoot with the strength of the sun. The world grows brighter and brighter, like it is about to explode, and Blaine's pupils shrink so drastically it's impossible to miss. I take a step toward him. My shadow falls across his face and his pupils grow. His eyes are normal again. They are normal but I swear I didn't imagine it before. He wasn't himself just earlier.

Blaine coughs—blood spatters the clay earth—and he collapses.

I run to him, roll him over, but he is already dead. There is an arrow in his forehead and around us, the clay earth has become snow. Bloody snow, starting beneath Blaine's skull and then blooming outward: searching, fanning, covering the world in red. And then the blood is everywhere. On my clothes, my hands, my face.

Blaine sits bolt upright and grips my elbow. His eyes are black now, every last inch of them, blood streaming from them like tears. "You murdered me."

I jolt awake—sweating, shaking—and bite on my knuckles to hold in a sob. In the darkness, all I can see is Blaine. My brother was in that Forgery I killed back near Stonewall. Just like Jackson, the real Blaine existed somewhere beneath his programming, and I killed him. I killed him before he could surface.

You didn't know, I tell myself. *And even if you did, it's not the same thing. It wasn't truly him.*

I close my eyes.

I can live with this. I *will* live with this.

I have to.

Titus and Bruno come to retrieve us in the morning, but only Clipper and I are untied and led from the room. I get an uneasy feeling that I'm in attendance solely in case Titus needs to revisit our bargain. I hope it doesn't come to this.

We pass a large group of Burg's citizens as we head for the Room of Whistles and Whirs. They are paired off as couples and filing into a separate hallway. Bringing up the rear is Bleak. I can see him properly for the first time and he looks different than he did under moonlight. He is definitely around my age. Unlike most of Burg's citizens, his hair hasn't given itself over to a matted mess; he's kept it incredibly short, as though he drags a blade over his scalp every few evenings. He walks with his shoulders held back, an almost bored look on his face, but the girl at his side doesn't seem to mind. She's smiling at him playfully.

Bleak's eyes find mine and before rounding the corner he gives me a small, indifferent shrug. I know exactly what he's feeling. I experienced it during every Claysoot slating. It's hard to hate what awaits, because it's far from torture, but the formality of the entire affair is both draining and depressing. I don't blame Bleak for his emotions. If anything, I'm surprised there aren't more people in Burg that share nicknames like his.

"Get to it, boy," Titus says, shoving Clipper forward.

We've reached the Room of Whistles and Whirs. The door is a heavy thing, thick and solid, no hinges or handle. Its edges are recognizable only because the door is recessed from the rest of the hallway, set back about a palm's width.

Clipper opens the small silver box mounted near the door to reveal what looks like a series of buttons. He pops these off, exposing a mess of wires and small panels that glint beneath the torchlight. This seems to make more sense to Clipper than the buttons, because he bends to retrieve something in the bag. Several moments later, he's attached his own wires to the box on the wall, and then attached those to some sort of thin, handheld panel.

The boy slides to the floor, the device resting on his knees, and waits. The screen keeps flashing sporadically, but it's not until it goes still, a constant blue light illuminating his face, that Clipper seems interested. He taps at the device frantically, tongue hanging out the corner of his mouth, eyes squinted in concentration.

"A knife," he says, jumping to his feet. "I need a knife."

Titus hesitates.

"Do you want to open the door or not?"

Titus snaps his fingers and Bruno complies. Clipper takes the knife and gathers the wires that spill from the silver box, flattening them into some semblance of order against the wall. He counts, recounts, moves his blade between them. Biting his lip, he puts the knife behind two of the wires and tugs. They split. He uses the blade to strip back some sort of casing on the wires and then twists two of them together. Bruno snatches back his blade.

Clipper returns to frantically tapping at the blue-screened device. I'm wondering why he bothered to cut the wires if he only wanted to rejoin them, when a deep, mechanical click echoes behind the door. Titus darts forward.

"Ya did it," he whispers.

And Clipper has.

The door moves. We stand there, breath held, as the Room of Whistles and Whirs opens.

TWENTY-EIGHT

IT SMELLS WEIRD.

Not bad.

Just weird. Like dead air. Like lost space. Like a place time forgot to touch.

And there's this noise. The steady whir that gave the room its name. Louder now that the door is open.

Clipper goes in first, using the illuminated screen of his device to light the way. Moments later there's a dull bang, like him throwing open a very stubborn window, and shoddy light fills the room.

The room is dull in color—grays and tans, like dead crop fields under a winter sky—and square. To our right is gear that reminds me of Crevice Valley's technology wing.

Computers sit on a long table gathering dust, and additional screens hang on the wall above them. The other walls of the room are lined with large, rectangular components, all metal and flush edges. The whirring noise is coming from one of them.

"Generators," Clipper says, looking them over quickly. "Just like I suspected. Not enough to power the whole town, though, so they must be for these computers. And the cameras, too, probably. Power and fuel lines must be underground—I mean, we didn't see any on the way in. The Tolling is the sound of generators kicking on and off while they take turns powering things, but I still don't really get it: Why waste resources keeping cameras on in a place you think is extinct?"

"Maybe Frank's not keeping an eye on the inside. Maybe he's watching the Outer Ring. Making sure no one wanders across his project."

"Destroying the place seems easier, although I guess that takes resources as well." Clipper's eyes go wide. "If they *are* monitoring the Outer Ring, wouldn't they have seen us entering the other day?"

I think the Order would have shown up already if this were the case, but I don't have a chance to answer Clipper, because Titus has started shouting.

"This was s'posed to be it!" he screams. "This was our way out. If it ain't, what's the point of the room?" He throws his knife in fury. It clatters off the wall and lands on the keyboard of one of the computers. Its screen comes to life, dim beneath layers of dust.

"Examine it," Titus orders Clipper.

"For what?" the boy asks.

"Anything. Find its secret. Find the way out of Burg."

"You have to climb the Wall. It's the only way out."

Titus punches Clipper so hard, the boy ends up on the floor.

"I ain't askin' for yer insight! I'm askin' ya to examine that thing and I ain't gonna ask again."

"Our deal was only to open the door," I say. "We've done our part."

But Titus doesn't acknowledge me. He grabs Clipper by the shirt, yanks him to his feet. The boy looks right at me, and though his eyes are wide, I don't find them filled with fear. They are stubborn, brave, willing to take a stand. I think back to what feels like years ago, an afternoon when I tracked Clipper in the woods. *I might get scared, but I'm not a coward.*

Even still, I can't stand the thought of him getting hurt because of my decisions. Bree said once that the Rebels trust people of skill no matter what their age, but no one should be asked to lay their life on the line at just twelve. I won't ask it of Clipper.

"Do what he says," I tell him.

He glares at me, but sits down at the computer.

A good while later, Clipper has confirmed that the generators do indeed power the cameras, whose video is backed up on the computers, which run off the same power source. He also discovers that the computers are networked with Taem. Workers there can send commands to the computers here, refocusing and repositioning cameras without an Order member ever having to set foot in Burg.

"Turn 'em off," Titus demands, twirling his knife.

"The cameras?" Clipper sounds downright terrified by the idea.

"Yes. I'll be rid of yer team of Reapers soon, but not yer eyes. I want 'em off."

"But I might not be able to do it without being detected."

"I don't care. Do it now."

"No, this is enough," I say, jumping in. "We've held up our part of the deal, and then some."

Titus is on Clipper in a heartbeat, striking him for the second time. He pulls out his knife and holds it before the boy's face. "Would cuttin' him be more persuasive than my fists?"

Clipper's lip is bleeding from the recent blow.

"If we turn them off, we're doing it our way, a safe way. And then you'll give us a few minutes in here—alone." This is a major change to our agreement, and I'm not letting Titus order us around for nothing. Especially not when we've walked into a room filled with so many assets.

Titus narrows his eyes. "What's the safe way?"

"If you want to work *with* us, we can manipulate the camera feed. Clipper would need some time, but we could fix things so the Order only sees what we want them to see—footage from a few days, on a steady loop. It was always our plan. We want to *help* you escape the Order, not bring them right to your door."

"I ain't working with anyone but my own people. I don't trust yer lot. Ya know too much to not be one of 'em: a Reaper. Turn it off right now, take yer alone time in the room, and then get gone from our home."

"I need hours," Clipper says. "To gather footage—different weather, night versus day. I can't do this immediately."

"Ya better kill the eyes now or yer gonna be dead within the next minute," Titus says, knife at the ready.

Clipper turns back to the computer and starts tapping

away at the keyboard. The screen before him is filled with line after line of words and numbers. Half the words don't even seem real. This must be *code*, as I've heard Harvey describe it, commands that tell the machine what to do and how to run. Something similar exists in Jackson, probably urging him to break the alliance we struck last night.

Clipper keeps typing and the lines of code fly by, on and on until the screen halts on a single question.

Terminate video link? Y / N

Titus squints at the prompt and I get the feeling that if he knows how to read, he doesn't know very well. He forms the words with his lips, no sound escaping him. Finally, as if it's all clicked, he straightens up and says, "Do it."

But Clipper's shaking his head, blood pooled in the corner of his mouth. "I've got a bad feeling."

"Now!"

Clipper glances at me for help. It's obvious Titus will never be our ally. We have to do this and pray it doesn't get us caught. Maybe we can salvage the act later. I don't want to give this place up—its underground passages, its computers and their connection to Order information. This is exactly the edge that the Rebels need, and Titus is forcing us to throw it aside. But Burg is worth nothing—can *be* nothing—if we're dead, unable to man it or tell Ryder of its assets.

And so I sort of nod and shrug at Clipper all at once because this is our only option.

Clipper punches in the command. The screen flashes some sort of success message.

We all hold our breath. We wait.

A minute, and nothing.

Several minutes. Still nothing.

"It's done," the boy says.

"Then it's yer turn," Titus answers, and he steps outside with Bruno.

I rush to Clipper, eye the damage from Titus's punches. I pull the handkerchief my father gave me so long ago from my pocket and wipe Clipper's mouth free of blood.

"You're ruining it," he says, watching the cloth grow pink.

"It was already ruined. It's been ruined for a long time." I tuck it back in my pants and put my hands on Clipper's shoulders. "I doubt he'll give us long, so don't bother with the cameras. Let's get in touch with Ryder. We need to tell him what we're up against here: how Titus won't budge but the place would make a great base, discuss if it's worth fighting for it or if we're better off continuing west to seek out the Expats."

Clipper shakes his head. "Ryder's unreachable. I can't connect to anything but Taem and the test groups."

I glance at the door. Titus is still nowhere to be seen, and I feel like I'm wasting a critical opportunity.

"So what *can* we do?"

"This connection is like being in Taem's biggest vault of secrets—a database of information—only we're invisible. We can look at almost anything we want and they'll never know we were here. It's when we take action, like pulling power to camera feeds, that they could catch on to us."

"So you could check if Frank has any records on Forgeries, then?" I say, an idea engulfing me.

"Sure. What for?"

"Blaine tricked us so easily in Stonewall, but if we *know* who exists as a Forgery, that will never happen again. Not to us. Or anyone in Crevice Valley."

Clipper nods and goes to work. I don't understand how it is possible for him to string words together so quickly; the letters beneath his fingers are painfully out of order—*q*, *w*, *e*, *r*. Code flies by on the screen, slipping out of view before I've even had time to read it. A moment later, Clipper lets out a small cheer. A list of names has appeared on the screen, a headline above them reading Forged Assets.

"Check Xavier, Bo, anyone who came from the Laicos Project," I say. "Start with Blaine, actually."

"His Forgery is dead."

"But Frank's goal has always been to create a Forgery that

could be replicated again and again. Last time I spoke with him, it sounded like he'd accomplished it. There could be dozens of Blaines for all we know."

Clipper shudders at the idea and jumps through the list, which, unlike the keys, is in alphabetical order. We find Blaine easily, in the *W*s.

Weathersby, Blaine

Model Type: F-Gen4

Models Forged: 1

Models in Operation: 0

These words are so welcomed, I let out a huge sigh. I've killed the only version of him. I won't have to do it again. I feel lighter. I feel so much lighter.

"Um . . . Gray. Did you see this? Here?"

I follow Clipper's hand farther down the screen. I was so focused on Blaine, I didn't even bother to read the following entry.

Weathersby, Gray

Model Type: F-Gen5

Models Forged: 1

Models in Operation: 1

My heart stops. It truly feels like it stops.

I'm out there somewhere. Me, just as I look right now, only it's not me—not really. It shouldn't be so surprising—if a Forged version of Blaine exists, why not me, too?—but I feel like there's not enough air in the room.

"And your model's newer," Clipper says, pointing at the 5 on the screen. "I wonder what that means in terms of its capabilities."

That *my* Forged counterpart is the version that can be Forged again and again? But no, there's only one in operation. It can't be. Unless there's simply one at the moment and hundreds are still being produced.

"Check Bree!" I say, now panicked. "Hurry. Bree and all the captains and Xavier and Bo and—"

"Time's up!" Titus announces, strolling into the room before Clipper can even bring a finger back to the keyboard.

"Wait. This is important." Bruno grabs my arm and starts hauling me away from the computer. "Dammit! You don't understand how important this is!"

But I'm shoved into the hallway despite my begging. Kaz is waiting with Sammy and Jackson. Sammy must read the panic on my face because he's searching the room, neck craned as we are jostled off.

We burst into Titus's quarters, and Bree is there. She's sitting on one of the crates, a single guard behind her. Her face is painted with bruises and scabs, but her eyes light up when we enter, and the injuries seem suddenly minuscule.

She flashes me a smile, and I don't return it.

I should. I want to.

But I get this feeling.

This horrible, viscous, vile feeling.

When I met Bree, she had long since run from Frank. She had already been Heisted. What if the girl I know . . . what if she's never really been *her*?

No. That can't be. I would know. I'd be able to tell.

Except you couldn't tell with your own brother, the doubt says.

But Bree was living with the Rebels for nearly a year when I met her. She would have compromised Crevice Valley's location already, figured out a way to reach Frank. Or she would have done it in person when we went back to Taem for the vaccine. She would have betrayed the Rebels a long time ago if she were truly a Forgery.

Unless she has her own motives, the doubt whispers. *Unless she's so strong she's loyal to herself before Frank. Like Jackson. He brokered a deal in Stonewall that went against his mission just to keep himself alive.*

I can't start thinking like this. Bree is Bree. That's all she's ever been. The way she's fought for the Rebels without hesitation since I met her. The way she feels about me—all that passion and anger and hurt when we argued on the beach. The way she cried just the other day in her cell. She's real. She has to be, because I'm not willing to leave her behind. I can't. Couldn't. It would kill me.

She'll kill you herself, if she's a Forgery.

But she's not.

She's not. She's not. She's not.

I've decided.

"Well, go ahead," Titus says, folding his arms over his chest. "Ya've got 'til the count of fifty."

"For what?" I glance at the team, but they look equally confused.

Titus jerks his head toward Bree. "To say yer good-byes."

TWENTY-NINE

BREE'S SMILE IS GONE, REPLACED immediately with a snarl. She jumps to her feet and the guard behind her grabs her at the elbows.

"Is this a joke?" I say, struggling to keep my voice calm.

Titus looks insulted. "I ne'er joke. Ya did yer job, and yer leavin' now, just as we agreed."

"We shook on it! In blood. The door for my team."

"Ah, see, that's the thing," he says, shaking his head. "We ne'er made a deal fer yer team. I said that if the boy opened the door, yer *men* would walk free. We shook on *those* words."

"I . . . you . . ." But I can't get out anything else because my lungs feel like they're about to collapse. I didn't catch his word choice originally, and even if I *had*, I might not have taken it so literally. It makes no sense, agreeing to a deal that ensures only part of your team's safety.

"Why?" I finally manage.

"Why *not*? A healthy female of breedin' age? We ain't stupid 'nuff to let that sort of resource wander off. It'd be wasteful, really."

No wonder they kept her separate from us, had nurses come to examine her. I can't walk out now, leave Bree to this sort of fate. I take a deep breath, tell myself that if I can only reason with him, everything will be fine.

"You know I wouldn't have agreed to this."

"Ain't my fault ya didn't analyze my words."

"You can't do this," I try again.

"Oh, but I can." He smiles and his eyes never leave mine as he waves a hand toward Bree's guard. "Take her to the Breeder hall and have someone introduce her to her new job."

Bree screams as she's tugged toward the doorway, a single word—*No!*—and it's her voice, uncharacteristically high and cracking, that causes me to abandon all reason.

I lunge at Titus. He pulls out his knife, but I don't care about the blade. I care only about Bree, because I realize a million truths in the blink of an eye: I need her and I trust her and I think I might love her and I saved her from a sinking ship and she reads me almost as well as my brother and can make loon calls with her hands and is stubborn and crazy and reckless and real and even if it puts my damn life on the line, I'm not leaving Burg without her.

Titus and I crash to the floor. I hear Sammy jump to action behind me, going after Bruno or Kaz. I think even Clipper joins in, but I don't dare turn my head to check. I claw the knife from Titus's hand, push it aside. I don't want to fight him with the blade because it will make it too easy. I want to feel every ounce of pain I inflict on him. I lose count of my punches. My hands are bloody, my knuckles on fire. Titus is moments away from passing out when someone—Bruno or Kaz—strikes me from behind. My world blurs. I fall to my knees, skull throbbing.

I look for Titus and find him already on his feet, retrieving the knife. He twists around and kicks all in one motion. My head whips backward. The world is white. And then Titus is above me, his knees against my chest and his blade right before my eyes. I spit at him. He lifts me by my shirt and slams me against the floor.

"Any last words before yer butchered, Reaper?" Titus's nose is gushing, his teeth smeared with blood, but he looks so happy in this moment. Proud. Behind him, Sammy is pinned to the wall by Kaz, and Clipper is slumped to the floor, dazed. Bruno towers over me, watching in amusement.

I catch Jackson in the corner. He's just standing there, motionless, watching us get beaten to death. I knew he wouldn't be able to fight it. It was wishful thinking to believe a Forgery could ever be my ally.

But then again . . .

Jackson's hands have become fists. They are clenched at his side, trembling. His lip twitches. His eyes dart between us all. It's like he wants to do something but can't find the courage.

"Now would be the time, Jackson. This is the moment we talked about."

Titus makes a face, confused with my seemingly odd choice of last words. Then he shrugs and brings the blade closer.

And Jackson springs to life.

He pulls Titus off my chest as though he weighs nothing and knees him in the gut. Titus coughs, buckles over, drops the knife. It is in Jackson's hand in a flash and before I've even scrambled to my feet, Jackson has dragged it across Titus's neck.

"Don't," Bruno pleads, as Jackson turns on him. "Please."

But the Forgery attacks anyway. He slams Bruno's head into the wall, and before the guard hits the ground, he turns on Kaz. Jackson brings the blunt end of the knife handle against his temple and the man goes still.

"You killed him," Clipper says, staring at Titus's body. "And the others."

Jackson shakes his head. "These two will live."

"What the hell just happened?" Sammy is looking at the fallen bodies in shock. "Did you?" He glances at Jackson, and then me, then the Forgery again. "You helped us. Gray said it was time and you *helped* us."

"We came to an agreement," Jackson says plainly. "It took me a little while to act on it, but I feel invincible now."

And maybe he is. Maybe he's broken down whatever greater power rules his mind and is truly free, but I don't have time to contemplate it. I brush by them.

They don't ask where I'm going.

They know, and they follow.

The Breeder hallway is quiet. The doors hang open, each room empty except for the random blanket or floor mat. My stomach rolls over. What if we're too late? What if we get there and it's already been done? I force myself to ignore the thought and push my legs faster.

The hall twists, and when we round the corner, I can make out a guard waiting at the far end. No, not a guard. Bree.

She's leaning against the wall nonchalantly, arms folded against her chest. I skid to a stop before her, startled.

"What happened?"

She looks up at me, eyebrows raised. "Nothing."

There are two men inside the room to her right, both unconscious.

"How did—"

"Knocked out the guy they shut me in with before he even saw it coming. The guard was so surprised when I stepped into the hallway he hardly had a chance. And then I waited. I knew you guys would come looking for me."

Sammy laughs. "You may be crazy, Nox, but you've got guts."

She grins proudly but I'm still staring at her, marveling at the fact that she is intact, untouched, unharmed. I grab her and pull her into a hug.

"I can't believe you're okay," I say into her hair. Then I grab her shoulders and move her away from me so I can look her in the eye. "I would . . . I'd have killed him, Bree. If he—"

She pushes me backward before I can finish. "That's insulting, Gray. That you don't think I can take care of myself."

How did I think, even for a moment, that she could be a Forgery? They are far more calculated and logical and precise, and here she is, yelling at me because I'd kill for her.

"I know you can take care of yourself," I say. "But that doesn't mean I'd stand here and do nothing if you needed help. I'd never force you to fight on your own."

"I'm strongest on my own," she says, her eyes narrowed. "You know, I can't believe I actually shed tears over you that night on the beach. You are such a liar. You *are* making me fight on my own. You have been since the very beginning, and even when I fight for us, you don't see it, because of Emma. And then when you do see it, it's in these small moments that never last and it kills me. I can't do it anymore. I'm on my own team from now on. I won't let you make me weak."

She means it. I can see it on her face, in her stance. She's leaning toward me just slightly, hands clenched in fists. The holding cell may have numbed her, but now that she's free, she's raging again. I don't know what to say. I've never known how to handle her in these states, in these moments that she's on fire.

Behind me, Sammy breaks the silence.

"Cried?" he asks doubtfully. "I don't believe it, Nox! You're human after all."

"Sammy, I will beat you to a pulp," she snaps. Her eyes drift to the blood on my hands. "Let's just get back to the others. I doubt we're welcome here anymore."

And then she knocks her shoulder against my chest as she passes by.

I hurry after her and take the lead because she has no clue where she's going. Sammy mumbles something about my priorities and I block him out. I can't deal with his criticisms now. Or Bree, who's not making sense. What's most important is getting out of the tunnels and back to the Wall and deciding on our next step: head west and try to engage the Expats as Ryder suggested, or start trekking home, failures.

When we reach the stairs near Titus's room, an odd sound breaks out overhead. An intense humming, like a hundred birds caught in a storm, their wings beating against a howling wind. The noise dies out abruptly and a moment later there is an amplified voice.

"Gray Weathersby!" Marco. Aboveground. Calling for me. "You will show yourself or the remains of this town will be destroyed as quickly as we sunk your puny ship."

Clipper's work with Burg's cameras was noticed after all. Frank must have been alerted, Marco called in to investigate. Given how quickly he arrived, he probably *was* waiting for us along the borderlines, just as Clipper suspected.

"I don't buy it," Sammy says. "He's not going to destroy anything. They won't waste supplies when they think this place is dead."

"It doesn't matter," I say. "They know we're here."

Marco's voice booms again above us. "We found your friends beyond the Wall. The men are dead. If you don't want your medic in the same state, you will show yourself."

Time seems to slow.

They can't be dead. Bo finally broke free of a life in Frank's prisons just months ago. And Xavier taught me to hunt, to gut and skin my game, to set traps and snares. How is it possible that these two men are gone?

"He could be lying," Bree warns.

But I can't take that risk, and Marco knows it. There is only one option. Just like when we were on the *Catherine*, the Order has pushed us into a corner of their choosing.

I move toward the stairs and Bree grabs my arm. "Don't. It's a trap."

"We're trapped as it is."

"I'll come with you."

Her eyes are softer now, filled with worry. How ironic for her to suddenly care, to no longer be furious with me. I shake her off.

"I'm stronger on my own, too."

These are her words, echoed back with anger and spite. I know they aren't true, but I say them anyway, just to watch her face go blank. I need her to know how ridiculous it feels to hear that lie.

"I'm going up," I tell the team. "Sammy, see if you can find Bleak. He's my age, dark skin, nearly the only guy I've seen who keeps his head shaved. He seems to want a better life for himself *and* the people here, so tell him what's happening. Make sure he gets everyone somewhere safe. They need to stay hidden.

"And Clipper, the radio's still with the other gear in the boiler room. Try to get in touch with Bo and Xavier. Maybe Marco's lying and they can help."

Clipper looks panicked. "I don't think—"

"Just try."

"And the rest of us?" Jackson asks.

"What? He's on our side now?" Bree looks shocked.

"You're out of the loop, Nox," Sammy says. "Shut up and listen."

But I don't know what order to give. "Just do whatever you think is right. So long as it doesn't include following me."

Clipper and Sammy race down the hallway.

"I'll be as quick as I can," I say to Bree and Jackson. "We'll meet in the Room of Whistles and Whirs. Tell the others."

"I could help if you just let me," Bree calls as I take the stairs two at a time.

But I keep climbing.

And I don't look back.

PART FOUR
OF ALLIES

THIRTY

IT'S SNOWING AGAIN, FREEZING COLD, and there are too many clouds for the moon to effectively light the land. The world is obscured by darkness save for a single light source ahead, barely penetrating the downpour of flakes.

I move toward it, feeling my way along the alley walls. The light is coming from a massive vehicle sitting just before the gallows, illuminating the ground around it in a gleaming ring. It looks like a wingless plane, vaguely similar to the metal birds I saw AmWest fly over Taem when I ran from Frank. This model stands on planklike feet, its body bulbous and proud. There are two more behind it, only they don't have their lights on. I squint, trying to take in more details, and notice the units *do* have wings. They are overhead, and numerous—more like a dragonfly than a bird. These must be helicopters. I read about them in some documentation about the Laicos Project. Something about this particular type of flying contraption makes it easiest for the Order to move over the Wall.

A figure moves, backlit by the helicopter's light. Marco. Even with the poor visibility, there's no mistaking that massive beard of his. A pair of Order members flank him. He raises something to his lips and then his voice is thundering through the evening.

"I have someone who wants to talk to you, Gray. Someone who wants you to know how important it is that you don't waste any more of my time."

I think I know what he means, and then I hear her voice, amplified.

"They're dead, Gray," Emma says. She sounds brave, her voice surprisingly steady. "Xavier and Bo. The Order didn't even hesitate when they took the shots."

I swallow, trying to push a knot out of my throat. There's an amplified sob from Emma, and whatever courage she was channeling just seconds earlier is gone.

"Please," she begs. "No. Please don't do this."

I realize she is no longer talking to me but to whoever is with her on the other side of the Wall.

Marco starts counting. "Five . . ."

Emma is sobbing now.

"Four . . ."

They won't do it. They can't.

"Three . . ."

I race forward.

"Two . . ."

"Wait!" I yell, spilling into the light of the helicopters. "I'm here."

A gunshot sounds in the distance.

I go rigid.

"Gray," Marco says. "I'm so glad you could join us."

"I showed myself! I came and you—"

"We gave you plenty of time. She didn't need to die, but you cut it too close. *You* killed her."

I sink to my knees, oblivious to the cold sting of the snow. I should want to strangle him, attack him, beat him until he begs for mercy, but I'm empty. First my father. Then Bo and Xavier. And now . . .

I can't think it. Can't even bring myself to admit she's gone.

One of the Order members checks me for weapons. "He's unarmed."

"Good," Marco says. He grabs me by the collar and hoists me to my feet. "Let's go for a walk."

I'm led into a ruined building by Marco, who leaves two guards stationed outside.

"Why stop here?" he asks. "You were trying to cross into enemy territory, were you not?" Even though he stands right in front of me, I can barely see him through the thickness of night.

"Why would I tell you anything?" I manage to say. "You killed her. You have no more leverage to use against me."

"I don't think that's entirely accurate. If you want to ensure the safety of the rest of your team, you will cooperate."

"They're dead. Drowned with the *Catherine*. I'm the only one left."

"We saw you lower a lifeboat—a *full* lifeboat."

"It got overturned," I say. "The three people you just killed were the only ones who didn't freeze to death that very night."

"You have a history of lying, Gray, and I don't believe you."

"That's not my problem."

It's so dark, I don't even see the blow coming. My face is suddenly burning, my mind blurry. It is the worst punch I've ever taken, but then I hear Marco reholster his handgun, and I know far worse than his fist struck me. I blink, move my head side to side, test my jaw. When I find it working, I toss a few foul words Marco's way.

He grabs me by the collar and shoves me. A shelf along

the wall hits my back and I cough in pain. I feel a deep, suppressed urge to push him off, but when I try to move, my limbs are too heavy. It's like I've already given up.

"Why are you here?" Marco snarls again.

"Seeking shelter on my way into AmWest. That was our goal, just like you suspected: cross the border."

"Then why turn off the cameras here?"

"I didn't."

"We know you did. It's the only reason we even found you!" I think he shakes his head, almost in embarrassment. "Sitting on the borderlines, waiting like idiots. I should be thankful you made such a stupid move." He shoves me harder against the wall. "Last chance, Gray. Give me the location of headquarters, and I'll spare the rest of your team."

"I already told you. They're dead. That threat means nothing."

"Have it your way. It makes no difference to me whether we get the location now or back in Taem."

And this is fine. Marco can take me to Frank, throw me in his prisons, torture me for the location. I'll die before I give it. At least Bree and the others can escape after I'm gone. I refuse to be responsible for the death of everyone under my lead.

Marco twists toward the doorway and shouts, "Get the choppers set to evacuate. And ready the weapons, too."

The guards' feet stomp off through the snow. Marco grabs my arm and tugs.

"I know your team is here somewhere, Gray, and I don't have the time to search them out. I'll let the bombs do that instead." He leans toward me. "But since you claim they're already dead, I guess you can just think of this as an unceremonious flattening of a deserted test group."

And at this, the numbness in my core melts, because I cannot be the only one to make it out of this alive. I twist when Marco least expects it, deliver a blow to his gut. He trips over something hidden in the darkness. I throw another two punches, grapple for his gun. It's so hard to see, though, and he's stronger than I anticipate. His elbow catches me in the jaw, then a boot finds the inside of my leg, near the knee. I buckle, and then collapse as I'm kicked in the stomach. Again, and again. I'm trying to scramble to my feet, trying to crawl to safety, but each time his foot finds me in the dark. I shield my face in my arms, try to protect myself from the blows. I feel his hands on the back of my shirt, flipping me over. His gun is right before me, the barrel pressed against my forehead.

"I know the posters ask for you alive," he sneers, "but believe me when I say I have no problem bringing back a corpse if you fail to cooperate. I can get the Rebels' location from someone else. It's only a matter of time."

"Good, then you do that," I say, positive he's bluffing. "Go on. Shoot me."

He flicks the safety off. Reaches for the trigger.

And then he does the unthinkable: He drops the gun. His eyes bulge. His hands fly to his neck.

I grab the fallen weapon and scramble backward, trying to make sense of things. Marco is sputtering, flailing, grabbing at something beneath his chin.

I step to the side and the figure comes into view: dark skin, dark clothes, almost invisible except for the whites of his eyes. Bleak. I don't know when he snuck out of the tunnels, or how he managed to get into this room unseen, but he's here now, a rope looped around Marco's neck. He pulls back on it with all his strength, and when Marco starts to go limp, Bleak lets him slide to the ground.

"If I can come with ya, I'll get yer team to the Wall. I swear it."

"Deal," I say immediately.

We shake at the same time Marco stumbles to his feet, coughing. He pulls a small knife from somewhere along his waistline and I turn on him, the gun aimed. We're little more than an arm's length apart, my weapon inches from his chest, his held out just as close.

"Don't even think about it."

"All I have to do is call for help," he says, voice raw.

"You make a sound and I'll shoot you."

"You won't pull the trigger."

"Are you sure you want to test me?"

"No," he says. "Maybe not."

But he doesn't lower his knife. He attacks.

I twist away instinctively, and as a cold sting rips down my thigh, I realize too late that I've missed my chance to fire. Marco darts for the door, but Bleak is quicker. He tackles him, loops the rope around his neck a second time, and drags him backward. Marco is gagging, making a scene that is sure to get us caught, but the pain blooming over my leg is so sharp and unforgiving that I barely hear him. I feel in the dark, wincing. The knife went in at the meaty part of my left thigh and trailed toward the outside of my knee as I twisted. It's dangerously deep for only an inch of the entire cut, but there's already a lot of blood. Too much blood. I shed my jacket and wrap it around the wound, tying it as tightly as possible by the sleeves.

There is a horrible screeching sound, and when I look up, Bleak has dragged something that looks like a short bookshelf to the center of the room. He throws his rope over a rafter, hauls a wheezing Marco atop the bookshelf, and tightens the looped section of rope around his head.

In a flash of recognition, I know what I'm seeing. Gallows.

Bleak pulls on the rope and Marco gags, toes barely reaching the wood.

"It's yers to finish," Bleak says to me.

I hobble forward. Marco mumbles something I can't quite hear. All I can comprehend is the gun in my hand and the fury in my chest, hot and rancid. I despise this man more than anyone I have ever met. He has taken so much from me, things that cannot be replaced or mended or rebuilt. He held invaluable pieces of my life in his palm and smothered them without hesitation.

I raise the weapon, aim directly at Marco's heart. I reach for the trigger.

It will be loud. The Order will hear. But I have to do this. I *need* to do this.

My hand shakes just slightly.

Marco chokes on his laughter, the sound escaping him broken and ragged. "And your father sacrificed his life for you! What a waste. Look how weak you are."

The shaking gets worse. I can't steady my arm.

"You don't have it in you!" The amusement in his voice is unmistakable. "You can't pull the trigger."

I lower the weapon. "You're right. I can't."

A triumphant smile spreads across Marco's lips.

"But I can do this," I say, "and it's for my father. For all of them."

I lift my good leg and kick the bookshelf from beneath him.

THIRTY-ONE

I DON'T LOOK BACK.

Bleak leads the way through a side alley. I can barely see where we're going, but he must have the town's layout memorized, because he plows ahead despite the darkness. I stumble after his form, not nearly as quiet as he is because my feet are unprepared for the sudden dips in the earth and my injured leg is throbbing. I hope I'm not bleeding into the snow, giving the Order an obvious trail to follow. They're bound to check on Marco soon. And that's if they didn't hear our struggle to begin with.

Bleak and I dart into a building with a collapsed roof and have to crawl beneath a fallen beam before we can stand again.

"This way," Bleak says.

I move toward the sound of his voice and find him holding back a raglike cloth that hangs against the wall. Behind it is a small room. He lifts something in the floor and reveals the top rung of a rickety-looking ladder.

He's halfway down it when the Order finds Marco. I can hear their shouts.

"Get him down from there! Do it quickly."

"It won't matter. He's beyond saving."

"Find the boy!"

Pushing aside the pain in my leg, I move after Bleak and pull the trapdoor closed overhead.

The passageway we drop into is in rougher shape than most of Burg's tunnels and only a fraction of the size. At the bottom of the ladder, we have to flatten onto our stomachs. I hear the sound of a flint striking, and then Bleak holds a feeble flame. The tunnel walls around us are dirt and earth and rubble. I instantly worry they'll collapse on us.

"Where are we?" I whisper as we begin shimmying through the tunnel on our stomachs.

"Underground."

"I know that much. Did you dig this?"

He nods. "So I could go above on my own terms."

"Is that what you were doing tonight?" I think of the

journal he keeps stashed in the schoolhouse, the girl's dreams that have become his own.

"No. Yer friend Sammy found me, told me what was happenin'. I locked Bruno and Kaz in Titus's room and ordered a few people I trust to spread the word: *There's a fight comin'. Stay hidden. Wait for me to come back.* Then I locked yer team in the Room of Whistles and Whirs." He glances over his shoulder at me, apologetic. "I thought ya were with them, ya know? The Reapers? I thought ya'd be up here tellin' 'em how to find us, but then I heard what that man did to yer team, Gray, even after ya showed yerself." A quick pause. "I'm sorry."

I should say something, but my tongue feels swollen and it's not like words will fix what's been broken. They won't bring back Emma or Bo or Xavier.

"I don't know if yer a Reaper or not," he continues, "but I know 'nuff to see that the ones out there are yer enemy as well as mine. And if yer fleeing from them, I wanna flee with ya, too. And I wanna make sure my people don't get the same fate they got last time those killers crossed our Wall."

We crawl in silence after that.

The tunnel is not terribly long, but the going is slow. I imagine it took several years for Bleak to dig. Eventually we spill into what must be his room, tumbling through a blanket hanging against the wall. The space is even more bare than Titus's. No table or chair-crates. No hammock. Just a mat on the floor. A blanket is folded and set to the side. Knives positioned with care hang from the wall. I spot the modified hayfork he mentioned the other day, its attached rope coiled into organization.

Bleak springs across the room and grabs it, followed by a pair of knives.

"Here," he says, thrusting one toward me. It's a good weapon, made of bone. The grip is smooth and slightly curved, fitting easily into my palm, and the blade, no longer than my forefinger, is sharpened expertly.

We slip from Bleak's room and through the halls, making our way to the Room of Whistles and Whirs. The door isn't locked as Bleak said, but in a manner, the team is indeed "locked in." Two people who must be Bleak's friends stand guard. They are armed with knives—in hand, strapped to their backs, hanging from their belts—and have stacked a series of crates in the doorway. Anyone exiting the room would be slow and easy to take down.

"They ain't our enemy," Bleak says, striding up to the boys.

He fills them in, and I scramble over the crates, too impatient to clear a proper entrance. The entire team is inside, huddled around the computers. Bree sees me first. Her eyes dart from mine, to my bloody leg, to my eyes once more.

"You made it back." She sounds like she doesn't believe her own words.

The rest of the team spins around, and their faces light up. Sammy embraces me the way Blaine often does, one hand clasping mine, the other smacking my back.

"The second Bleak shoved us in here, I thought you'd chosen the wrong guy to trust," he says, "but it looks like he saved your skin after all. Although dammit, Weathersby, you really cut it close."

"Close?"

"Marco's countdown," Clipper says from near the computers.

"Sammy nearly wet himself with relief when Marco stopped at *two*," Jackson says.

I force a smile but can't bring myself to tell them the truth. If they heard the countdown, they must have also heard Emma confirm that Xavier and Bo are dead. But Sammy still seems relieved, the Forgery is cracking jokes, and Bree is scowling only semifiercely so she might as well be smiling, all of which means that they couldn't possibly have heard the gunshot. They think Emma's still alive, and that small victory seems to have rendered them hopeful. I can't ruin that by telling them I was too slow, that I am the reason Emma is dead like the others. I need their hope to fuel us all, because I've run dry.

"I sent out a distress call," Clipper announces. "I couldn't reach Xavier and Bo and then when we got locked in here, I started thinking: about these computers, all the AmWest rumors, that message from Ryder to *engage*."

"What are you saying, Clipper?"

"You were up there with Marco and we didn't know if you'd make it back. The Order had us surrounded. Still do, actually." Clipper's eyes move from the keyboard, to the computer screen, and finally back to me. "I thought they'd be our best shot. I couldn't reach them directly, so I just . . . I sent out a broad call. Addressing the Expats. Hailing them for help."

"What?" A wave of panic rushes through me. "I thought you said the computers were only networked with Franconian technology."

"They are. But the Rebels had spies at the source. Remember Christie, who helped you and Harvey get the vaccine? Who's to say there aren't Expats in important places? With access to Franconian information?"

"But if you sent a call in the open, doesn't that mean that the Order could pick it up, too?"

He frowns. "Well, yeah. It was always a risk."

"A risk?" I shout. "Could you have done anything more stupid, Clipper? If the Order hadn't called for backup already, some will definitely be sent after they hear your 'distress' call. And why would the Expats even *think* of helping us now? We're surrounded, with more Order forces likely on their way. Aiding us would be like walking to their deaths!"

"Screw you," Clipper says, so quietly I almost miss it.

"Excuse me?"

"Screw you!" He stands, pushing his sleeves up to his elbows. "You gave me an order and I took a chance. Just like you did when you went above to face off with Marco. That's what happens when stuff doesn't go as planned. You take chances and hope they pay off. Harvey would have done what I did. He would have made this same call—I *know* it—and I'm pretty sure you wouldn't be yelling at him the way you're yelling at me. I might be young, but I'm not stupid."

He stops, out of breath, and I'm so startled by his outburst that I have absolutely no idea what to say. For the first time since setting out I see him not as an almost-thirteen-year-old boy, but as a member of our team. Ageless. Titleless. And he's right. There are risks to every action and sometimes the actions we think are best backfire. After all, I did what I thought was necessary just earlier, and it got Emma killed.

"I guess we'll just hope your call gets to the right people," I say.

Clipper doesn't look as sure of himself anymore, but I would love for him to prove me wrong. To go aboveground and find allies waiting to usher us to safety would be a dream come true.

"Puck's rallyin' the others," Bleak says from the doorway. "They're gonna sneak above and spread out on the opposite side of town, try and create a distraction. That'll give yer team a chance to run fer it. I'll get ya to the Wall and then I'll lead my people after when the fightin's o'er. It ain't gonna be safe for us here no more."

"You know you're outmatched, right, Bleak? The weapons these people have . . . We're grateful and all, but—"

"We know what we're up against from the stories of our grandparents," he says to me. "And it ain't like no one here don't want a little revenge."

The stairwell we take above dumps us at the edge of town, right where the overrun livestock fields begin. Glancing over my shoulder, I can make out the lights of the Order helicopters near the gallows. I cringe at the thought of what awaits the Burg citizens. Half of me wants to stand with them, but I have to make a decision, and as ugly as it is, I'm putting the lives of my four remaining team members above the hundreds who will fight as we run. Maybe this makes me horrible. I don't know. And I don't have time to assess it.

Bleak points ahead. "We'll run, and once we start we ain't stoppin' 'til we reach the Wall."

Bree groans. "How can you even see?"

She has a point. It's pitch-black.

"I *can't*," Bleak admits. "But there ain't no trees, and the land is mostly level. Just keep yer feet movin' and trust yer balance. We take off soon as we hear the signal."

Just then, there's an outburst behind us. Order members shouting in confusion. Flashlight beams bouncing off the buildings, the snow, the cloud-socked sky overhead. The citizens of Burg have sprung to action.

"Now!" Bleak whispers, and we all break into a sprint.

We're clumsy in the snow, and loud. I can hear the Order fighting Burg's people in the distance, but I swear some of their voices grow nearer. And that the beams of their flashlights are flicking against the snow around us.

"There!" someone shouts, and my suspicions are confirmed. We've been spotted.

"Call the others. Give the order."

"Now! Hit the lights now!"

A wall of light appears ahead. Helicopters, so many more than the three that were originally in Burg's center. I think I can hear a distant roar, too, and I know in an instant that the Order called for reinforcements. After finding Marco, maybe. Regardless, we are trapped, surrounded with nowhere to run. We skid to a halt.

When the first Order member leaps down from one of the helicopters, I feel like someone has shoved a knife between my ribs.

He has the same broad shoulders and lean build. Same dark hair and quiet gait. Same chin and nose and ears and mouth and deep-set, colorless eyes.

It seems impossible, even when I'm staring at the proof.

But it's not.

This is my one operational model, just like Frank's records said, and he's standing before me.

THIRTY-TWO

BLOOD POUNDS IN MY EARS.

I take back everything I thought about wanting to save the small piece of Blaine that was in his Forged version. Because a Forgery is not the real thing. This replica, this reflection— it is not me. I want it dead. I want it gone. I want it to have never existed.

It motions, a fist in the air, and a small army of what I assume to be more Forgeries emerges from the helicopters to join him in the snow. They are a diverse group. Varying heights and builds, hair and skin color. Some are female, but most male.

Forged Me is staring at our team with a terribly calculating look. He inclines his chin just slightly, eyeing me over the bridge of his nose. It's an acknowledgment of my presence. A nod that he sees me.

For the briefest moment, I have the delusional thought that he will help us. That they all will. But unlike Jackson, these Forgeries didn't see the Wall. They didn't touch it, climb it. They flew overhead, and the structure—if it was visible at all in the darkness—was likely nothing but a blur. These Forgeries are not going to break down or malfunction. No matter how hard I wish it, they will not end up on our side.

As if he can hear my thoughts, the faintest smile tugs at the corners of Forged Me's lips. He points his handgun in our direction and says, "Hi, Gray."

The distant rumble is more of a roar now, additional reinforcements bearing down fast. There is no way we are getting out of this.

"What do we do?" Sammy asks frantically, but I'm too busy grabbing Bree and pulling her into my chest to answer.

"I'm sorry," she says into my shirt.

"Me, too."

Forged Me to his soldiers: "Ready."

They raise their weapons. The roar of the approaching enemy grows louder.

"Aim."

Sammy again: "Gray! What do we do?"

I rest my chin on the top of Bree's head and close my eyes

because the answer is nothing. We have lost.

"Fi—"

There is an explosion of brilliance and I'm thrown off my feet. The world goes silent.

I'm dead.

I'm dead. I'm dead. I'm dead.

But I can still feel, and there is pain.

Everywhere.

I force my eyes open. One of the helicopters is in ruins, its metal frayed and scattered. The earth around it has been upheaved, dirt staining the snow in violent spatters. There are bodies in the mess, black and bloody and pieces of a whole. Those still alive are running for cover, but I can't hear them. I can't hear anything except a hollow echo in my ears.

The world smells of fire and smoke and burning flesh. Shadows pass overhead, casting bold patterns on the snow. The world goes brilliant again.

For the second time, I'm thrown aside as though I weigh nothing. I put my arms overhead, protecting myself from the random chunks of metal that rain down. When I look up another two helicopters have been destroyed.

I catch Bree in the corner of my vision. She's crawling toward me. Her mouth is moving, but no words come out. Nearby, Jackson is pulling Bleak to his feet. They, too, are yelling, and I still can't hear them. I try to stand but my balance is off.

Sounds return slowly.

First comes the roar of aircraft overhead, retreating, followed by the blurring screams of the Order scrambling for cover. And then, finally, Bree.

"Gray!" Her voice is murky and muffled, like she's calling out to me underwater. "Dammit, Gray!"

And now it's crisp and urgent as she grabs my wrist. I force myself to my feet, my balance poor and my bad leg hot with pain. I feel like I might fall over, but the roar overhead is growing louder yet again.

"Quick!" I shout to the others. "Before they come back."

Sammy looks at the sky and I know he's pieced together what I have. Clipper's distress call reached more than the Order after all. Someone in AmWest heard our cry for help and the infamous Expats are flying overhead right now, giving us this small window of opportunity to escape. Of course, they may very well kill us in the process.

Jackson hauls Clipper to his feet—the boy's shoulder is so bloody I'm amazed he's still conscious—and we run. Every step burns my leg. We dart between the burning wreckage of two helicopters, Bree grabbing the rifle of a fallen man in the process. There are limbs scattered among the remains, fragments of soldiers that have been ripped apart as though they were paper. The snow beneath our feet is a million shades of pink. I force myself on, gagging.

Just as the lights from the still-intact helicopters begin to fade behind us, the sky goes brilliant for a third time. The explosion is thunderous, even from this distance. We sprint into the safety of darkness, and for the first time since arriving in Burg, I'm happy for such little light. We are temporarily invisible. But then I hear the pounding of footsteps behind us: the Order—or worse, the Forgeries—on our tail.

I skid to a stop when we reach the Wall. It seems especially massive tonight. Bleak slings the coils of rope off his shoulder and tosses the hooked bit of metal at the Wall. We hear it scrape on the surface, anchor in place as he tugs down on the rope.

"What is that? A homemade grappling hook?" Sammy takes the rope and tests its strength. "Genius!" A moment later he's climbing as fast as possible, feet against the facade.

"Got it," comes his response a few grunts later, and even though I can't see him, I know he's pulled himself atop the Wall. "Put a lasso knot in the bottom and I'll help pull you up. It'll be quicker than climbing."

I turn to Bree.

"You first," she says.

"Bree, don't even argue with me about this."

Even in the darkness I can sense her scowl, but I grab her

arm and tug her toward the rope. She puts her foot in the loop that Bleak's tied and Sammy pulls her to safety. Clipper goes next, his shoulder looking like a piece of poorly butchered meat. I've never seen a weapon that could do that sort of damage, and wonder if it was the scraps of helicopter that mangled his skin or fragments of the exploding weapon itself. Clipper somehow manages to remain conscious as Sammy hauls him up.

"You have to climb," I say, turning toward Bleak. "If you go back for your people you're going to be killed before you can even reach town."

I can't make out his face in the darkness to gauge his reaction, but he grabs the rope. The shouts of the pursuing Forgeries can be heard easily now. A sea of flashlight beams bob up and down as they close in, their brilliance bouncing off the smooth surface of the Wall. I motion for Jackson.

"No. You go," he says.

I can see how close the lights are, how there's barely enough time for even one more person. And we were supposed to be allies. How can I just leave him here after everything?

"I'm one of them, Gray," he says as if he's read my mind. "Maybe they'll recognize that. Now please go. Before all of this was for nothing."

I find the rope in the dark and step into it with my good leg. My shoulder bangs against the Wall as Sammy pulls, and while I try to use my injured leg to help scale, it's too painful. A moment later Sammy's hands hook beneath my shoulders and I'm heaved atop the Wall.

I look back just in time to see the lights descend on Jackson.

Even though he has his arms raised in surrender, the Forgeries do not slow. There must be a dozen of them, and my Forged counterpart is leading the charge, arms pumping. Just steps away from Jackson, he throws what I think is a punch.

But then I see the weapon in his hand: a knife held in reverse grip, the blade exposed and gleaming.

Jackson's hands go to his neck.

And then he collapses in the snow, dead.

THIRTY-THREE

I'M SCREAMING AT MY FORGERY, cursing him. How could I be capable of that? How could some piece of me kill a man who had his hands up in surrender?

Sammy pulls the rope up before anyone can grab it. Forged Me turns to the others, starts shouting orders, instructing them to form a pyramid so they can get into the Outer Ring. Over half of them seem distracted, though, staring at the Wall the way Jackson did when he first saw it.

I look between the few Forgeries at work and the group at a standstill. I'd bet almost anything that Jackson was an older model, an F-Gen4 like Blaine, and that these Forgeries, pausing to admire the Wall rather than trying to scale it, are the same. The towering structure is causing something to flicker in their programming. But Forged Me, and the handful that must be F-Gen5 models, are stronger. Nothing seems to faze them.

Sammy nudges me into action. I take one last look at Jackson's crumpled body, and we drop safely into the Outer Ring. There's a small fire burning ahead in camp. We sprint toward it.

My run is becoming more and more of a limp, but I push myself harder. I can make out Bleak helping Clipper, and Bree approaching with her rifle at the ready. I have no idea how many Order members found our team here, but our car is the only one in sight, so at least they are only on foot.

When I've almost caught up to Bree, she comes to an abrupt halt. She spins, a look of horror on her face. Shakes her head. Waves for me to stop. And I see why.

Emma.

She's not dead. She's alive. Xavier, too. But she has a gun to his head. Emma is holding Xavier at gunpoint and Bo is facedown behind her, the snow beneath him dark.

"That's close enough," Emma says calmly.

I must be seeing this wrong. I must. She gives me her customary half smile. Instead of the typical ache in my chest, the expression makes my stomach clench.

"There was never an Order member out here, was there?" I manage. "You killed Bo, jumped Xavier, used the radio to get in touch with Marco."

"Very good, Gray," she says. I realize, as the knot in my stomach twists even tighter, that this is not the first time she's betrayed us.

"And it was you on the boat, too. You said you were getting bandages but you called the Order."

"I was worried you'd doubt me from the moment you saw me bent over Isaac's maps," she says, smiling even wider. "But love's a funny thing, isn't it? It makes us blind."

"Gray," Xavier begs. "Please—"

Emma presses the weapon against his head a bit harder, and he falls silent. The rest of the team spills into camp behind me and I hear them freeze in their tracks.

"Emma, why are you doing this? Did Frank promise you something? Did he say he'd let Carter go? Free Claysoot?"

"You think I don't *want* to be doing this?" she sneers. "You think I'm experiencing some moment of weakness?"

It's like I'm talking to a stranger. "There's no way you actually want to do this, Emma."

"But I do!" she practically shouts. "I've wanted this from the moment you took me out of Taem, and I can't even tell you how hard it was to be so patient, to wait for exactly the right moment. And that's why it's so surprising, isn't it, Gray? Because unlike Blaine and Jackson, you didn't even think this was possible."

My breath catches and I see the truth.

This isn't Emma.

This was never Emma.

Emma is still in Taem. Or worse, dead. The girl standing before me only looks like her. I was foolish—so, so foolish—to assume that a Forgery would only be made from a Heisted subject.

"I could have ended it all that morning on the *Catherine*," she adds, "but no, you had to come barging in, forcing me to drop my call the very moment I was able to make contact. I was *so close*, and I just had to quit. Get all shy and meek and bat my eyelashes and act flustered by your presence."

She looks disgusted by the idea. The expression triggers a handful of moments, all of which now seem painfully obvious. How she hasn't shed a single tear since I rescued her from Taem, despite all she's been through. Her annoyance when I let Jackson speak to the Order in Bone Harbor instead of her, and her offhand comment about his speed when he opened the Outer Ring, because maybe it really *could* have been done faster. And her eyes. They've seemed so lifeless and dead lately, so emotionless. So unlike Emma. She even pointed out that sign to us, told us how to identify her own kind, and I was too blind to see it.

I feel like the wind has been knocked out of me.

"But you never gave us up when we were at Crevice Valley,"

I say. "And it wouldn't have been hard for you to sneak into the technology wing, figure out how to contact the Order."

"I wasn't going to call them when I was *there*, and they were foolish to think I would. Why would I willingly give them a read on my location—the *Rebels'* location—and let them end my own life with the bombs they were sure to drop? How dumb do they think I am?"

She's just like Jackson in Stonewall: putting her own life before her mission. Self-preservation is the strongest of motivators.

"So now we're here," she says, "and I've finally gotten through to them. Granted, Crevice Valley is just a damn nickname and I don't know exactly how to find it, have no direct coordinates to report. I've told them to check where my tracker last transmitted. It should be enough for them to find your precious headquarters, but just in case, we'll wait. As soon as the Order isn't quite so busy"—she tilts her head toward the Wall as an explosion momentarily lights up the sky—"you can confirm things, Gray."

I'm starting to feel sick. From blood loss. From her. From everything.

"Emma, I can't just wait and let you hand us over. You have to know that. But if you put the gun down, we can figure something out." I move toward her cautiously.

"Not another step."

I take one anyway.

"You think I won't do it?" She pushes the barrel harder against Xavier's skull.

"I know you won't." Another step. "Because you're in there somewhere, Emma. And you're better than this. You can help us. Like Jackson."

"If he helped you, it means he's an older model. I'm stronger than him."

She's a mere arm's length away now. One more step and I can grab the gun. One more step and everything will be fine.

"If you don't stop right now, he's dead."

"You're not a killer, Emma. I know you."

She looks right at me, and for the briefest moment, I think she hears me. I reach for the weapon and the recognition on her face vanishes. Her eyes narrow and her nostrils flare and she says, "I'm not your Emma. You don't know anything about me."

And she pulls the trigger.

And the blast echoes.

And she points the weapon at my chest.

And there's another gunshot.

I paw at my front.

But I'm not bleeding. I'm . . . fine.

Emma looks down to find her jacket blooming with darkness. She falls to her knees, and then sideways, legs bent beneath her.

I spin around, searching for the shooter. Bree is lowering her rifle. Her eyes are impossibly heavy as they meet mine, her lips pressed together as though they are stitched shut. Sammy is staring at the dead bodies as though he's seen a ghost.

There's noise behind us. Distant flashlights.

The Forgeries.

Everyone bolts for the car but I check Xavier. He's gone. He's gone and it's bad and I want to unsee it, but can't. I throw up in the snow.

"Gray?" Emma coughs.

And even when I know it's not her, I move to her side. I go to her because she's saying my name and her voice sounds exactly like Emma's and I can't ignore it. She reaches for my hand, grabbing, fingers sticky with blood, and she smiles. She's dying but she's beaming like it's the best day of her life.

"They're coming."

The sound of Bree opening fire makes me flinch, but even still I can't move.

"Where is she?" I ask hurriedly. "The real Emma?"

She takes a few shallow breaths. "I don't know."

Sammy shouts for me from the car.

"Dammit, Emma." I shake her hand. "Is she alive at least? Tell me she's alive!"

"I don't know," she repeats. "But it was so easy to be her . . . to pretend I loved you." She coughs up a small amount of blood. "Her memories . . . emotions . . . I felt them clear as day."

I pry her fingers from mine. "Don't act like you know her. You are nothing like her. The way you deceived us, what you did here tonight."

"But you never . . . suspected me," she says between gasps. "Not once." A smile. "Maybe *you're* the one . . . who doesn't know her."

And I have nothing to say because I worry it's true. First with the Forged version of my brother; now Emma. How can I claim to know these people and not be able to sense such a foul wrongness in them?

Sammy is cursing, waving his arms like a madman from the driver's seat. I look at Bo and Xavier in the snow. They won't even get a proper burial.

"There's no time!" Sammy shouts, and I know he's right.

I turn my back on Emma, and sprint for the car.

THIRTY-FOUR

BREE CLIMBS INTO THE FRONT seat, and me, the rear. We've barely shut the doors when the Forgeries enter the extended glow of the campfire, Forged Me still in the lead. We pull away and he loses it. Screaming, shouting, kicking at the snow. His back is arched in rage, his arms outstretched.

He scares me. He scares me more than anything I've ever faced.

He waves the other Forgeries after us. Bree leans out the window, firing as they chase us, coming blindly, fearlessly, endlessly after our car. The ground is slick with snow, but Sammy must be driving fast enough, because Bree ducks back inside a moment later. Even though it is too dark to properly see anything, I stare at my hands.

How did this happen? I couldn't sense that something was off with Emma and now Bo and Xavier are dead as a result. Clipper may as well be. I've seen the blood. I know he won't last long.

And then everything seems to crash on me at once. I see the Forgeries torn apart, smell their burning flesh. I see Emma dead, Isaac dead, my father dead. I see Forged Me aiming his gun at my chest and slashing Jackson's neck and screaming after our fleeing car. How could I be the basis for that? Why was Jackson able fight his orders, and my Forgery was not?

I punch the seat in front of me, cover my mouth with my hands, and shout swears into them.

"Not now, Gray," Bree says from the front. I want to scream at her lack of emotion. I want to call her heartless. I want to tell her she might as well be a Forgery for how callous she is. But then she says, "Later—I promise later—but not now," and I realize she's saying exactly the words I need to hear. It's not that I can't feel these things; it's that I can't let them own me in this moment.

"Clipper," I say, flinching at the sound of my own voice. It is uneven and I struggle to steady it. "I'm sorry about earlier. You were right to send that distress call hailing the Expats. It's the only reason we're alive right now."

I don't mention that I'm rushing to apologize because I fear I won't get another chance, that he'll be dead if I put it off.

"Right or not . . . I still . . . got punished," Clipper gasps. "Shrapnel to the shoulder."

"We'll get you to a doctor. Maybe in that town you spotted beyond Burg." I wanted to head west immediately, toward the Expats, but Clipper isn't going to last long. "Which way was it again?"

"North," he wheezes. "Head north."

And then he passes out.

The sky outside the car illuminates with another explosion and I swear I can hear the Forgeries shouting even though we are too far for this to be possible. My thigh is throbbing, my pant leg heavy with blood. I wonder if I'm starting to lose my sense of reality.

"We're coming up on the exit," Sammy announces. I see the Outer Ring whiz by outside my window but before I can feel even the slightest wave of relief, Sammy slams on the brakes. We all lurch forward.

"Sammy!" Bree yells. "What the—"

But she doesn't bother with another word because it becomes very obvious what Sammy has stopped for.

A barricade of light appears before us. We're trapped. Again.

Sammy curses luck and the heavens and odds and a number of other things, smacking the steering wheel in rage as he does so. Bree twists around to face me and the light from outside the car is so bright I can see every inch of her expression. Determination in her brow. Worry in her eyes. Fear at the corners of her lips.

"What now?" she asks.

But dark figures are already descending on the car, ripping the doors open. They leave Clipper untouched, but Sammy and Bree are yanked from the front, followed by Bleak and me in the rear. I stare at how white the snow is. How crisp and perfect and pure. This is the end for sure. If it's the Forged version of myself who will do the deed, I don't want to look.

A pair of boots steps into my vision, but they are not the typical Order model. I glance up, startled.

The man before me wears thick pants that tuck into the boots, a woolen hat, and gloves that are cut away to expose his fingers, and even though it's freezing, he's opted for a bulky sweater instead of a jacket. He looks about my father's age and dark stubble covers his jaw. The attire of the woman with him is just as mismatched.

I peer at the vehicle behind them. It looks something like the Order's helicopters, only a bit more battered. The emblem on its side is familiar: a blue circle positioned inside a red triangle, with a pale, unadorned star at its center.

It's them. AmWest. The people whose ancestors started the Second Civil War and released a virus on millions of innocent lives. The people who today saw reason to answer our call for help, even when just months earlier I watched their planes attack Taem.

"Who's in charge?" the man asks. His voice is low and raspy, like he doesn't use it much.

I raise a hand and he tilts his head to the side and looks us over, something like curiosity and doubt flicking across his expression.

The woman motions at us with a knife. "They don't look like much, Adam."

The man, Adam, doesn't take his eyes off us as he answers. "Neither did we."

There's an explosion in the distance and I'm pulled back into the moment, hyperaware that the Forgeries are still chasing us, that Clipper is bleeding out in the car.

"One of our team needs a doctor." As I say this, my leg spasms with pain and I realize I need one as well.

Adam simply raises his eyebrows. "How many are you?"

"Five."

He motions a forefinger in a small circle. "*All* of you."

"We lost four just earlier, and another on the Gulf. Split up with one more before setting sail."

Adam inclines his chin, still waiting, and I throw my hands up in frustration. "I have a boy on the verge of death in this car! If you have a deeper question, just say it. I don't have time for games, even if you did save our asses back there."

Adam smiles at this: a wide, brilliant smile that is so white it matches the snow. "I meant what I said: All of you. Your people. How many?"

Bree seems to hear the heart of his question because she answers for me. "Last time there was a head count we were just over two thousand."

Adam purses his lips, like he's tasting the number and finds its flavor rather curious. What had Isaac said? *If you have good information—methods of undermining AmEast— AmWest is always willing to make a trade or strike a deal.* Could this be true now? They answered our distress call only because they thought we might be beneficial to their cause and now Adam's sizing up the Rebels' numbers to see if those assumptions were correct?

"Someone told us the real patriots are Expats," I say, repeating words I first heard from Isaac.

Adam's eyes light up.

"I was thinking we could maybe work together. Your people. Our people. We might have more success united."

"You know," Adam says, a small grin appearing, "I had the same thought when we decided to answer your call."

We reach for each other, and in one curt handshake, I strike an allegiance with the Expats.

THIRTY-FIVE

WE LIFT INTO THE SKY and I instantly feel nauseous. I keep a hand against the window, watching Burg disappear from view. It is still bursting with explosions of light and chaos. I worry about the rest of Bleak's people, wonder how they are holding up. At least with the Expats' aid they stand a chance of surviving. There are others still fighting by air behind the Wall, and just before we took off, I heard Adam give an order to keep it that way until the Order was defeated.

Clipper is conscious again, clutching Sammy's hand beside me. He keeps making these horrible noises, gasps of pain so unbearable I wish a bomb could go off and temporarily deafen me again. The boy's face looks hopeless. Like he just wants it to be over.

I press my head against the window and will the pain to pass. The pain in my leg, my chest, my mind. I start drifting in and out of consciousness, reality and dreams blending.

I see the Forged version of Emma in the clouds, her jacket dripping with blood. *You have to wonder about that day you found Emma with Craw,* she says. *Was it really her? Or was it me? Is your Emma even alive?* She giggles lightly, and carries on in a singsong manner. *I won't tell. Never. Not ever.*

But I already know. I don't want to admit it, but I know it was my Emma, the *real* Emma, that day in Taem. I was disguised as Blaine, and yet she touched my face and knew it was me. She was crying, full of emotion. And I screwed everything up by not taking her with me right then. I bet Frank even saw that reunion—his cameras are everywhere. By the time I returned for Emma, he knew the truth: that I was Gray, not Blaine. That I'd take Emma back to Crevice Valley with me. That he could plant a spy right into my eager, outstretched hands.

So clever, Emma sings among the clouds. *Only it's too late. Far, far too late.*

Bree's voice in the distance: "Keep your eyes open, Gray."

But Emma is morphing into the girl from Burg's tunnels. *My children ain't old 'nuff to die,* she says. *Nobody here asked fer this and ya brought the Reapers right to our door.*

I blink and she's Xavier, a hole clear through his skull. *You pushed Emma too hard. You didn't think she'd do it, and now look. Look!*

But I can't, and when I don't, there's Jackson, a line of ragged red across his neck—*Some ally you are*—and Bo—*I was finally out, finally free. It wasn't supposed to end like this.*

The world shrinks, narrowing like I've set foot in a tunnel. Bree's hand is in mine. I feel her fingers, miles away, but squeezing. No words, just a reassuring grip. My vision steadies slightly as the helicopter greets land.

I'm off the vehicle somehow, an arm wrapped behind Bree's neck. We're moving, but she's doing most of the work. There's a squat white building ahead. And a woman with auburn curls, running to meet us.

The ground shifts beneath me. It happens slowly, like I'm suspended in time. I turn to Bree because I want to warn her of what's coming, but I manage to say only her name before collapsing in the snow.

I wake in a foreign bed, feeling thirsty and downright exhausted. Bree is asleep in a chair beside me, one hand resting on the mattress near mine, almost as if our fingers were laced together before she drifted off.

By the look of the place, we're in an average home. The bedroom's walls are a dusty peach, the windows dressed with curtains so thin the first light of dawn filters through them. There is a nightstand beside the bed, a glass of water sitting on its worn surface. I grab the drink and down it in several gulps. The liquid sloshes in my stomach, which has been empty for too long.

Gritting my teeth, I sit and push back the sheets. The leg of my pants has been cut off high around my injured thigh, the wound seen to and bandaged. I climb out of bed. Putting weight on my leg is unpleasant, but I manage.

It's not until I'm standing, bracing against the steady ebb of pain, that I notice how small and vulnerable Bree looks. I haven't seen her sleeping before, not in such clarity, and now the morning light is basking over her and all I can see is this calm, peaceful girl, so different from the one I usually face. Her forehead is smooth because she's not scowling it full of wrinkles. Her eyebrows arch elegantly; her lips part with grace. Everything about her is softer when she dreams. I feel like I'm witnessing some great secret, seeing this gentle side she never shows the world.

She flinches; makes a small, tiny sigh. She's going to wake with a horrible pain in her neck if she stays in the chair, so I lift her and transfer her onto the bed.

"Gray?" she murmurs. She's still dreaming and my name comes out tinged with panic, like she might be having a nightmare. She's even scowling now.

"I'm here," I tell her. "I'm here and we're fine."

Her lips twitch into a smile and her face goes still, like the dream has steadied.

And in that moment I forget everything she said to me below Burg, because this is what I want: to make her fears melt away. To calm her and steady her and to simply be there when she needs me. Always.

I watch a few strands of blond hair flutter in rhythm with Bree's exhales. I know I should go find the team, but all I want to do is climb into the bed. I want to fall asleep with Bree's back against my chest and my arm around her waist, because if we're together we'll be okay. I've known her barely five months, but it feels years longer. When I wasn't looking, she became my second half, and now the thought of braving the storm raging around us seems impossible if I have to do it alone. Truthfully, the thought of braving anything without her seems utterly absurd.

She was right. About us. About the fact that I was fighting it. Why does she always have to be right?

I put a hand on her shoulder, but I don't wake her. I don't know how to even begin to apologize. *I was wrong about everything . . . I do need you, us, the fire, to be scared and challenged and pushed . . . I was wrong and I'm sorry.*

None of it seems like enough.

So I kiss her forehead, tuck the blanket beneath her chin, and leave to find the others.

THIRTY-SIX

THE AMWEST WOMAN IS WAITING when I step into the hall. She introduces herself as Heidi and tells me Clipper's injuries have been seen to and that he and the rest of the team are sleeping. I ask to see them, and she insists Adam needs to talk to me first. When I press the issue she tosses around words like *urgent* and *imperative*, so I reluctantly follow her.

We head through a sitting room littered with books and plush couches, a kitchen that smells of warm bread and soup, and down a flight of stairs before finally entering a large, windowless room. It's packed with computers and displays and other devices I'm sure Clipper would know how to use blindfolded. Adam is standing in the center with his back to us, talking to the woman I remember rushing to greet the helicopter before I passed out last night. Her curls are pulled back and her freckle-covered cheeks are flushed.

"Sylvia," Heidi says to the woman. It's a dismissal of sorts, because Sylvia leaves, followed by Heidi, and then it's just me and Adam.

He sits in a chair, drinks from a glass on the table, and then leans back, arms hooked behind his head.

"How's the leg, Gray?"

"How'd you know my—"

"Bree told us. Then proceeded to order us around like she owned this place, made sure you and Clipper were seen to, requested food and drink for your team." His eyebrows flick skyward. "Quite a girl."

I smile, feeling proud—of Bree, *for* Bree.

"I never thanked you for helping us," I say. "Earlier, with the Order. And here. Wherever here is."

"I owe you thanks for sending that call as much as you owe me one for answering it. What happened in Burg benefited us both. As for the state of your team, that was all Sylvia and her husband. They man this refuge."

I eye the displays on the wall behind him. *Refuge.* A home filled with a bit of everything—medics, computers, extra beds for the Expat in need.

"How'd things turn out in Burg?"

Adam's face hardens. "I'd told my pilots to eliminate the

Order at all costs, and the results weren't pretty. I didn't know there were civilians fighting on the ground, or living beneath all those buildings. We only managed to save about half of them."

I'm not quick enough to keep the horror from showing on my face.

"But the Order was annihilated, and we cleared out before additional forces arrived," Adam says. "Plus, the remaining Burg survivors were ushered west to Expat safe houses. That's success in my book."

"But all those other people. Dead. Because I called you. Because we—"

"A person can go crazy thinking like that, and sacrifices must be made in battles like this. Besides, do you think all the Order members my men killed in the process of saving yours deserved to die? Could it be possible that some of them are blinded by Frank? Think they are doing good? Willing to change if they were shown the error of their ways? Perhaps, but I gave orders to eliminate them, no questions asked."

I pull up a chair and join Adam because the thought that Burg is destroyed, and so many people dead, has made my feet weary.

"Humans are complex creatures," Adam adds. "We are not all good or all bad. We are shades. Many, many shades. Surely you understand this, Gray, with a name like yours."

I do. Practically everyone I've met these last few weeks has been fueled by complex motives: Jackson, Titus, Bleak. Not to mention the fact that I'm the biggest contradiction of all. I killed a version of my own brother in order to save what I thought was Emma. I took advantage of a relationship with Bree in the hopes of repairing a childhood one. I treated Jackson as less than human because I assumed him a threat, and I left so many people in Burg to die. I tossed aside hundreds of lives to save the handful I knew.

"More sacrifices will likely be made in the process, but setting things right, removing Frank from power—*that* is an act that needs to happen," Adam says. "So how about you put me in touch with your leader back east?"

Even with all the gear filling the room, I know only one way of reaching Crevice Valley.

"I can't do it. But Clipper probably can."

"I thought that might be the case."

Just then, Heidi appears with Clipper in tow. His bad arm is in a sling, his shoulder heavily bandaged. He takes the room in slowly, gazing over the equipment before finally making eye contact with me.

"What's going on?"

"You're getting us in touch with Ryder," I say.

He grins, pulls a chair up to one of the computers, and is in his element.

Seeing Ryder's face come up on the display, knowing that Crevice Valley still stands, is an immense relief.

I give Ryder a quick rundown of the team's current status. Despite Emma's betrayal, Ryder explains that Order activity in the forest has been no better or worse than usual. Much of Crevice Valley's electronic equipment would have produced magnetic fields interfering with Emma's tracking device, and Ryder claims Harvey had even set up some gear to scramble signals at a distance—near the interrogation center and beyond—as additional precautions. I smile, recalling something Bree said to me once about the Rebels having defenses even if they couldn't be seen.

"I want to talk with Adam," Ryder says. "Alone."

I can tell arguing will be futile, so I head into the hallway.

"What are they going on about?" Clipper asks.

I slide to the floor, back against the wall opposite him. "I wish I knew. How's your arm?"

He shrugs. "Sylvia said some of the metal will be in me for life, but I'll be fine."

I want to tell him that he did well and I'm proud of him, but it all sounds so lame in my head.

"I've been thinking about that Forgery of Emma," he says. "She took care of Aiden so genuinely. Rusty never seemed to suspect her the way he did Jackson and Blaine. She even feared the two of them initially, just like us, and when she *did* spot them for what they were, she stayed quiet. She sold them out only when it benefited her most. It's like she was on another level. Like she was one of those newer models—like your Forgery."

"She *was*. She told me so right before she shot Xavier." I pause for a moment, staring at my feet. "It scares me how convincing these newer ones are. And how they can't be reasoned with. This changes everything, doesn't it?"

"Yes," Clipper says. "And no. We just stay vigilant. Trust our instincts. Work together. That's what Harvey would do."

"How old are you again?"

He breaks into a wide smile and it's when his teeth show—unruly and proud—that he actually looks his age. In a flash, the smile is gone, replaced with a look of horror.

"Harvey tested everyone who walked into Crevice Valley, but Emma was the first to arrive after his death and I only clipped her," he says. "In a way, this is all my fault."

"You can't think like that. It's no *one* person's fault. I brought her back, after all."

He eyes the stairwell, looking unconvinced. "Yell for me if they need anything else, okay? I'm tired."

I nod and he's gone, taking his guilt with him. Muffled voices still converse from behind the door. And I'm just sitting here. Waiting. Clueless.

How can Ryder kick me out of a meeting like this? Be so focused on business and alliances? He didn't even flinch when I listed my father, Bo, and Xavier as deceased. I wonder, suddenly, if Ryder is numb with shock. He was best friends with Bo—practically brothers.

And then my chest flares because I realize if Adam is talking to Ryder, back in Crevice Valley, I can talk to Blaine. Everything else becomes unimportant. I jump to my feet. The door is pulled open before I get to it and Adam steps into the hall.

"He wants to talk to you again."

I slip past him. Ryder is still on the display, rubbing his eyes like he desperately needs sleep. I don't bother with greetings.

"Is Blaine there? Can I talk to him?"

Ryder looks up and sighs. "That's not what's most important right now."

"Not important?" I erupt.

"Gray—"

"No. Don't you dare tell me what's important when I hiked across this damn country only to lose half the people I love. My father is dead, Ryder. He's dead! Bo and Xavier, too. Oh, and Emma? I don't even know if she's alive, and that's almost worse than the alternative. So excuse me for wanting to talk to my brother. I'm so sorry I'm not focused on the right things after this stupid, *wasted* mission!"

I want him to yell back, scream at me, but he has the nerve to calmly place his hands on the table and say, "We can talk about your brother later. Right now, we're discussing this new alliance."

"Dammit, Ryder. I just want to see Blaine. I—" Everything seems broken. So many people are dead, and I'm here, separated from Blaine, feeling lost, sick. "How did this happen?" I mutter. "This wasn't supposed to be my life."

"And do you think I wished this to be mine?" *Now* he decides to yell. Not before, when I wanted it, but now. "I haven't let my guard down since I was eighteen! My best friend is now dead. I've lost one of the finest captains I've had under my command. Is it terrible? Yes. Does it hurt? Worse than I can even begin to describe. But I square my shoulders, hold my head high, and carry on. Moving forward is the only option."

I'm glaring at him now, because I can't push feelings aside the way he describes. I don't work that way. I don't know how to exist if I don't feel.

"Here's what you're going to do," he continues. "You're going to take some time to mourn for those you lost and then you are going to realize that this mission was not a waste. Look at all you've accomplished. You saved Bleak from a life underground and Adam's men freed half his people. You met a Forgery that fought against his programming—bent his will to help you! Above all, you have given us our best edge in years: an ally. Adam has assured me that the Expats will put our numbers to shame, that together we will be unstoppable."

I can see the logic to his words, but the price paid in the process of gaining these assets seems unjustly steep.

"Now as for this alliance," Ryder continues, "I'm sending a captain to help oversee things out west. Elijah will meet Adam at neutral ground—about a three-hour hike north of Crevice Valley—and he should be to you by tomorrow evening at the latest."

"And Blaine," I say. "Send Blaine, too."

"That was not a part of our agreement."

I slam my hands on the table. "I don't care, Ryder. Just send him!"

As if on cue, there is the sound of a door bursting open on Ryder's end, and then Blaine, speaking from out of view.

"Is it true? I heard you made contact with them!" And then he's stumbling into the frame, pushing against Ryder, who is trying to restrain him. "Gray!"

His hands go into his hair, like he can't believe what he's seeing, and I don't know how I ever mistook a Forgery for him. *This* is Blaine, so real and alive I can feel it even though he's only on a screen. Ryder is pointing back toward the door, asking Blaine to leave, but Blaine pulls up a chair.

"You look horrible," he says as he sits down.

"Thank you?"

He laughs and I can't help but laugh, too. It fills an empty space in my core.

"I'm coming," Blaine announces. He says this so surely it's almost as if he believes he can blink his eyes and be next to me.

"You are not," Ryder says.

"Ryder, I'm going and that's the end of it. I sat here when Gray went into Taem to get the vaccine and it nearly killed me. I spent the last month chewing my nails and worrying nonstop while he trekked across the country. You keep us apart again, and I'm just going to hike there myself. You know I can do it. I'm well enough now."

I'm speechless. I don't think I've ever seen Blaine disagree with someone so forcefully. Ryder opens his mouth, closes it.

"Fine," he says eventually. "You two are as stubborn as your father."

I'm beaming, because this seems like the very best kind of compliment, and Blaine thanks Ryder profusely.

"Gray, be sure Elijah gets in touch with me when you're all settled over there," Ryder says. "Until then, I'm sure you have some things to attend to."

He stands and moves out of the frame. I hear a door close a moment later and I'm left with my brother. All I wanted was to see him, and now even this is not enough. Tomorrow seems terribly far away.

"Pa's dead," I blurt out.

"What?"

"He jumped in front of a bullet. To save me. And . . . it's a long story. I'll tell you everything when you get here. I promise. I just couldn't keep it from you and I'm sorry it happened."

"It's not your fault."

"Everyone keeps saying that."

He's making one of his big-brother faces now, something like parental concern mixed with sympathy. "You're okay, and that's what matters."

"He mattered, too, Blaine."

"I'm not saying he didn't. It's just that you matter more."

I shake my head. Blaine's always doing this: weighing outcomes as though every piece of life is either more or less important than another. I don't think he realizes that in no way does my living make our father's death any easier to accept.

When I look up, Blaine's hand is resting against the display, like he wanted to grab my shoulder and forgot we were on opposite ends of the country.

"I'll see you real soon, Gray," he says. "Promise."

"If I've learned anything these past weeks, it's that you shouldn't make promises. Not ever. Nothing is so certain you can guarantee it."

He smiles. "Oh, I'm guaranteeing this. There is nothing more important right now than getting to you. You come first. Always."

I feel like we've had this conversation before, but I can't help repeating his final word.

"Always."

THIRTY-SEVEN

I ROUND UP THE TEAM so that we can properly say good-bye to our dead. It is a crisp, clear afternoon, the sky so cheerfully blue I swear it is mocking us.

We walk behind the house and form a half ring around a small fire pit, the wind at our backs. I clear away the snow and nurse some flames to life. Sammy says a few words the way he did that day in Stonewall. A funeral should make you feel at ease, help you move on, but I just keep feeling guiltier and emptier and unworthy of being alive. I made it and they didn't. That's the bit that kills me most, but that's how it is with death: It doesn't care if you deserve to face it or not. It comes of its own accord and it takes life without considering how those left standing will feel. Death is a greedy, selfish thing.

Sammy brings things to a close and Bleak, Clipper, and Bree head inside, shivering.

"You going to be here awhile?" Sammy asks.

I stare at the flames. My legs feel like roots, suddenly, reaching deep into the earth. "I guess so."

"Great. I'll be right back."

When he returns he's clutching a near-empty glass jug, amber liquid sloshing in it as he walks. He takes a swig and passes it to me.

"Swiped it from the kitchen pantry."

I take a drink and the burn of the alcohol is a welcome distraction. We pass the jug back and forth a few times, watching the fire like it's doing something interesting.

"I loved her," Sammy finally says. I have never before heard him say three words with more sincerity.

"I know," I say, because I've suspected it for a while.

He seems startled by my answer and coughs on a bit of alcohol. "Was it anything like her, or did I fall for an illusion?"

"Sammy, that Forgery was so much like Emma it terrifies me. It had her personality and her voice and her mannerisms. I mean, it fooled me, and I grew up with her."

We both take a few more swigs from the jug.

"I hope she's okay," he says. "I can't lose them both. God, I can't." His eyes grow glossy and I realize he's mourning not only for Emma, but for Xavier, too. They were best friends, always walking around Crevice Valley like they were each other's shadow. And Sammy watched that friend die at the hands of a thing he thought he loved. He might be as messed up about Emma as I am.

"She has to be alive still," I tell him, because the alternative is unthinkable. "We'll find her somehow. I have to find her."

"I feel the same way. It's just that . . ." He takes a deep breath and looks right at me. "You don't deserve her, Gray. Not if you can't see her, and it's so damn obvious that Nox is the only thing you really, truly see."

"I know," I say again. Deep down, I think I've known all along.

"That's it?" Sammy looks confused. "I was sure you'd be furious with me for saying that."

"Last week I might have been. Or even yesterday. But now I see what everyone else already knew, what Bree's been trying to tell me for ages." He still doesn't look convinced. "I've loved Emma since I was six, Sammy. It's sort of hard to admit you might love someone new more than the person you've loved for forever."

He nods at this, stares at the fire.

We keep drinking and the ache of sorrow steadily surrenders. I grow warm despite the setting sun. We don't exchange any more words. We don't need to. Maybe I have a friend in him now. I'm not sure if it's a real friendship, or something forced upon us from everything we've been through. Maybe the details don't matter. Maybe a friend is a friend.

By the time we are called inside for dinner, the jug is empty.

Sylvia's cooking is the best meal we've had in ages—some sort of meat stew with fresh bread. My head is humming, my body warm. I imagine Sammy is the same. We're not belligerent by any means, but we keep laughing at things that aren't very funny and fumbling with our spoons. Sylvia's looking pretty annoyed and I start feeling bad about the whole thing. She did patch up our team and give us beds and agree to keep us under her roof until Adam returns with Elijah and Blaine. So I apologize for being rude, only to have Sammy tell her we're not being rude at all. I knock over my bowl while trying to punch his arm.

"Dammit, I am so sorry," I say, sopping up the mess.

"I've got it," Sylvia says. "Just stop. I have it under control."

"No. I'll help." I manage to knock Sammy's bowl askew as

I try to clean quicker than her. More stew floods the table.

"Why don't you just excuse yourself," she says to me sharply.

Everyone at the table is glaring at me and I have the foresight to not push things. I get up, leave. I have no intention of falling asleep, but when I lie down on my bed, the weight of the last few days is suddenly unbearable.

I wake to a knock on my door.

I'm cold now, the pleasant hum of alcohol replaced with guilt and regret and things I wish I could change. It's dark out, the sun still hours away from rising. I couldn't have been asleep long.

Another knock, less patient this time.

"Come in."

Bree enters and tosses something on my bed. "I was going through the gear and found that in Owen's pack. I thought you might want it."

My fingers close around the handle of a small knife sheathed in leather. I pull it from the case. A couple of shavings fall onto my lap and the memory of a wooden duck Blaine and I played with as children hits me. It was a gift from our father, a product of his work with this very blade. *Weathersby* is carved into the handle.

My breath snags as I exhale, and I'm caught between wanting to laugh and needing to cry. I look at Bree and I can't seem to get my mouth to form the words *thank you*, but she must hear me anyway because she says, "Don't mention it."

My eyes trail over her. The angle of her brows, her slender neck, the shape of her collarbone, which has been hidden beneath bulky attire for what feels like a lifetime. Bree turns to leave and I grab her wrist, pull her toward me.

She frowns. "I have to go now."

"No you don't."

"Yes. I do." She twists free of my grasp.

I sit up, swing my legs over the mattress. "Bree, I was wrong. About us. About everything. I should—"

"I'm not your consolation prize," she snaps.

It takes me a long moment to realize what she means.

"No. It's not like that. I always needed . . . I just . . . I thought . . ." But I know I'm not making sense. I'm still half-asleep, flustered from being given Owen's knife, aching from how much I need to pull Bree into my bed, to strip her bare and touch her everywhere and use my lips to tell her all the things I worked out earlier and am currently grappling for so poorly.

"You told me you needed *her* more than you needed *me*,

Gray. That's what you implied that night on the beach. So what happens when you see her again? The real her? What then?" She folds her arms across her chest. "If I wasn't enough for you before, I don't see why things would be any different now."

She heads for the hallway and I'm left gaping after her, still trying to process her words.

"But we're stronger together," I say. "We both know it."

She pauses near the doorway. "Yeah. We are."

"So what's the problem?"

"The *problem* is I told you things I've told no one else. I let you get close to me. I stopped protecting myself all the time and dropped my guard. I trusted you to not shatter what we had, and when you did I felt so vulnerable, so exposed, so foreign in my own skin that I couldn't think straight. I still feel this way and I hate it, Gray! I hate that you can make me so weak."

So *this* is what she meant when she spoke about weakness in Burg. I think I understand her now, because a piece of who I am is so tied up in her that she's made me feel weak, too. Weak when I'm without her. Never stronger than when we're together. I want to tell her this but the concept seems too complex for words.

She pulls the door open.

"Don't go," is all I manage to say. "Please?"

But Bree just shakes her head.

"I already gave you everything, Gray, and I'm not doing it again. I'm putting myself first."

THIRTY-EIGHT

IT IS MIDDAY WHEN ADAM returns.

Our gear is packed—the team, restless. I'm sitting on my bed, sharpening Owen's knife and replaying my conversation with Bree, when I hear the helicopter approaching. I slip the knife into its sheath and race from the room.

Adam is jumping from the vehicle when I burst outside. Elijah comes next, and finally, Blaine. He has a bag slung over his shoulder in this carefree manner, and he's smiling so wide that I remember it is possible to be happy. We collide, our greeting a series of playful shoves that are punctuated by moments when one of us breaks down and clasps the other around the back.

This is my brother. This is what I should have felt that day back in Stonewall: complete ease and sureness. I still don't know how that Forgery fooled me for even the briefest of moments.

"I hope this isn't too much for you," I joke, shoving him. "Given your fragile, recovering state and all."

He shoves me back. "I'm in working order again. Might even be able to outrun you if you don't watch yourself."

"I don't doubt it. I took a knife to the leg two nights ago."

This news seems to startle him, and never missing a chance to play big brother, his face flushes with concern. "You doing okay?"

"Yeah. My leg is the least of my worries."

"Anything you want to talk about?"

Bree steps outside with the rest of our team, carrying our remaining supplies. She shoots me a scowl, and I turn back to Blaine.

"Maybe later."

He winks, like he already knows everything I have yet to say, and then moves to say hello to the rest of the team. While Adam and Heidi thank Sylvia for her assistance, I help Elijah load the helicopter with our gear.

"New year, new start," he says after we shake in greeting.

I pause, trying to recall when we fled from Burg and the number of days that have passed since.

"Today's January first," Elijah clarifies. "This is the year things turn around for us. I can feel it."

A new year. What would have been Year 48 in Claysoot. The year I was supposed to be Heisted. The year I grew up fearing because it marked my turning eighteen. But no, I'll be nineteen this summer. It's like I blinked and missed twelve months of my own life.

I'm somewhat overwhelmed by it all. Here we are, going west again, moving even farther from the thing we have to fight. But I need to trust that Ryder and Adam know what they are doing. Clearly, I can't be trusted with heavy things. Not missions, or lives, or people's hearts.

I glance at Bree. Sammy's heckling her about something. In fact, he's been back to his sarcastic self since this morning. I think it might be the armor he's chosen to wear as he recovers from the shock of the last few days. After a few foul words from him, Bree finally snaps.

"You know I can take you, so don't push me."

"Aw, you're just looking for an excuse to wrestle," he responds. "I don't blame you, really. Girls can't keep their hands off me."

Bree rolls her eyes and I wish I were Sammy. She used to make that face at me, too. We used to be nothing but playful banter and ridicule. We used to be easy. But I don't want easy anymore, because I want all of her. Every last drop. Even the pieces that terrify me.

Bree catches me watching her, and her mouth twitches into a tiny grin. She looks away even quicker, but the glance was there, mischievous rather than hostile, and it makes me think I can fix things between us if I try hard enough.

I hear footsteps in the snow and Adam is suddenly at my side, tossing the last few bags into the rig.

"So what happens now?" I ask him.

"Elijah has the details."

"And I don't get to know anything?"

"Guess that depends. Sometimes when a person has details, they end up running operations they never intend to."

I could nod and let it lie. It would be easy enough, and I'm not sure I'm cut out for this type of stuff: knowing specifics, being trusted with missions and things of importance. But I think about my father, how he told me that I am stronger than most, and I feel like I should do this: stay involved, *be* involved. I owe him that.

So I look at Adam and say, "No, tell me. I want to know."

"We'll fly for about an hour to a refueling station. Then we'll head to Pike." A quick raise of his eyebrows. "Frank isn't the only one with a domed city, after all."

Sammy and September mentioned that domed cities sprang up around the country before the War split the land in two. It shouldn't be surprising to hear that AmWest has one, or that Adam and his Expats seek refuge beneath its dome, but I'm still caught off guard.

"The ocean is right at our door," Adam adds. "The *real* ocean. Puts that gulf you sailed across to shame."

I instantly want to see it.

"I think you'll like it. When the sun hits the water in the evenings, the entire thing lights up orange. But summer is the best: warm winds, calm evenings, loons that can be heard for miles."

"Loons?" I ask. "Like the bird?"

"That's the one."

Adam climbs into the front of the helicopter, and I step into the rear. I take a seat beside Blaine, but I don't join him when he falls into conversation with Sammy. I'm staring at Bree, who is sitting across the way with the others, staring back. I'm thinking about how trust is delicate but repairable, about how the loons sometimes get separated but then they cry and cry and don't let up until one hears the other. They always reunite, two halves becoming one.

I cup my hands together and try to reproduce a call. I fail.

But Bree makes one.

The eerie cry fills the space between us, somehow as beautiful and reassuring as it is mournful. It is instantly drowned out by the roar of the helicopter, but Bree and I share a small, knowing smile as we lift into the uncertainties of an overcast sky.

ACKNOWLEDGMENTS

I thought writing these the second time 'round would be easier than with my debut, and I thought wrong. (Turns out everything about sequels is a challenge.)

So much time, attention, and care is required to put a book into the world, and while my name is on *Frozen*'s cover, a small army made the bound product possible.

First and foremost, the wonderful team at HarperTeen/Harper-Collins Children's. My editor, Erica Sussman, continues to ask all the right questions—sometimes queries I don't want to hear, but always ones that make the story stronger when I roll up my sleeves and put in the work. Erica, I am forever grateful for your keen eye and sharp intellect. Tyler Infinger, it has been an absolute privilege working with you on this series. Erin Fitzsimmons (and the rest of the design department), you exceeded my expectations once again, and gave *Frozen* a cover I love even more than my first. (I didn't think it possible.) Christina Colangelo, Casey McIntyre, and all the other dedicated, astute minds who worked tirelessly to bring this sequel to readers: thank you!

My agent, Sara Crowe, whose steadfast guidance and savvy business edge have proved invaluable assets countless times over: thank you for fielding all my ridiculous questions, securing foreign rights, brainstorming everything from plot twists to marketing possibilities, and fighting (when necessary) on my behalf. Every author needs such a champion, and I'm so fortunate to have you in my corner.

Writing is a lonely endeavor, complete with unexpected panic attacks, waterfalls of self-doubt, and lots of staring out windows. (Perhaps enough to rival the time spent staring at blinking cursors.) I've found fantastic support groups in Pub(lishing) Crawl and Friday the Thirteeners. Ladies, thank you for talking me off ledges and keeping me sane. Especially Sarah J. Maas and Susan Dennard. You two are my rocks. Of the diamond variety. No, *crystals*. Kat Zhang, I'm still suffering writer's envy from the prose you churned out during our workshops while on tour. (This is a good problem. You've made me raise my bar.) Alex Bracken and Jodi Meadows, I'm requesting another breakfast and coffee date, respectively. One can never talk books for too long or too often. Marie Lu: you read *Taken* well over a year ago and sent me an email filled with so many kind words upon completion that I'm still grinning. We were mere internet acquaintances back then, and this then-debut was extremely grateful for your time. (I'd hoped to put that in *Taken*'s acknowledgments but missed my window. You know how publishing timelines are.) I'm honored to now call you a friend.

April Tucholke and Jenny Martin: many thanks for critiquing and beta reading. You guys have been on this journey with me (and Gray!) from the beginning, and I'd be scratching my head more than I already do without your advice and cheerleading.

Speaking of encouragement . . . Rob, the dedication for this novel couldn't be truer. Writing this book wasn't easy, and you pulled me back to reality when I required a break, and understood when I needed to be locked away in my office, typing by the light of my screen. I'm not sure how many times I said *just five more minutes*, and you nodded, well aware it would be closer to fifty. I'm a lucky girl to have such a patient husband.

Mom and Dad: you guys remain the greatest teachers I know. I owe you so much more than words can adequately express.

Kelsy, who knew I could find a best friend, first reader, and sounding board all in my sister? Love you to the moon and back.

Additional love to my friends (both online and IRL) and extended family (aunts, uncles, cousins, Grandma, in-laws). The support you have shown me and this series is truly remarkable. I need to hire each and every one of you as my backup marketing team. Your guerrilla tactics are gold.

To all the librarians, booksellers, and educators who put young adult novels on their shelves and in the hands of teens: you are real-world superheroes.

And last but certainly not least, a million *thank-you*s to you. Yes, *you*—holding this book and devouring every last word. Thank you for following Gray on this journey. Thank you for your emails and tweets and support and time. Sharing this story with the world is an honor, and none one of it would be possible without readers. Without you.